Running up the Score

Jacky De Groot

Books by Jacqueline DeGroot

Climax
The Secret of the Kindred Spirit
What Dreams Are Made Of
Barefoot Beaches
For the Love of Amanda
Shipwrecked at Sunset
Worth Any Price
Running Into Temptation with Peggy Grich
Tales of the Silver Coast, A Secret History of
Brunswick County with Miller Pope
The Widows of Sea Trail-Book One
Running up the Score with Peggy Grich

To contact the author or find out about her other books,
please visit
www.jacquelinedegroot.com

Running up the Score

by
Jacqueline DeGroot
with Peggy Grich

©2008 by Jacqueline DeGroot and Peggy Grich

Published by American Imaging
Cover design: Jim Grich
Format and packaging: Peggy Grich

Printed in the United States of America

First Edition 2008

ISBN 978-1-60702-590-0

Dedicated to the millions of people who have embraced a lifestyle that allows them to live and travel on their own terms.

You deserve an adventure written around your experiences. Although RVing isn't always easy, your home on wheels, no matter the size, is truly the best of all worlds.

There's something about giving in to a sense of wanderlust that is appealing and basic in all of us..

Acknowledgments

Thank you to my proofreaders:

Bill DeGroot
Regina Flemion
Peggy Grich
Sharon Markatos
Pam McNeel
Martha Murphy
Diane Stander
Brenda Tew
Becky Upton

Miller Pope for the cover illustration (Love the lizard!)

Peggy Grich for providing so many insights into the world of a full-timer and for taking the time to provide local color as she travels. She also holds my hand through the publishing process by formatting and packaging the final manuscript—then goes on the road and sells the books! She's an amazing team player, and a cherished friend. I'm glad she's on the road seeing the country, but I miss her greatly.

Jim Grich for his technical advice, cover design, and attention to detail. If there's something about RVing Jim doesn't know, then it's probably not worth knowing. I count on him for so many things, and he's always there for me.

Running up the Score

Chapter One

My name is Jenny now. I was Debbie when I left Virginia and Carrie from North Carolina to Utah. I wish it wasn't necessary to keep hiding like this, but it is. I haven't quite accepted the fact that it could always be like this, that I might never be able to stop running, but like it or not, this is the life I was forced into. I traded my old life for a role similar to Julia Robert's in *Sleeping with the Enemy*, except that I escaped from my abusive husband in an RV, and I am blonde instead of brunette. Now I am Jenny, and I am in Oregon, and I'm trying very hard not to be lonely or afraid as I point my new RV toward a place I never thought I'd see.

As soon as I come over the rise onto Rim Drive and look down on Crater Lake, I know that Oregon is going to be a wonderful place for me to hide and heal for a while. I've run from my husband for close to two months now—a miracle in my mind, and I have solved a four-year-old missing persons case in the interim. I believe I also have the beginnings of a wonderful new love blooming inside my heart, but I'm not ready for it now and neither is Brick. We're in a holding pattern as we both deal with the dramas life has thrown our way.

I gingerly pull my new Class A motorhome, the most

luxurious of RVs, into a lovely scenic overlook, careful to pull all the way to the end so no one can park in front of me. I have not yet backed this little behemoth up and I sure as hell don't want my first time to be on a narrow ledge thousands of feet up from the floor of the valley, a drop-off not even protected by so much as a primitive split rail fence.

The lake below is pristine, an amazing deep blue color, glittering in the sun and without a single ripple. I am in awe of the beauty all around me. The stands of pines covering the sloping sides are a vivid green. They are standing sentinel under a pale blue sky and so thickly enmeshed that the only grass I can see is close to the top. Some places make you feel reverent; this is one of them. I walk closer to the edge and stand on the new summer grass.

It's as far as I dare to venture and I spend long minutes taking it all in. It's odd to see so many signs of spring, yet still see clumps of snow scattered everywhere.

I don't know how long I stood there admiring the scene in front of me but I knew it was time to move on when I heard the slamming of car doors and the running feet of children. I looked over my shoulder and sighed. This wasn't a view that I wanted to share with a group of boisterous boy scouts.

Twenty minutes later I pulled into Mazama Campground. Each site promised an incomparable view and I liked their website, so this was home for a while. The website described a lot of the activities in the region and had links for more information on each. The campground also had a pool and wireless Internet, something I was coming to appreciate and regard very highly. Brick and I usually made some kind of contact every day, and wireless connections made life a whole lot easier for a fledgling computer user like me.

Driving out of Utah, I decided to settle in one spot for at least two weeks. There were several reasons for this, not the least of which was my budget. Even though I had earned a nice reward for solving the missing persons case, I used most of the proceeds to trade up to a larger RV. It had been a necessary thing to do if I wanted to continue to elude my husband, Jared.

Unfortunately, Jared had found out about my old RV, my wonderful Atlantis, rather early after my hasty departure from our Virginia estate. In plotting my carefully planned great escape I hadn't factored in his resourcefulness thoroughly enough. Implanting a tracking device in my never-to-have-again navel piercing led him to my first campsite near Black Mountain, North Carolina. And after discovering I fled in an RV, he circulated a nationwide flier describing my Atlantis and offering a reward for information leading to me. So, in Provo, after Brick and I had come to the conclusion that I could no longer hide in my Atlantis, we went to an RV dealer and traded it in. So now I own a Dolphin. Brick was a federal or state agent of some kind. I hadn't been able to figure out which exactly, as each time we'd had a run in, a different group of cops had accompanied him. If he hadn't been so attracted to me, and I to him, I'd probably be in jail right now for the wild chase I'd led him on.

The money that was left over from the reward had gone into an account in a Nevada bank where I opted for a debit card that I could use at any ATM in the country. My chance meeting with a little girl named Angelina at a K.O.A. pool, two months ago, had netted me enough to cover living expenses for two years; three if I was careful. The reward money was a windfall that I truly needed. I had expected to get a job somewhere on the road, but now couldn't as I had to keep running and stay out of sight.

The price I was paying for gas now was so much higher than it had been in the East that it scared me, made me almost want to rethink this great adventure. As it was nearly summertime, I found premium prices at the pump as well as at the campgrounds. It was still amazing to me that in less than three months I had gone from the trophy wife of a millionaire to a penny-pinching, coupon-clipping vagabond. I had to smile. I loved it! I absolutely did. However, for the first time in my life,

I had to be frugal.

Being independent was a heady feeling for me as it had been over six years since I'd been free to do anything on my own without repercussions from my domineering and obsessively possessive husband. As each day brought new surprises and decisions, I relished the uncertainty and the excitement of what turning the next corner would bring.

As far as I could figure, my new RV was getting nine miles to the gallon. With the price per gallon close to $3.50, every five hundred miles I drove depleted my reserves by close to two hundred dollars. Added to that, campsites with hookups had been running close to thirty-five dollars a night. Once I discovered that most campsites gave discounts for longer visits, I decided to take advantage of the reduced rates and extend my stays.

After extensive research on the Web, I chose Mazama Village. It seemed to have everything I needed and promised serenity, which I desperately wanted, and obscurity, which was critical right now. I wanted to lay low, be unobtrusive and pull myself back together. The fact that Brick was also in Oregon was a bonus. It cheered me just knowing that he was so close.

It didn't take long to check in and set up camp. The site I had been directed to was lovely, high on a ridge overlooking the rich green forests that surrounded the area. I had been told that I could either back in, or pull in, and use the hook ups on either side. A huge tree, whose root system had become so extensive that it had to be cut down, was on the lot to my left. As long as they were waiting for a crew to come section it off and haul it away, I essentially had the use of both lots and their connections. I opted to pull in so I could see the panoramic view out of the windshield.

I was pretty much on my own, with no other campers in sight unless I walked back to the main road. I was in a secluded section of the park, with the highest elevation and the most amazing views, but I knew it wouldn't be long before I had neighbors.

The rigmarole of setting the hydraulic jacks and connecting the sewer, electric and water lines, was becoming rote. I hardly ever needed the checklist, but diligently used it, just in case. I was thrilled that I didn't have to constantly search out the manual for each appliance to figure something out. But I have to admit when it came to the electronics above the dash, I was still hopeless. I was hoping that in a few days I would come across a really nice, geeky man who would show me how to set up and use my new DVD player and satellite dish. The entertainment system in the Atlantis hadn't been quite as complicated. I admittedly wished that I had paid more attention when the salesman had shown me how to use things before pulling off the lot in Utah.

When Brick helped me trade my Atlantis in on a new Dolphin, I wasn't really able to concentrate on anything the salesman was saying. Brick had stood so close that I got lost in the warmth and sexuality he radiated. I didn't know what was going on with us, but the attraction we had for each other could not be denied, even after I had embarrassed him and put him in several difficult situations with the powers that be—namely his bosses.

After tying my hammock to some nearby trees, a final look at my check sheet, and a quick walk around my motorhome, I was assured that all was well and that I could go inside to relax. Setting my laptop up on my new Corian tabletop, I checked to see if I could get a decent signal so I could check my e-mail. Angelina's family and Brick were the only ones who knew how to contact me, and at times I felt as if they were my only connection to the world. I looked forward to hearing from all of them, but Brick especially. Often I laughed out loud at his comments; his biting humor and teasing manner entertained me and lifted my spirits. I went online to access the Yahoo account Brick had set up for me and was delighted when I found that there was a message from <u>BTyler5wheel@yahoo.com</u>, Brick's cyberspace address that referred to his impressive fifth wheel trailer.

Brick: Any sign of you know who? I'm running into a dead end here. You would not believe how many RVers are camped here. This RV Rally has by far the biggest crowd I have ever seen in one place. The brown and green-eyed monster has not made himself known to anyone I've talked to so far. I'm getting desperate, this case is taking too long to solve. I'm coming across too many dead ends and it scares me to death. I am beginning to wonder if I will ever see my sister alive again. I hope you have found that special place you said you were looking for, to unwind, settle some emotional issues and to wait for God's providence to guide the next step in your life. I worry about you and think about you (far more than I should!). Keep an eye on your rear since I'm not there to do it for you, and that's a real shame as it's a very nice rear. Brick

Jenny: He wasn't behind me, no one was. For the last twenty miles or so I was the only one on the road, so I know I wasn't being followed. Stop worrying, I'm fine. I did as you said and stopped at the place you recommended in Nevada and bought a little Vespa to tool around in. Your friend Marty arranged to have the lift installed while I waited and I was out of there in time to set up camp a few miles outside of Klamath Falls. I arrived at Crater Lake this afternoon and all I can say is this isn't a lake to pee in, no matter how big it is! I had to laugh at myself today when I remembered how seriously I used to take my mother's admonitions when I was kid, that I not use our municipal pool as a bathroom. When I was a teenager at summer camp, it took my

girlfriends a whole week to convince me that it
was okay to let loose in the lake, rather than
walk all the way back to the cabin. Today when
I looked around this huge crater I felt the
solemn quality of this place and I knew that
any thought of polluting it should be banished
immediately. Surely, God would smite anyone for
doing the deed in this magnificent water! You
should see it; it is this incredible shade of
blue, a blue so vivid it takes your breath away.
Wow is the first word you think of when you first
see the lake. When the sun is shinning on it
it's iridescent, jewel-like. The color varies
from navy blue to violet and it appears as if
there's a sheen of oil on the top that reflects
the sun's rays, But of course there's not, the
water is actually the purest in the world. Isn't
that awesome? When the wind blows the ripples
move the color across the surface of the water
and the longer you stand looking at the water,
the more awestruck you are. I think I'm going to
be happy here at Mazama Village. I have a lovely
view of the mountains and I'm rather secluded
and off to myself—until the weekend when I'm
told they're expecting a big crowd. I think of
you too, and wonder how you manage to keep sane.
I read the file you sent and I will be looking
for the man with different colored eyes. I pray
every night that you find your sister soon. Jenny
(a.k.a. Carrie, a.k.a. Deborah, a.k.a. . . .who
knows!)

Chapter Two

I was reclining in my hammock, reading a wonderful Regency romance when a humongous Class A motorhome pulled into the lot beside mine. It was the prettiest RV I had ever seen. The highly lacquered paint dazzled and drew the eye with its muted shades of browns, beiges and golds, all tastefully layered in large stripes with wispy silver and black ribbons of paint as accents woven throughout. It screamed money, and lots of it.

I watched, a bit enviously, as the driver unhooked his "toad" car, a matching Jeep Cherokee, and confidently backed onto the lot and snugged his rig between two towering trees. With two years of practice, I told myself, maybe I would be able to park my home-on-wheels in under two minutes.

I listened to the low throaty hum of the diesel pusher at idle, and when I heard the engine shut down, it reminded me of the sound Jared's jet made when his pilot flipped all the switches, ending with one last deafening surge before there was total silence. I watched as two slides expanded the unit on my side. I imagined there was at least one on the other side, and together they were turning what was already a spacious motorhome in to a traveling estate.

The door to the right of the front wheels opened and

a man and a woman stepped out. They were an older couple, both on the short side, ample, with fuzzy flyaway graying hair, the woman's with touches of red in it. They were not casually dressed, as one would expect for campers this time of year. Squinting from the setting sun so I could assess them better, I judged them to have an academic appearance. Something about them reminded me of dry English Literature classes and Algebra tutors who thought what they were sharing was nirvana.

They didn't acknowledge my presence even though the woman and I made eye contact for several seconds. They busily set about rolling out awnings and retrieving lawn furniture, picnic items and a large grill from under the floor compartments around the bottom perimeter of the RV. In RV lingo I knew this area, often quite spacious, was referred to as "the basement."

I watched them putter around, setting up their makeshift camp, in awe of their synchrony. It was as if each had an assigned task, and having done it moved to the next. Ten minutes later, this was a campsite worthy of an RV sales brochure. I had never seen anything like it. These were some serious campers.

They both went back inside. I went back to my book, one ear and one eye trained on the little patio area they had just set up. The carpet they had rolled out even had flagstones drawn into it. I didn't doubt that it was the indoor/outdoor type and the best that the industry offered. Minutes later the man came out and lit the grill. It was a gleaming stainless steel job with two side burners and a huge dial centered on the cover. I was impressed; this was state-of-the-art stuff.

Madam came out next with two whole chickens on a tray. They were coated with what appeared to be barbecue sauce. The lid was lifted, the chickens skewered on a rotisserie spit that was fitted into side slots, the lid lowered and the dial adjusted. This was done so efficiently that I thought this might be a nightly ritual. Maybe they were retired chicken farmers dedicated to the poultry association. It was hard not to admire their proficiency.

They went back inside, toddled really, as they were both

a bit on the heavy side. I was reminded of the Weeble Family; they wobble, but they don't fall down. That was mean I told myself, not everyone was blessed with an overactive metabolism as I was, and not everyone considered exercise fun, as I did. I readjusted myself in the hammock, fitfully repositioning the canvas pillow for what must have been the hundredth time. I listened to the steady hum of the rotisserie as it spun and the chickens as they periodically hissed, and went back to my book.

Not ten minutes later, I heard a car door slam somewhere behind me. Then I heard low voices arguing. A tall man in a business suit pulling a young girl behind him came into my line of vision. I watched as he hissed through his teeth at her then shoved her toward the mammoth RV. He had her by her elbow and it looked like he was hurting her.

"This is all your fault, and this is how we're going to fix it! Now stop whining and grow up!"

The venom I heard in the man's voice caused my blood to chill. His tone, and the way he gritted the words out through clamped teeth, reminded me of Jared and the way he would admonish me when he was angry, when I wasn't cooperating, when I wasn't being the ideal, biddable wife.

"I don't want to do this! It isn't right!" The girl whispered harshly.

"Well, you didn't leave us any choice in the matter now, did you?" Again, his words were gruff and spoken with disgust.

"We're going to get caught."

"No, we're not. You just do as you're told. And I don't want to hear any more about it."

They were walking just ahead of me now, almost to the "staged" patio when the man saw me. I closed my eyes and tried to hold myself perfectly still, as if I was asleep. But not too many people sleep with a book held high over their head.

"Shhh!" he hissed again.

Then I heard them knocking on the door of the poultry farmers' mini-mansion. The door opened, the man and girl were greeted warmly, then the door was shut with everyone inside.

I let out the breath I had been holding and opened my eyes wide. *Just what the heck was that all about?* And then for the next twenty minutes I tried not to think of all the things that could be going on inside that luxury RV.

Were they abusing that girl? She was being made to do things she clearly didn't want to do, that had certainly been more than evident. My mind shuddered at what those things could be. Oh, good Lord! Who was the man who had pushed the girl ahead of him? Was he her father, or someone else? And those scholarly looking people, what were they up to that "wasn't right" according to the girl?

I hadn't taken a good look at either the man or the girl, but the vague impression I had was that the girl was in her teens and that the man was in his forties. I strained to hear sounds coming from the Shangri-La on wheels but all I heard was the steady whir of the rotisserie as it spun on the spit and the sound of tires on gravel as some boys rode their bikes on the road behind me.

I let out a big breath and told myself not to let my imagination run away with me. I tried to figure out scenarios where everything fit and made sense, and where no one was getting hurt but nothing I could come up with justified the words I'd heard. Nothing legitimized the conversation and explained away my fears.

I went back to my book and re-read the same paragraph for perhaps the tenth time. I closed the book; there would be no more reading right now. My mind was jumbled. I felt just like I had when I'd seen Angelina's face on a missing persons flier at Wal-Mart all those weeks ago—sick to my stomach, scared and unsure what to do next.

The door to the chicken farmers' hut opened and the tall man came out alone. He walked briskly to his car without acknowledging me in any way. I am a very attractive blonde, I am wearing skimpy cut-offs and a low-cut halter-top. I have fairly long legs, which are shapely and nicely tanned. If that man was ignoring me, there was a reason, and I almost didn't want to know what it was.

Scant minutes later a pickup truck pulled up, dropped another young girl off, and spun on gravel as it hastily pulled away. I watched as the girl almost trotted alongside the lengthy motorhome. She was focused on the door and breathing heavily, walking quickly as if she was late. The door opened before she got to it, and she was admitted without knocking. She didn't receive the same effusive welcome the first girl had. She was unceremoniously pulled into the camper and the door was shut behind her. I heard the locks click.

I flipped over to the other side of the hammock, grabbed the lemonade in the sipper cup that I had barely touched, and carried that and my book inside. My new RV, which had seemed so big just an hour ago, seemed rather puny next to the Chicken Coop next door. I went inside to start my own dinner. The smell of chicken barbecuing had permeated my nose, but I knew I didn't have a roasting chicken or a fancy grill to cook one on, so I had to settle for Stouffer's Lean Cuisine Chicken Parmesan. That, and some Black Cherry non-fat yogurt for dessert would have to suffice for tonight.

When everything was ready I took my dinner out to my tiny collapsible camping table. Even with a tablecloth, or should I say tablevinyl, I felt inconsequential next to the new neighbors' set up. I noticed that the lid was now up on the grill and that the chickens had been taken away. Lights were on all over the RV, but as all the shades were drawn, there wasn't anything more to see in that arena. I dragged my table over the lumpy grass until I was only a few feet from the ledge that overlooked the rising foothills. As far as I could see, I saw trees. Everything was a deep shade of green, the shadows of impending nightfall flitted as the sun fell. Streaks of pale yellow slivered between stands of trees, giving everything an ethereal glow. It was a view that cleansed my mind completely. As I watched the sunset spread its pastel palate over the entire area, I picked at my meal. Two thoughts played in my mind and I had to sigh out loud. One, was how unfortunate it was that I had no one to share this lovely view with, and two, what the heck was going on in that extravagant motorhome next door?

Chapter Three

A restless night had me waking at 5 A.M. As usual, the circumstances of my being on the run were causing me to have anxiety attacks that woke me with a galloping heart and an unsettled stomach. I was becoming accustomed to them and had a system: If one occurred before 3 A.M., I took a Lunestra sleeping pill to get back to sleep; if it happened after that, I got up, ate some crackers and cheese, and started my yoga or Pilates regimen.

Not wanting to miss the opportunity to combine exercise with the visual of watching my first sunrise over the mountain, I grabbed my mat and went outside. The pastel tints of a new day were just beginning to creep around the edges of the horizon. I took deep breaths, stretched, and pretzeled my body while I watched the world around me come alive.

I thought for a few minutes that I might be the only one awake in the Village, until I saw a sliver of light shining under the drawn shade in the Colossus next to me. Maintaining *Downward Facing Dog*, I watched as the door to the unit opened and the young girl I had seen yesterday slipped out and hurried to the road. I tucked my head under my arm, and upside down, I was in time to see her get into the pickup that had dropped her off yesterday.

I didn't think much of it, except that I thought she had been the one who had come with the tall man in the car. I went back to breathing, twisting and scanning the vista as I watched the shadows of night lift. My neck and shoulders weren't cooperating with my loosening efforts, so I blamed Jared for that too.

It had been a mistake to marry him. A woman swept off her feet by a man so sure of himself, so taken with the rapt attention he showered on her, she deserved what she got, I told myself. A smart, savvy woman did not commit herself to a man as quickly as I had. But he had fit the criteria most young, dating-to-find-a-mate women had: handsome, self-motivated, successful, confident, and with kisses that unsettled and threw caution aside.

When Jared had discovered that I was still a virgin at twenty-two, he had produced a ring and proposed. I thought he was perfect, so I accepted. Look where it had gotten me—six years of isolation, devotion so pervasive it bordered on obsessive, and verbal abuse I hadn't recognized for what it was. I had been progressively stripped of my independence and coached into a decadent lifestyle I didn't want before I finally opened my eyes and realized I had married a despicable, evil man.

The fact that I had made a plan, bided my time, and followed it through in order to leave him, warmed me. I was coming back to life, to my life, to the person I truly wanted to be, needed to be—not the person he had been trying to turn me into.

Had Helen Reddy been singing *I Am Woman, Hear Me Roar*, as the sun made its debut, I didn't doubt I could have cartwheeled all around my campsite. It felt good to be alive again and I lived in the moment, cherishing the simple, everyday occurrence of night turning into day. The Stepford zombie Jared had been trying to turn me into was gone; she had been defeated by reserves I had finally mustered. I was always and forever going to be my own woman, no one was going to own me or use me ever again. I smiled at the winking sun as it filtered through the trees and made the dew on the grass sparkle. Yes, the sun was out, and so was I. I stood tall, grabbed my heel from behind and struck a perfect *Natarajasana*, or *Lord of the Dance* pose. It was going to be a beautiful day.

I heard a door slam and watched Mr. Tall guy of the BMW sedan get out of his car and stride over to the Mega RV. The door opened before he got there and the young girl of the day before slid out to meet him. A few words were whispered, then he led her to the car.

Hey, wait a minute, my mind screamed. Wasn't that the same girl who left not an hour before? I made slits of my eyes, straining to take in her appearance. The girl had the same build, same hairstyle and color, same porcelain skin with freckles, same pointed chin and pert nose. The girl who had left this morning had been wearing an identical headband and bracelet as this girl. This girl even carried the same purse, tightly clenched in her fist. Even so, I did not think she was the same girl who had arrived with this man late yesterday afternoon. And just why was that? Why did I think that?

Manner of walking, tilt of the head, something had clued me in, but right now I couldn't place it. Of course, I could be mistaken. But I didn't think that I was. Were they twins? I hadn't noticed any resemblance at all yesterday in the two girls. What was going on here?

My presence and avid attention didn't go unnoticed. The man and girl could be heard arguing in loud whispers as they scurried to the car, hurriedly got in and sped away. How odd I thought, as the one word I deciphered easily from their tirade echoed in my head: "Caught."

Chapter Four

I laced up my Garmont Flash XCR boots and grabbed my REI Venus backpack. It was full of all sorts of handy things: a Leatherman multi-tool, Kashi Honey Almond Flax snack bars, my cell phone, which was technically Brick's, a Highgear TrailPilot 2 Compass, two bottles of citrus-flavored water, an ultra light Packtowel, and my iPod. I was taking a hike, my very first solitary hike, and I was as excited as a kid on summer vacation. Of course, I wasn't leaving anything to chance; I wanted to be prepared for whatever came along.

I could not wait to go exploring, to see the Wild West in all its glory. I had a map in my hand and a camera around my neck. The only thing I wished I had, but didn't, was a set of binoculars; but I figured the zoom on my camera would do in a pinch. I locked up the Dolphin and made a beeline for the hiking trail beside the camp entrance and headed into the woods. Classical music was playing through the earpieces of my headset and I couldn't think of anything better than listening to Rachmaninoff, while inhaling fragrant pine and walking on cushy beds of spongy moss.

I had read that as the nation's sixth oldest national park, Crater Lake National Park had a lot to offer other than the lake itself. I had an activity planned for each day, and today was all about hiking and enjoying the view from different vantage points along Rim Drive. I wasn't up to taking on the whole thirty-three miles, but I knew I was good for at least three out and three back. The trail was marked on the map I had received at the Rim Village Visitor Center on my arrival and was rated as moderately difficult, so I plodded on.

Mountain hemlock, noble fir, and too many varieties of spruce and pine to name, gave the air a heady, tangy fragrance that intensified the further I walked. The day was sunny and a balmy sixty-eight degrees so I was removing my vest not twenty minutes into my hike.

Cobalt, sapphire, indigo, navy and azure came to mind as I looked to my left and tried to think of words to describe the bluest blue I had ever seen. The lake was breathtaking and, as I snapped branches under my boots and left them in my wake, I felt at peace for the first time in years. I was refreshed and euphoric as I climbed, and I knew it wasn't all due to the endorphins of the rigorous exercise. I was losing some of the worry I had been carrying around and I was excited about what the future held for me. In short, I was energized. Like a kid on her way to camp, I couldn't wait to see what was in store for me when I got there.

The caldera below kept me centered and acted as a lodestone as I ventured on and off the path to sigh at the beauty of meadows filled with wildflowers, to watch adventurous chipmunks and to seek out views of the neighboring Cascade Mountains. I stopped to sit on a boulder to pick out the volcanic spires shown on the map and looked up just in time to see a bald eagle soar right past me. I was so stunned that it took me a few seconds to remember my camera, but he was kind enough to take a second pass and I got a great shot of him winking at me. I was thrilled beyond belief. The only thing that could have made the day better was to have had someone to share it with. I thought of Brick and the Great North American RV Rally he was attending in hopes of finding his little sister.

The way his voice had cracked when he had spoken to me about her made me close my eyes against the sadness, just as I had then, on the last day we had been together. He had told me about the tragedy of her kidnapping four years earlier in a mall food court. She was his stepsister and he was watching her for his parents while they were on a cruise celebrating an anniversary. She had only been five when she had been taken right from under his nose. He'd been standing in line for Asian food, and had looked away from where she was sitting eating a cheese steak sandwich to pay for his meal. When he'd turned back to their table, she was gone. He'd been looking for her ever since.

As an officer of the law, specifically assigned to a federal task force that was dealing with issues relating to just this kind of thing, he had quickly become frustrated with his inability to find her. The one clue he had came to him in the mail months later. A paper plate folded into an envelope with a realistic-looking stamp drawn in the corner had begged him to find her. She had written that the man who had her went by the name Snooks, and that he had one blue eye and one brown one. That had been four years ago, and he'd told me that not a day went by that he didn't feel guilt like a heavy cloak weighing down his soul. It was the reason Brick and I couldn't be together now. As attracted to each other as we were, we both had things we had to settle before we could concentrate on us. There'd be a time for us, he had told me, and I was happy to wait.

I gave a great sigh, grabbed my water bottle, tucked the wrapper from my Kashi bar into my backpack, and pulled myself up from the ledge. From the angle of the sun, I figured it was time I started heading back—it would not do to be lost out here in the dark. Even though it was summer, the temperature could go as low as the 30s at night, and the animals who owned these forests were a lot bigger than the chipmunks I had been watching.

Two hours later I walked up to my Dolphin and put my

key in the door. I noticed that all was quiet next door, but the faint light coming from under the large window shade on the slide made me confident someone was home. Turning my back to go into my RV, I thought I could feel whoever it was watching me.

I took a nice long shower, my elbows thankful that my new shower had a bit more room than my other one had. In my Atlantis, I'd had to remember to turn sideways to shampoo my hair or bump them on the sides of the shower each time I moved. The Dolphin, although not spacious by any means, was quite an improvement.

After drying off, I dressed in a jogging set and went to the kitchen to fix a snack. As I sat at my dinette eating my PB & J on Ezekiel Sesame Bread, I noticed a rather obese young man puffing his way to my neighbor's door. He had short dark hair, an obvious acne problem, and he was perspiring heavily. I could see sweat soaking the back of his shirt. His thick-framed black glasses slid down his nose and he swung his arms as he walked heavily onto the faux patio. He reminded me of a tuba player in a marching band. He was certainly big enough to carry such a large instrument and he was already puffing as if he was practicing a Souza march. He knocked and the door immediately opened for him. He managed to squeeze his way inside and the door quickly closed. I saw the madam look over toward my RV, but I didn't think she noticed me sitting in the dark, several yards back from the window, watching. But I thought it was interesting that she'd bothered to look.

Half an hour later, another young man went to the door and gained entry. He was medium height with a wrestler's build, he had big shoulders and muscled arms, with a nipped in waist. He had a cute button nose that looked like it might have been broken somewhere along the line. This was certainly curious, I thought as I took my plate to the sink.

I decided to jog over to the camp store to see about renting a DVD to watch so I grabbed a peach from the fruit bowl along with a Handi-wipe from underneath the sink and headed out.

Kim Bassinger was hugging her young rescuer in the movie *Cellular,* and the ending credits were just beginning to pop up on the screens of everyone's cell phones during the finale, when I heard a car pull onto the lot next door. That was odd, the lot was one of the largest the Village had, but it didn't have room for ancillary parking. I slid over to the bedroom window that fronted my neighbor's RV and lifted the edge of the blinds so I could look out.

A small pickup had pulled alongside the RV, backing up to the edge of the quasi-patio. A tall man got out, walked to the bed of the pickup and removed a large box. He took it to the door before coming back for another one. The door opened for him and he carried them both inside. Moments later he was gone and all was quiet again. I looked at the alarm clock that I had velcroed to my nightstand so it would stay in place when I was driving. It was 12:30 in the morning. I rolled over, hit the button on the remote to turn off the DVD player, and then I turned off the light and went to sleep. My long hike had exhausted my body, and my wandering thoughts about what was going on next door had taxed my brain, too.

I don't know exactly what woke me: a full bladder, hearing myself snore as I often did after a day spent outdoors, or the wind rustling the branches overhead. But it was 4 A.M. and I was wide-awake again. I decided to read for a while, as I wasn't quite ready for exercise of any kind. Thanks to my overlong hike, my calves were like iron knots and my inner thighs were telling me I should have "gotten off the horse" a lot sooner than I had. I was content to just sit back against the headboard with my Regency romance. It was beyond me why the rakish Duke couldn't figure out that the woman behind the mask was the exact same girl he'd kissed two weeks ago—especially since she had the same amazing violet eyes and compelling scent that reminded him of jasmine. That, and the fact that she was setting his insides on fire with a kiss that tasted of wild raspberries, reminiscent of the other woman's, should have been the second clue. Anyway, I was wide-awake when I heard the door open next door. Boy, the people next door kept strange hours, I thought.

I slid off the bed and went to the window in the main living area. It was dark in that room, so I could see out the window with no problem. I was off to the side, looking between the gap in the blind, when I saw the oddest thing. The young man I had seen yesterday, the really big one, was walking down the path with what could have been his twin. I squinted and tried to see their faces before they passed by the window and I thought I recognized the nose of the one who I had thought resembled a wrestler. Something about the way he walked looked familiar, even though apparently he had gained well over a hundred pounds since I'd seen him this afternoon.

As he passed my window I saw his face in profile and I knew without a doubt that the nose I was seeing was the very same one I'd seen earlier, the one that looked like it had been broken. Hurriedly, I tried to take both men in as they walked by, one with a practiced lumbering gait, the other as if just learning to walk with his new girth. *Were they going to some sort of costume party as twins? Was that what this was all about? Were the people next door making clones of the people coming to see them?* This was really strange. My curiosity was peaked. I couldn't fathom what in the world could be going on in the RV next door to mine.

The words that girl had spoken the other day flashed through my mind as they had several times since I'd heard her say them—*We're going to get caught.* I spun around and walked briskly to my room to get my phone. I couldn't wait to tell Brick what I had stumbled on to and to get his opinion of what the heck was going on in this quiet little village on the rim of a crater in Oregon.

Unfortunately, I had forgotten just how early it was and

his first words to me were mumbled curses that made me feel guilty as all get out.

"I'm so sorry Brick. I forgot the time. I'll call you back later."

"No, no. You got me up, might as well talk. Say something sexy."

"Is there a demand for young, overweight porn stars that are twins?"

"What! That's not sexy! Boy, you sure can kill the mood. What the heck are you talking about?"

I told him everything I could remember about everyone I had seen enter and leave the RV next door.

"Well if it weren't for the words you overhead from the girl being tugged into the motorhome, I'd say you were imagining things."

"I'm telling you exactly what I've seen and heard. Something weird is going on next door. And whatever it is, it's not kosher. I wish I could be a fly on the wall over there so I could see what's up."

"Well you can't, so just let it go. It's probably nothing. I certainly don't think you've run into a porn ring. I don't think there's a market for overweight look-a-likes. The only porn I've seen with twins featured girls looking more like the Doublemint twins, wholesome and stunningly beautiful. Which reminds me Gorgeous, say something sexy. I sure do miss you."

"How often do you watch porn?"

"Only when we confiscate it. I have to watch it to see what we've got."

"Yeah. Uh huh. So, you want me to say something sexy, huh?"

"Yeah," his voice had softened and he drawled the word out in anticipation.

"I'm naked and on my way to the shower."

"The one in your RV I hope, not the public ones in the center of camp?"

"Of course not. I'm not that brash."

"Good, because I'm beginning to think of you as my woman, and I don't share."

I felt a tingle travel through my body as his possessive words seeped into my brain. "Wow, that sent sparks through the line."

"You want sparks? Wait until I see you again. I'm going to build a wildfire in you, and then I'm going to make sure you burn *real* slow. And when the fire's almost out, I'm going to blow on the embers and heat you up again."

"Mmmm. You say the headiest things. And just when might that be?"

"I'm leaving here to go to Montana to help search the woods for a felon, then I have to head back this way for a conference. In the meantime there's another rally I have to check out, and two hikers I arrested last night need to be interrogated after their lawyers get here."

"What did they do?"

"A teenager's missing. They have her iPod, but they say they haven't seen her."

"Boy you do have an interesting job."

"Yeah, so I don't need my girlfriend looking for more work for me. Keep your nose clean and give your neighbors some space. That's why people go RVing, to get away from nosy neighbors and to have some privacy off on their own."

"I am not nosy! And you must admit it's all pretty strange. Twice now, a second person has gone into that RV and come out looking exactly like the first."

"Let me know when they look like the Doublemint twins, I'd fly in for that."

"Yeah like I'd tell you about that. I'm not into sharing either."

"Goodbye sweetheart. Have a nice shower. Alone." I heard the line go dead and I smiled. Even though he was miles away, he still managed to tug on my heart.

Chapter Five

After showering I decided to try out my new Vespa. I had written down every word Brick's friend had said about operating both the lift and the mini-scooter when I had purchased both before leaving Nevada. I thumbed through my notes, which I kept in a large file along with the instructions for everything else in my house. Boy, if you couldn't read, you'd have a hard time RVing—there is so much to know!

I decided to wear jeans in case I took a tumble, and I put on a heavy denim shirt over a tank top since the day promised to be a warm one. Patches of snow still peeked out in places, but they didn't fool me anymore, the afternoons got plenty warm. There was a little basket in front of the tiny handlebar and I stuffed it with my camera—wrapped in a towel—a water bottle, a sandwich, some fruit, and my wallet. I had learned how to travel light. Just a few months ago I would have lugged around a suitcase-sized Gucci or Fendi bag. My, how my lifestyle had changed. I thought of Jared. Had he given up trying to find me? I truly didn't believe that to be the case, and that was unsettling. But I had to admit, I wasn't being as diligent as I should have been about keeping an eye out for him. I felt safe in this little mountain campground. How could he possibly find me here? I mean this really was out of the way.

Driving around the winding road, I kept my ears tuned to the sounds around me. I wanted to make sure I heard the engine noises of any vehicles coming my way over the high-pitched whine of the Vespa. Rim Drive slopes away on each side, sometimes quite dramatically, and with no shoulders and crumbling edges, I often found myself encroaching into the oncoming traffic's right of way. After a few minutes, I was comfortable with the handling of the scooter and sped up a little. My hair, in a loose braid, flew out behind me and when I slowed down, I felt it slap against my back. This was fun. I was having a ball.

Back out on Rim Drive I took in one scenic overlook after another until I finally realized that at this rate it could take five or six hours to do the circuit before returning. So I found a nice boulder to sit on at an overlook known as The Watchman which gave me a view of Wizard Island, a volcanic island near the southern end where you can see the cone shaped depression at the top. I ate my turkey sandwich and nibbled on a pear, enjoying the amazing view. I was washing it all down with water when I felt a presence behind me. Nothing that alarmed me, just an awareness that someone was behind me, someone rather tall judging by the shadow cast over me. I assumed that whoever it was, was looking over my head to the view beyond. Water bottle still in my mouth, I turned to see who the interloper was. I was surprised when I saw a soldier staring not at the view, but at me.

I felt water dribble down my chin and I hastily removed the bottle and swiped at it. "Uh, hi," I managed.

"Hello, had to take in this particular view." He was looking right at me and I wasn't sure exactly what he meant by that. It was the crater he was referring to, wasn't it?

"Nice, huh?" I mean what else was I supposed to say?

"It is that." He walked closer and the shadow elongated. Some detached part of my brain wondered if it was mathematically possible to figure out a man's height by measuring the shadow he cast. Of course you'd have to know the angle of the sun, and how fast the train was going, and what time it left Chicago. Okay, it was just an idle thought, things your mind plays at when stressed.

"Mind if I join you?" he was indicating the boulder on the other side of mine.

"Sure, it's a bit hard, but it's all yours."

"Thanks."

As he climbed over and nimbly sat on the edge of the boulder, I took in his appearance. His hair was short, military short, probably not even half an inch long. He wore camouflage fatigues and shiny lace-up boots, and under it all I was betting he was lean and muscled. His hat was folded and tucked into his waistband, and he wore aviator-styled mirrored sunglasses. He was G.I. Joe in the new millennium. It was hard not to admire the full, smiling lips on his clean-shaven face, but something tuned me in to the fact that he was probably younger than he was trying to look. Maybe it was his smooth unlined features, the overdone cologne wafting over with the breeze, or the telltale splotches of flesh-toned acne medication on his neck.

"Is there a base around here?" I asked.

"Not one close. I'm on leave. Gotta report back in three months."

"Why the uniform, surely it must be hot?"

He looked over at me and snickered agreement, "Yup, but it's all I've got right now, my clothes are back at home, and there's no point going there as no one's home. Mom, Dad and my sister, Karen, are on vacation in Germany."

"Ah," I said, as if I understood, but I really didn't.

"I just got in, came into San Diego and made my way here."

"Is this home?"

"Nah, I'm from Georgia."

"What did you do with your southern drawl?"

He smiled over at me, "Never had one, my dad was a lifer and I've lived all over."

"Lifer?"

"Slang for career soldier."

"Oh. So what brings you to Oregon?"

"Looking for my girl." And as he said it I sensed pride. "I'm waiting to find out where I need to go; the Army will fly me there when I'm ready."

"I'm sorry if I'm asking too many questions."

"It's quite all right. I don't mind. I could stand someone to talk to actually."

"Yeah, me too." I realized instantly that I should not have let on that I was alone.

He just looked over at me. There was interest, but not the way I had originally thought. He was polite and friendly, but it wasn't like he was flirting, not since he'd commented on the nice view. But I certainly could have mistaken that, maybe he *had* really meant the scenery.

"I've never met her."

Her who? "I beg your pardon?"

"I've never met my girlfriend, least not in person. She's like a pen pal, only more so, if'n you know what I mean."

Yeah, I knew what he meant. I had one of those too. Brick and I were using e-mail to keep our budding romance alive. "How'd you meet?"

"They had this project at her school. They handed out soldier's names and everyone got one. They were supposed to wish us a Happy Valentine's Day and send a picture of something from their hometown for us to relate to. She sent me a picture of her with her arm around a snowman. I took one look at her smile and I was a goner. She was beautiful, with big-eyed innocence and she reminded me that there were places that weren't 120 degrees under the shade of a Hummer. I was in Iraq at the time."

"I guess it was nice to be reminded of home."

"Yeah, and it was real nice knowing that there were pretty girls who cared about the guys over there."

"No pretty girls in Iraq?"

"Are you kidding? No, none in Iraq. A few WACS caught my eye from time to time, but most of them were either spoken for, butch, or too free with their wares, the rest were clingy, looking to set up house."

"Truly?"

"It's a strange world over there. It changes you. Most of the women I met couldn't wait to get home. A few were even on a mission to get pregnant so they could get shipped back. It's really a man's world over there. I hated seeing the women struggle so much just to survive."

I was going to say something about his being sexist, but I kind of agreed with him. I thought war was a man's game, and couldn't understand why women would even want to be involved, but that was just me. "So you kept writing?"

"We weren't supposed to. In fact Diana, that's her name, wasn't supposed to send anything personal. But yes, we started e-mailing. I even managed to call her on her friend's cell phone a few times from a base phone. We got to know each other fairly well, and rather quickly. Aww hell, I might as well tell you, we fell in love."

"Well, that's wonderful!"

"Not exactly."

I held my breath.

"She was sixteen at the time."

"Oh my."

"Oh my, is right."

He reached into his pocket and pulled out a picture that was worn around the edges and had a crease where he'd had to fold it to fit. "Tell me you'd have pegged her at sixteen."

I took the picture from him and studied it. Smiling eyes looked out from under a pink ski cap and full lips, open in what was surely a delightful laugh, curved up. There was mischief in her stance and upon further scrutiny, I spied the snowball partially hidden in her hand. She was tall and slender in a white parka and ski pants, almost as tall as the snowman and no, she didn't look sixteen.

"Eighteen, nineteen, somewhere in there I would have guessed," I said.

"Yeah!" he said as if vindicated.

"So how old is she now?"

"Eighteen next week."

"When did you find out how young she actually was?"

"When her dad found our e-mails, about six months ago."

"Uh oh."

"Mmmhmm. He wasn't happy. She was told not to communicate with me anymore. I was told not to communicate with her. Her dad even had my C.O. dress me down."

"C.O.?"

"Commanding Officer."

"But I gather she continued to e-mail?"

"Yeah, from the library, and her girlfriend's house when she went off restriction."

"What's her father's objection? You seem to be a pretty clean-cut, all-American kind of guy."

He smiled over at me and shook his head, "If you had a daughter who was a high school senior would you want her involved with a twenty-three year old, nevertheless a military man of dubious character?"

"Dubious character?"

"I said some things in those e-mails I shouldn't have."

"How bad were they?"

"Let's just say they might not have been proper had she been twenty-one."

"Things of a sexual nature?"

"Itemized lists of places I wanted to visit."

I simply tsked and shook my head.

"Well he did what he had to. Now, I have to do what I have to."

"Which is?"

"I don't know, probably kidnap her for a while so I can at least find out if the feelings we have for each other are genuine."

I had to laugh—it was so absurd. But then I studied his face and saw he was serious. I raised both eyebrows in censure.

"Don't look so shocked, I'm sure it's what she's expecting me to do."

"You don't know?"

Sheepishly, he shook his head. "We've been incommunicado for almost two months. She was caught instant messaging me on prom night. She went out to dinner with her friends and then on the way to the prom they dropped her off at the university library. She was supposed to meet them at eleven but got locked in instead. They locked up early while she was in the rest room. When she didn't make curfew everything came out. The police chief was a friend of her dad's and he had his techs find everything we had written. I got an e-mail directly from him that said if I attempted to contact her again, I would be picked up by the M.P.s."

"M.P.s?"

"Military Police."

"So you're waiting until she's eighteen?"

"Yes. She graduated last week and five days from now she turns eighteen."

"And you're just going to snatch her?"

"Well yeah, that was the plan." There was some hesitancy in his voice, I keyed in on it.

"Don't tell me, let me guess. You don't know where she is?"

"Bingo. He's moved her. Reconnaissance of the address I had shows no one living in the house."

My thighs were beginning to cramp and my butt was

falling asleep from the hard boulder, so I stood up. He stood, too.

I was just about to ask him his name, but then I read it on the white tape sewn above his pocket. "Well, O'Reilly, just how are you going to go about finding her?"

He walked with me around our little area of the park as I listened, asked questions, and threw darts at all his ideas.

He only had her address, which was now a house standing empty. The name of her school wasn't much help either. They had no forwarding information and apparently the guidance counselor had been alerted that he might inquire after Diana. So there was no help in that corner. O'Reilly knew she had applied to six colleges and been accepted by four, but at the time of their last communication she hadn't made a decision about which one she planned to attend. Even if he'd known which one, it wasn't likely she'd show up on any campus until late August. He didn't know her father's name, who, as it turned out, was actually her stepfather, so he probably had a different last name altogether. Knowing *her* name, Diana James, was of little help. There were no accounts in her name, no phone listings in her name, nothing to hone in on, nothing to lead him to her.

Every idea he bounced off of me, I found a hole in, everything I came up with, he had already tried. She had no car; she hadn't shared her plans with the friends he had contacted; she'd had no job; there were no siblings; there was no trail that he could find. To make matters worse, the Army had closed his military e-mail account with his deployment home, so even if she wanted to, she couldn't contact him.

As we were walking back to the parking lot, he asked me if I'd like to go to dinner with him. I thought about it for a moment, and then nodded. *Why not?* I was lonely, and apparently, so was he. We were both sort of involved with others, so clearly it wasn't a date, and I was intrigued by his problem. Concerned that he was a strange man on his own, I asked to see his military I. D., which pretty much verified everything he had told me. His name was Connor O'Reilly and he was a medic, the military's equivalent of an E.M.T. He was a corporal in the U.S. Army, fighting for my freedom, the freedom I was just beginning to appreciate.

We agreed to meet at the Mazama Village Registration Center. I was still a little wary of him knowing exactly where I was staying. I didn't want him coming to my campsite, but since he had a Jeep, it made sense to use his vehicle to get around. He suggested the Lodge at Crater Lake and, as our restaurant options were limited in this wonderful wilderness, I heartily agreed. I had read on the website that they used only fresh Oregon-grown organic foods and that they had a wonderful selection of seafood from the coast, so I was anxious to try it out.

Connor said he would take care of getting a reservation, and we arranged to meet at seven, which would give us plenty of time to get there, and to enjoy a cocktail in the great hall before dinner. We had planned what seemed to be a very romantic evening, but it was obvious that we were both going to be thinking romantically of others. He was steadfastly determined to find his Diana, and I, well, I was waiting until Brick and I were ready for the next step.

I backtracked along the now familiar area of Rim Drive and chugged into the Village smiling at everyone as I wound around the curves to my campsite.

It looked pretty quiet in our little section. The "toad" my neighbors had parked on the spur was gone so I assumed they were off on a day trip somewhere, and I was glad about that. There were certainly more questions than answers about their bizarre behavior and odd guests.

I unlocked my Dolphin and went inside for a cool drink and a warm shower. My Dolphin didn't have its own washer and dryer but I didn't mind using the laundromats at the campgrounds when I amassed a pile of dirty clothes. Fortunately, most of my clothes were knit or nylon so I was often able to soak my undergarments and tops in Woolite, and then clip them to a clothesline strung between the trees. I was hanging up my tank top when I heard the neighbor's car turn into the drive. As I hung the rest of my clothes, mindful to clip my thongs and bras behind a t-shirt for modesty's sake, I watched as the scholarly duo unloaded bag after bag of groceries. How two people could eat so much was beyond me, but then I remembered that often their "guests" arrived before the dinner hour, and remained until the wee hours of the morning. They must be expecting more teenagers to tutor. In my mind, I had decided they were teachers, and that in order to afford their monstrous motorhome, they spent their summers tutoring. Why late into the night? That part I hadn't figured out yet.

I was on the bottom step propelling myself upward and into the RV when I had the sensation of stepping on something not quite solid, but not quite soft either. I looked down just in time to see a stumpy lizard scurry out from beneath my sandal. I was stunned for a moment as I realized I had stepped on it. Then I felt something tapping the side of my foot and I screamed. The lizard was gone, but his tail was still on the step, rapidly pulsing back and forth like a metronome gone haywire. I shrieked and bounced backward off the step, mesmerized, as that black appendage twitched and slithered seemingly oblivious to the fact that it was no longer attached to a body. I stood fascinated as my neighbors came up behind me, curious to see what the commotion was about. I was heaving big sobs now. I had murdered a lizard, a rather big one it seemed by the tail that was still flailing on my step.

The man grunted and shrugged, "It's just a skink. The way you hollered I thought you'd seen a snake."

The woman sniffed, "He's going to be a bit unbalanced, but it'll grow back."

"What?" I asked unsure what she was talking about. "What'll grow back?"

"His tail. He'll get a new one."

The "old" one was beginning to lose momentum, but it still had quite a bit of life left to it.

I grabbed at the absolution offered, "Really, he's not going to die, it'll grow back?"

The man stuck his thumbs in his pockets and rocked back on his heels and I could just see him in front of a podium winding up for a two-hour lecture. If he wasn't a college professor, my name was not . . . what the hell was it this week? Jenny. Yeah, that was it. Then the lecture began.

"Designed to do just that. In nature a lot of things have tails that regenerate. A predator can grab hold of it, but as long as the little critter keeps on moving, he's not lost much. Not his life at least. From what's remaining, I'd say you have a member of the Gekkonidae family there. They're usually found in tropical areas but it's not unusual to see one here. Side-blotched specimen if I'm not mistaken. Judging from the stumpy tail he left behind, he's decent sized, eight or nine inches maybe." Then he looked at me rather sheepishly, "Well he used to be, he's maybe half that now."

I cringed. "You're sure he'll grow it back?" I needed my guilt assuaged.

"I don't know, it looks like you got a bit more than tail there, but it should. He'll be unbalanced, not able to run up and down as he's used to without his tail to stabilize him, but he'll get used to it. He's still got four legs to get him around, and his tongue is long and sticky, so he shouldn't find it *too* difficult to find food while he recovers."

"Food? What does he eat?"

"Bugs, insects, mostly the flying type. Don't see how he's going to climb trees for a while though. He may have to do with grasshoppers and fleas."

I shivered. The tail was only twitching intermittently now.

"Uh . . . what do I do with this part?"

The man clamped me on the shoulder and threw his head

back in laughter. "Cook it if you want, I don't think he's going to come back for it!"

He hadn't taken the hint. I was asking for assistance, manly assistance, kill-the-spider-in-the-bathroom assistance. He wasn't in tune to me or my feminine wiles. He and his wife simply turned and went back to unloading their car.

I waited until the tail was "dead," until it didn't twitch, pulse, or throb. I had to move it off the step, but I certainly didn't want to touch it while it was still in action. I looked around for something to move it with, even debated as to whether I should bury it. It occurred to me that maybe when the tail died so did the other part. I went back to the clothesline and took an unused clothespin off the line. How was I going to do this? I tried three times, each time jerking my hand back before the clothespin even met the mottled skin. I dropped the clothespin and walked around the campsite. Then I looked out at the road and saw a young boy on his bike. I waved him over and offered him five dollars to move the tail for me. He smiled, shrugged and grabbed it between his chubby fingers, then he walked it over to the edge of the cliff and heaved it off. I closed my eyes tightly and said I was sorry as I imagined it plummeting down the side of the mountain. Then I went inside to get some money for my rescuer.

I filled a small bucket with water so I could clean off the step, then went inside. I was in a funk. I knew I'd killed that lizard, and it depressed me. I certainly hadn't meant to.

I plopped lengthwise down on the sofa, threw my arm over my forehead and gave a great sigh. Within minutes I was asleep conjuring up the *Geico* lizard with his twangy Aussie accent, going into a diatribe, "My mum, bless her soul. She was just out for a walk on the Oregon coast . . ."

I woke to the sound of my cell phone ringing. I rarely kept it on, but it was in its charger, so it was on now. My heart sped up. Only a handful of people had the number. My first thought was that it must be Brick. I ran to the bedroom to answer it.

"Hi!" I recognized the young voice immediately. It was Angelina, my little imp, the little girl I had reunited with her mom and dad. They were just settling into a new home in Austin, and she was very excited.

"Mom and Dad said I could!"

"Could what, sweetie?"

"Have a puppy!"

"Oh, that's wonderful! But I'm supposed to be the one to get you the puppy when they say it's okay."

"I know. So when are you bringing him?"

I laughed. She was always forthright. I missed her, she was such a delight. "Well, let's see . . . I'm in Oregon now. That's a long way away." It was June now, but one thing about being on the road, I had no ties, no job, nothing holding me here, except possibly the chance encounter with Brick I was counting on. "Are you sure your mommy and daddy are ready for company?"

"You're not company."

She couldn't have said anything else that would have made me smile more. "Let me speak to your daddy."

She must not have moved the phone far from her mouth, because I heard her call for Daniel. Seconds later he was on the line.

"She says you're alright with me bringing a puppy?"

I felt the hesitation. "We're alright with her having a puppy."

That was odd phrasing. "But I can't bring it?"

"It would be best if you didn't."

"Daniel, what's going on?"

I heard him tell Angelina to go check on Lula Belle, her doll. He told her he thought he heard her crying.

"Daniel?"

"He's here, Carrie."

My heart started pumping harder. With a calmness I didn't feel, I said, "Jenny."

"Oh, yeah, I keep forgetting."

"How do you know?"

"The neighbors. They're asking very peculiar questions. I think he was here this week asking around and offering a reward. He probably figures you're bound to show up here to visit."

"Hmm. Well I sure don't want to disappoint Angelina. I promised her a small white dog."

I know. And that's all she talks about."

"Maybe we can meet somewhere?"

"He's watching, I can just feel it."

"Damn!"

There was silence for a few seconds, then I heard him talking to Julie.

"We all want to see you. It's just not safe right now. And, Carr—Jen, I wouldn't underestimate him."

"Has he approached you?"

Again, a long hesitation, "Julie went to the grocery store yesterday. The man in line in front of her used his charge card to pay for her groceries. Then he told her he'd buy her a house too, if she told him where he could find you. She was so upset she left the groceries in the store. Thank God Angelina was with me."

"Oh Daniel, I'm so sorry."

"It's okay. We'd never take that man's money, you know that don't you?"

"Of course."

"We'll just have to wait."

"I'll figure something out Daniel. Just tell Angelina to be patient."

"I will. You take care."

"You guys happy?"

"Deliriously." He laughed and I could hear Angelina squeal as he tickled her before disconnecting.

Jared! Damn his soul! So he hadn't given up.

I walked up front to the kitchen and opened a bottle of wine. Sitting at the dinette in front of my laptop, I went online to check out breeders in the Austin area, ones who bred small, white dogs. There were many, and I smiled as I clicked from link to link, imagining Angelina's face when each arrived on her doorstep. I was bummed that I couldn't take Angelina a puppy, as I'd so dearly love to do. But there was more than one way to skin a cat. Ugh! That thought made me think of the gecko, and I cringed. A big gulp of wine followed.

I broke out of the search and went into my e-mail program. I figured that before dinner, I'd better tell Brick about Corporal Connor O'Reilly.

Chapter Six

Connor and I had a lovely dinner in the lodge. I had the Seafood Risotto and the Lodge Salad, and he had Wild Mushroom Brushetta and the Crater Lake Greens Salad. Then we opted to share an entrée, and decided on the Alaskan Halibut Fillet. We were so stuffed that we couldn't even look at the desserts, which were presented tableside. But we did enjoy a wonderful cup of coffee as we stared out the window at the eerily shadowed mountains. Fully satisfied, we pushed back our chairs and lumbered out of the restaurant into the chilly summer evening. It wouldn't be unusual for the temperature to dip into the thirties this time of the year, but thankfully, right now, it was only a brisk forty-six.

I smiled over at Connor, who had practically talked non-stop about his Diana and the plans he had for them. He saw a future that most women dream of—a happily ever after, filled with kids, dogs, and white picket fences. It was hard for me to resist smiling at his optimism, and his unflagging drive. He was one determined soldier. As I tossed one negative comment after another his way, he merely shrugged his shoulders and waved it away. He was going to find her no matter what. In his mind, the crusade had begun. All he needed was something akin to a scent, and he'd turn into a bloodhound, off and running.

But despite many hours of banter and deep thought, neither of us could come up with the starting point he so desperately needed. I let him walk me to the door of my RV. After getting to know him, I had decided he was one of the good guys, so I no longer worried about him as a threat to my safety. And although he sure was cute, he was certainly not a threat to my newly-foresworn chastity—he was way too young—and only Brick had a chance at that. But still I kept my distance as we walked; I did not want to give him the wrong impression, or encourage anything so lame as a goodnight kiss. Although, after all the talk about Diana, I would have been sorely disappointed if he had made any attempt at anything more than a peck on the cheek. Diana, wherever she was, owned his heart whether she knew it or not, whether she wanted it or not.

"That was a great dinner. Thanks for suggesting the Lodge, and for taking me," I offered, as I fished through my purse for my key. My eyes were averted, straining to see through the meager light of the moon, so I didn't see what made Connor jump back three feet.

"What the hell was that?" he cried out.

All my nerves tensed as one thought raced through my mind, *Jared.*

Then I saw him stoop and cup his hand against the ground. He came up seconds later with a lizard, or the better part of one—a side-blotched lizard missing one very long appendage. I swallowed a lump of guilt.

"Well look what I found," he said in a tender voice that told me that this man loved all God's creatures, perfectly formed or otherwise.

"That's my lizard," I mumbled. "Wonder what he's doing here," I asked, as I peered down into his palm at the small reptile enjoying the single stroking finger gliding down his long back.

"He's your pet?"

"Well no, actually I'm the one who disfigured him, well

sort of." I explained my traumatic experience of this afternoon, noting over and over again that it really had been an accident, that I hadn't even seen the little critter until it had been too late. Now he was tailless and possibly homeless because of me. Without his tail, he probably couldn't even get back to his family.

"You should keep him and take care of him until he grows his tail back."

"What? Are you nuts?" Then I saw his big grin and I knew he was teasing.

"You keep him!" I looked down into his hand again. The lizard was licking his palm, his long, dark tongue taking languorous forays against the calloused skin.

"He's hungry," Connor murmured softly, almost cooing. In that moment I saw him as a dedicated, caring medic, anxious to soothe and calm not just a wounded soldier, but also anything that was hurting. I experienced another pang of guilt, because clearly, it was my fault that the lizard was hungry.

"He can't climb trees, he's temporarily crippled," I said.

"Then it's up to you to feed him. I'd say you've found yourself a pet," he returned.

I could visualize the smug smile I couldn't see, but knew was there, as his head bent over the small, black, wiggling body.

"Pet? Who makes a pet out of a tiny forest denizen like that?"

"You do. You were the one that hurt him. Now it's your duty to feed him, and to help him get better. You have no choice, those are the rules."

"Rules? Whose rules?"

He looked up into my face and I saw what might have been tears filming his eyes. Lord, what this man must have seen over there, I thought. And here he's worried about this one tiny little lizard.

As if reading my mind, he said, "I couldn't do anything about injustice over there, here I can."

I sighed, and slumped in defeat. He had me there. "Okay, what do I have to do?"

He smiled and held the lizard up to my face. I squealed and jumped back. Then he reached out and grabbed my hand and drew me back. "First, you give him a name, that honors him and makes him yours. Then you touch him to show you care. And then you feed him."

I gulped. "Are you really going to make me do this?" I whispered.

"Yes," he whispered back, "I am. I most certainly am."

I just stood there looking at the lizard that was now circling his palm and wandering over the edge of his thumb.

"A name . . ." he prompted.

I hesitated and said the first thing that came to mind. "Stumpy."

"Okay, that works. I've actually known a few amputees that answered to that name."

I knew then that he was deadly serious, and that this wasn't a game. Stumpy was my new pet, my companion until his tail decided to make a grand re-emergence.

"Touch him . . ."

"I can't. I just can't." I tried to work up a shiver to show my revulsion, but he didn't give me a chance. His hand still gripping mine, forced it open and dropped the lizard into it. "If you drop him, he'll probably die," he warned. Every impulse I had came to life, with gut-wrenching fear. I had to tense every muscle to inhibit my desire to sling the beast far, far away. I stopped breathing and lowered widened eyes to my open hand. Then an odd thing happened, Stumpy looked up at me and blinked, and I calmed. I watched him crawl around and actually enjoyed the tickling feeling his tiny feet made against the pads of my palm. Then I felt something wet and slimy slither out of him. If Connor had not grabbed my wrist, that lizard would have ended up at the bottom of Crater Lake. As it was, we were struggling, the three of us, to keep Stumpy from falling four feet to the hard ground.

"Good, I was afraid he wouldn't be able to do that anymore, so it was only his tail that was affected. That's great news." Connor slid him from my hand to his, and I ran for the closest water spigot. I shoved my hand under the hard spray, not caring that my dress was getting splattered. I let the water run until I was sure there was no evidence of the thin black turd that had just been gifted to me.

"If you're going to have a pet, you can't be squeamish about the messes they make."

I wanted to hit him over the head with my purse, and he knew it. He gave a hearty laugh and tried to hand him back to me.

"No way. Un unh."

"Well you've named him, and touched him, now it's time to feed him."

"And pray tell, just how do I do that?"

"I think you have to catch some bugs for him."

"Are you trying to ruin my dinner?"

He laughed again. "Here, I'll help you. I see some lightning bugs over there. That ought to do for now."

"How many does he need?" I asked as I followed him closer to the trees.

"I really don't know, but more than usual I'm sure, after all, he has a mighty long tail to grow back."

"Here, take him while I catch a few bugs."

Given the choice of either holding him or catching bugs, I tentatively eased my hand out. But before I could connect with Connor's, the lizard jumped; he actually jumped onto my hand. I stood there amazed as it crawled back and forth, pumped the flesh of my thumb like a cat trying to flatten a pillow, and sniffed at my fingers while Connor caught bugs.

I wondered what would happen if I dropped to my knees and put my hand on the ground. Surely he'd scamper off. *And would that be such a bad thing?* I bent my knees.

"Don't even think about it," Connor said. "He's your responsibility now."

I straightened. I had to admit he was right. And besides, I didn't want to disappoint Connor. He was a decent, all-American guy, and Diana could do a whole lot worse. I certainly had.

An hour later, I sat with Stumpy nestled in a small storage bin. There was a jar of fireflies on the kitchen counter—the leftovers from Stumpy's dinner. Fifteen had been more than ample. I was tempted to let the others go, until I remembered that he'd be hungry in the morning, and then where would I be?

I turned back to my laptop and started typing an e-mail to Brick. I told him about my dinner with Connor, Connor's dilemma regarding Diana, and the pet that had been morally thrust upon me by him. Had I re-read my missive before sending it, I might have noticed that I had overdone the use of the word "Connor."

I found out at four in the morning that Brick had noticed that fact, and had reacted unfavorably to what he perceived as a challenge toward my attentions.

Chapter Seven

Ironically, I was sleeping soundly; not something I often did in the wee hours of the morning. But the incessant tapping of a key on my bedroom window finally jolted me awake. I sat up, ran my hand through my hair, and attempted to get my bearings. Often I still awoke and questioned my surroundings. For almost seven years I had lived in a master bedroom so sumptuous that it was on three levels; my current bedroom could not even do justice to one of the closets from my former life.

Shaking my head, I quickly registered who I was, where I was, and what that continual, irritating tapping sound was. I lifted the shade, pulling first the room darkening one up before the lighter, light emitting one, as I had found you had to be Hercules to pull them both up at one time.

Brick's stern upturned face greeted me from the ground; his fingers were gripping the back of a small flashlight he was using to tap on the window. He stopped as I managed to get the blind up. I smiled, and was taken aback when he didn't return it. With the hand holding the flashlight, he jerked his thumb toward the front of the RV, indicating I should go open the door for him. Despite his grim countenance, I hopped off the bed and ran for the door. My heart was doing triple time. No matter the reason,

I was delighted he was here.

He was there when I opened the door and then up the step and into the RV before I could fully step back from the door. An arm, hard and masterful, snaked out and encircled my waist like a band of steel, and he brought me in close to his body. I could smell that delightful woodsy cologne I liked so much; it was at once elegant and all male, and I knew I would never smell it again without thinking of him. I noticed him take a deep breath and wondered if he was scenting me, too. The thought was some kind of erotic.

In a voice husky and deep, he informed me that, "You are mine. I may not be able to do anything about it, because on both sides of the fence, there are still things that need to be ironed out, but never doubt that you are mine. I want you and I am staking my claim. So, tell your soldier boy to back off and go home, you hear me?"

My eyes were wide, taking in the words spoken so gruffly, with a command that brooked no insubordination of any kind.

"He's not my soldier. For God's sake Brick, he's just a kid."

"He's twenty-three, graduated college at age twenty as a Rhode's Scholar, and has a very bad habit of running stop signs."

I was continually amazed at Brick's resources. "A Rhode's Scholar, huh?" I was impressed, and since I knew that had not been Brick's aim, I couldn't help needling him. "Wow, that's really something, he's apparently very smart then."

"He's not smart enough to take you away from *me.*" His arm around my waist tightened and then his lips lowered. In the meager glow from the nightlight in the refrigerator door, I saw bright flinty shards in his eyes. The thought occurred to me that this was a man set to make a conquest, as he paused to rake me from head to toe. "You forgot your panties," he murmured as his mouth captured my lips. While his lips crushed and masterfully took mine, I remembered that I had on my usual bedroom attire, consisting of only a soft t-shirt—a concession to my health-minded mother who insisted that a woman's privates needed a nightly airing. As his firm lips urged mine to open to his, I felt the hand around my waist loosen and slide up my back taking a fistful of t-shirt with it in an effort to uncover more of my bare bottom.

Mortified that Brick had seen evidence that I was pantyless, I managed to free a hand and tug my shirt down. I could feel his chuckle as his teeth nibbled at my bottom lip, then soothed it with his tongue. His hand continued its soft caress up my side and to my shoulder, and from there to my neck and cheek, while his other hand followed a similar path on the other side, until my face was in a firm vise between both hands. Rapturous kisses rained on my lips as he held my face close to his. Inch by languorous inch, he threaded those long, capable fingers into my hair. My lips were captive to both his gentle and savage kisses while he took possession of my mouth. I whimpered from the onslaught and felt my knees soften. All I could think was that I wanted to be swept off my feet; I wanted to be prone, under him with his pelvis grinding into me. It was as if he was reading my thoughts because I was suddenly gathered into his arms and carried sideways through the hallway toward my bedroom in the back.

As I was gingerly placed on my mussed, still warm-to-the-touch bed, I was keenly aware that one hand was supporting my back, while the other was hugging me tightly behind my knees. Within seconds of being deposited all that changed. The hand behind my knees slid under my t-shirt to grasp my hip, fully exposing me, while the other slid up to cup the back of my head. He lowered his body over mine, matching each body part to a corresponding one of mine. I felt the stiff fabric of his jeans covering me and abrading my thighs, his zipper placket, and all that was behind it, was pressing into my mons. And oh, did he grind himself into me. It was a testament to the bed that it was well made because it did not creak or groan, although Brick most assuredly did. The RV, on its stabilizing jacks, shuddered at about the same time I did. I could hardly believe that the simple act of him pressing himself against me so intimately had made me come.

"Let that be a lesson to you," he whispered, as he looked down into my slumberous face and kissed the tip of my nose.

"Oh, I've learned my lesson all right." I pushed a curl off his brow.

He chuckled and ran a finger down my cheek. "I wish I could stay. I could give you a few more *lessons,* but I've got to get back. I left my team five hours away, setting up surveillance at a rally."

"You just got here."

"This was not a planned trip. I just had to see you and to impress upon you my feelings in this matter." To emphasize his words, he pressed his hips into my pelvis again. I felt those wonderful stirrings begin to fire up again.

"Oh, I'm impressed."

"Be sure you stay that way. Now, just where is this Corporal O'Reilly? I need to have a word with him before I head back."

"You don't have to worry, I'm kind of stuck on you at the moment."

"I believe that leaving Connor O'Reilly with a healthy dose of fear, garnered from a swaggering suitor toting a gun, would be in my best interests."

"Swaggering?"

"It's only because of your recent history that I don't take you right now and settle any future issues, but he doesn't need to know I haven't had you yet."

His lips sucked on my bottom lip, when he pulled on it until it released I asked, "Is that important?"

"A man will hesitate to take a woman if she's accommodating someone else, especially if that man has made it known he intends her to continue doing the same." He paused for effect, "However, one who hasn't, ummm . . . succumbed shall we say, can be considered still available in the weird ass way that men think. In other words, you'd still be up for grabs."

"Hmmm. Interesting, these mating rituals."

"I *will* mate with you," he whispered hoarsely, as his lips followed the line of my jaw to my ear. "And you will be very accommodating, won't you?" he prompted.

I laughed as he tickled me and began a chorus of, "Won't you? Won't you? Won't you?" that alternated with me saying, "I'll think about it," "Maybe I will," and finally my surrender with, "Yes! Yes!"

He left me moments later to find Corporal O'Reilly, which caused me a few seconds of consternation, because I did not remember telling him where he could be found.

Chapter Eight

The sun came up as I lolled on the sofa watching Stumpy doze in his plastic terrarium. In an effort to make it homey, I had found a few small rocks and twigs he could climb on, and unearthed a swatch-sized section of moss to fool him into thinking he was outside. It could have been my imagination, but it seemed to me that his tail was already showing signs of re-growth. Or was I just anxious to be done with my latest houseguest?

Stumpy didn't chatter and run on about everything imaginable, as Angelina had, which I dearly missed; but then she hadn't required anything more than Cheerio's for breakfast either.

The fireflies in the jar had not made it through the night and I didn't know whether I should feed them to him or not. I reasoned that people food was killed prior to our even buying it, so I dumped them in and waited to see what he would do when he awoke.

I made some coffee and took some into the bathroom where I forced myself to shower. I was reluctant to wash off the last vestiges of Brick's cologne. As long as I could smell him, it made me feel warm and sappy, and giddily aroused. The man had done little more than press me into the mattress and

I'd had an orgasm that had lit up the back of my eyes like a kaleidoscope. And he'd left without even taking his pleasure in me. In the world I was from, that was unheard of. It was odd to think that his needs had not only not come first, but that he'd foregone them entirely.

Jared would never have allowed such a thing. He had trained me to secure his release before even trying to seek out my own. Often, I didn't have the heart for it after what he put me through. The scenarios, where I was either his captive or his adolescent student, had left me cold and emotionless, and the farthest thing from feeling sexy that I could possibly imagine. Reaffirmed that I had done the right thing by leaving Jared, I put all thoughts of him aside.

The idea of taking a boat ride on the lake suddenly appealed to me so I dressed in capris and a sweater and went to see about both my breakfast and Stumpy's. He was awake, but he wasn't having anything to do with the dead fireflies. I had expected as much. Great, I would get to go bug hunting before enjoying my own breakfast.

I opened the door and stepped off the step just as Connor stepped out of his Jeep at the edge of the road. He had a small container in his hand and waved with it. I watched him as he walked down the worn pathway. He really was young looking. He and Diana sure had that in common; they both looked like kids on a high school varsity team.

"First, I want you to know that this is not a gift, that you should not attach any romantic sentiments to it whatsoever."

"Brick found you?"

"Oh yeah. He makes Diana's father look like Ozzie Nelson."

"What'd he say?" I was curious to say the least.

"Off limits—head on a pike—entrails entrailing . . . things like that."

I smiled and tenderly said what I was thinking, "What a sweet guy."

"Yeah, right!"

"So what's the gift?"

"Chiggers, aphids, lady bugs, roly-polys, a few spiders—a real smorgasbord. For the critter," he added as if I needed that spelled out.

"Well aren't you thoughtful. I was just about to go scavenging. He apparently doesn't like leftovers, especially once they've died."

He chuckled and handed me the container before turning to go. Impulsively, I blurted out, "You want to go down to the lake and take a boat tour?"

"What about Medieval Man?"

"He didn't say we couldn't be friends. I never thought we were going to be anything else anyway, did you?"

"Hell no!"

Well that hurt my feelings. "Why not?"

"Correct me if I'm wrong, but as you've been married, and are now *clearly* involved, you're probably not a virgin. I'm looking for a virgin."

I blinked wide at that. "You're not serious?"

"Yeah. I am."

"You know you're really limiting your choices. There are probably only a handful of virgins on the planet. And isn't that, uh . . . pretty arrogant, using the old double standard and all?"

"No. I'm a virgin. And so is Diana. We both pledged abstinence in high school. It's one of the things I love about her, her sense of self worth and piety."

Miffed with the unfavorable comparison, I tossed out, "Well, I was a virgin when I married."

"Bully for you. No offense, but now look at you, technically you're an adulterer."

Ah, so Brick *had* embellished, if not outright defined our supposed relationship by insinuating, or actually stating, that things were further along than they were. I wasn't about to contradict him for there was no point. "Do you want to go for a boat ride or not?"

"Are you going to try to toss me over board?" he asked with a widening grin.

"Possibly."

Chapter Nine

It took us a while to get down to the lake, but once we were on the water it was worth it. We were anxious to get part way out so we could look up at the sides of the crater and get some perspective. While admiring the scenery all around us we were nonstop with our queries about each other. I learned more about Diana than I knew about my own sister, and after a while I finally opened up a little about Jared. Until then, Connor thought I was just a divorcee striking out on her own. Now he knew I was haunted and hunted. We joked that maybe Jared would be able to find Diana for Connor.

I thought of several things we could look into to try to find Diana. I knew there was a registry for class rings, in case they became lost or stolen, but Connor had already called Josten's and had no luck. He'd even contacted the company who'd taken her class picture; they still had her previous address on file. He'd called all the dentists in the area where she'd lived, and managed to locate her dentist, but they had no forwarding address. He knew who her medical doctor was, as she'd joked once that his name was Dr. Flew, but his office staff wouldn't even talk to him because of the H.I.P.P.A. regulations. It seemed hopeless.

After two hours we'd both had enough sun and decided

to call it a day. Our muscles were cramped from walking back up the side of the mountain to the rim, the equivalent of 65 flights of stairs. We were walking toward a concession stand when I froze. Not ten feet in front of me were neighbors from my old, very exclusive neighborhood in Great Falls, Virginia, Jocelyn and Gene Abramson. And it was too late to duck them. I saw the moment they recognized me, and then the moment they realized what this could mean to them. In cartoons they draw dollar signs in big, wild eyes—Jocelyn and Gene's expressions were as close to that as I was ever likely to see outside of animation. As far as I knew, the hefty reward for information leading Jared to me was still being offered. I pasted a smile on my face and pretended everything was as normal as it could possibly be.

"Debbie!" Jocelyn called out, putting her arms out for a hug.

"I'm all sweaty," I said as I backed out of the full embrace. "We just came off the lake and made that steep climb."

"Really?" She looked directly at Connor, expecting an introduction. I wasn't about to give her one.

"It's quite beautiful here isn't it?" I said, trying very hard to figure out how to play this. Gene shook Connor's hand and leaned in to give me a kiss on the cheek. Then the silence became awkward.

Gene cleared his throat. "You know, Jared is pretty upset about . . ." He obviously didn't know what else to say.

It would be pointless to explain anything to these people. They'd never believe me for one, and two, since they ran in the same circles as Jared, who had a lot of influence in our little community, it would be hard for them to accept that he was less than stellar, and practically impossible to accept that he was an abuser with carnal appetites that would compete with a world-class hedonist.

So I just shrugged and said I was sorry I had to leave without saying goodbye. They asked where I was staying, where I was going next, and what I was doing here in Oregon.

I answered all their questions with lies, instantly made up and obviously insincere. I said we had to go, and Jocelyn and I fake-cheek kissed. Then I grabbed Connor's hand and together we fast walked toward the parking lot. Connor looked behind us as we turned down a path leading behind the gift shop.

"He's using his cell phone. And she's looking in her purse for something."

"We've got to get out of here without them seeing us."

"Too late, they're following."

"Jared must be telling them to keep track of us. What am I going to do?" I was afraid to get Connor involved, yet unsure what I could do on my own without any transportation.

"I think you're being ridiculous about this, but I have an idea," he said as he pulled me along with him.

Minutes later, we were in the parking lot asking a Mom and Pop couple if they could take us down to Mazama Village, as our vehicle had run out of gas. We really did look wholesome, and the way we were dressed didn't allow for too many surprises. Idiotically, I wondered if Connor had a virgin card he could flash.

They hesitated for just a moment before saying, "Sure thing."

We hopped into the back seat of their Buick, and as we exited the parking lot, we looked out the window and waved to the Abramsons, who had just come running around the corner. We watched as Jocelyn wrote down the tag number, then asked the older couple where they were from. They said they were headed back to Minnesota in the morning and we told them we hoped they had a wonderful, uneventful ride home. I didn't think it would be uneventful, but I didn't think they would be put out too much when Jared showed up demanding to know where I was.

They dropped us off at the Mazama Village gas pump and Connor paid a tow truck driver fifty dollars to tow his Jeep from the parking lot to the Village Store. We sat on a bench in the office hiding from view in case the Abramsons happened to drive by.

I was scared, but was trying not to show it. Connor smiled apologetically, and with a sheepish grin, commented that it was pretty ironic that I was trying to hide from someone while he was trying to find someone. He was so obviously in love that it pained me to look at him. I was more determined than ever to help him find his Diana.

Chapter Ten

When the Jeep was towed into the Village and taken off the lift, Connor drove me home. I surprised him when I asked him for an umbrella before getting out of the car.

"The sun is shining full bright, why do you need an umbrella?"

"To get inside my RV without being spotted."

"You are beginning to sound like a loon. I would think an umbrella open on a clear day like this would certainly make you more noticeable."

"Just humor me, please." He fished around in a bag on the back seat and handed me an Army issue umbrella in camouflage earth tones. It had apparently seen lots of use, as it was bleached out by the sun in several places.

"Perfect," I said as I took it from him. I opened the door just enough to pop open the umbrella. "Wait a few minutes and follow me. I don't imagine they have a good description of you. Here, this'll help," I said as I grabbed his hat from above the visor and shoved it onto his head.

"Lady, you are wacko."

"I'll explain more inside, but trust me, this is necessary."

I made my way quickly to the door of the RV, scampering under the awning the last few feet before hurriedly dropping the umbrella and using the key so I could get inside. A few minutes later Connor followed, tripping over the umbrella and up the steps.

"You know, you're doing a very bad *Bourne Identity* scenario here. Aren't you taking this obsessive husband thing a bit far?"

"I know this is hard for you to understand, but Jared has money, and friends in high-tech places. And my gut tells me that he hasn't given up. The fact that those two were on the phone before we even turned the corner, and then came looking for us should tell you something."

I did not want to mention the reward. It was a lot of money and could be life altering for most anyone, and since I really didn't know Connor well enough to discount him being tempted by it, I kept my mouth shut.

"The umbrella?" he prompted by waving it in front of my face.

"You were in the Army, surely you know all about satellites and spy-in-the-sky technology. Now that he knows I'm in the area, he'll be able to use Google Earth, or programs like it, to try to find me."

"You've got to have some pretty sophisticated equipment to do that, and government connections."

"Believe me, he has both."

"And you really think he's going to go to all this trouble and expense to find you, just for you to inform him you're not interested in going home with him?"

"You don't understand. He's not about to ask me anything. When no one's around, he'll suddenly appear and then *I'll* disappear. And no one will ever see me again."

He shook his head, "And you don't think you're being a bit over dramatic here?"

I started to answer him but my words were drowned out

by a series of loud thumping sounds accompanied by vibrations that shook the RV. For a military man the sound was instantly recognizable, and for Connor in particular, just back from the war, it triggered something in him. "Choppers Overhead!" he yelled as he grabbed me and threw me on the kitchen floor.

We lay there on the floor, him covering my legs and back, his hands crossed over my head as we listened. There were two distinct rotors causing alternating vibrating sensations that I could feel to my teeth, as both helicopters flew low enough to fan the branches of the trees and to cause great clouds of dust and to billow up to the windows around us. Singularly, they swept the campsite, hovering and then moving on as if examining each unit as they went. Then they were gone.

"What do you suppose that was all about?" Connor asked as he stood up and pulled me with him.

I gave him an I-told-you-so look and shrugged sheepishly.

"Nah! That couldn't be . . ."

"I'm telling you, it was. Fortunately, he thinks I still have the old RV, and that's probably what they're looking for. So for now, I'm safe. I just can't leave the RV."

"It's supposed to rain for the next two days anyway."

"Great! Good thing I've got some movies on DVD and some new books."

"I'll bring you food and whatever else you might need."

"That's sweet Connor, I really appreciate it, but you really need to concentrate on finding Diana."

"I know, I just don't have a clue where to start." He sat on the sofa and his whole body sagged as he bent forward and covered his face with his hands. "I find the one woman who's meant for me, and then I lose her. How did this happen?"

His frustration was palpable and I wanted so much to be able to help him. He left a few minutes later, totally dejected, and I settled in to watch movies and eat frozen Asian dinners.

I was enjoying the classics, running through my small

collection of Hepburn favorites, trying to decide which one to watch when something on the cover of Breakfast at Tiffany's made me freeze just as I was inserting the DVD. I sat back on my heels on the bed and stared at the picture—Audrey in very fashionable clothes. Fashion, one of the things that was of utmost importance to young high school girls. Diana . . . just what had she been wearing in that picture? I had seen it, even stared at it for several minutes at a time over the last two days. What was it? The parka, yes, there was something about the parka. I tried to picture the logo. Was it one I was familiar with, but had not readily recognized? Just what the hell was it? I eased back and closed my eyes and tried to conjure up the picture in my mind. Everything came to me in snatches, like pieces of a quilt coming together. The snow on the ground, the snowman, her cute little hat, the hand hiding the snowball, the endearing smile, the North Face parka . . . I sat straight up and whooped. I knew how to find her. I suddenly knew exactly how to find Diana.

Chapter Eleven

"You're saying she couldn't have bought this in a store?"
Connor said.

We were in my RV, sitting on the sofa, staring at Connor's
one and only picture of Diana.

"Well she could have, but it's not likely."

"And why not?"

"She's tall, she has long arms and a long torso, and she's
wearing it loose, not snug across her chest. She would most
likely wear a large. The stores just don't stock many larges,
everything stylish is for 2's and 4's these days, basically your
small to medium gals."

"So how'd she get it?"

"I'm betting she ordered it, online. It's sometimes the
only way to get the color you want in the size you want. If
memory serves this was a hot item a few winters ago, the stores
were probably sold out of most colors and styles. If she was
particular, she would have had to go online to get the jacket she
wanted."

"You're sure of this?"

"I used to wear only couture. But now I'm a Mart Girl,
K-mart, Wal-Mart, Steinmart." I laughed at my own joke. "So

no, I'm not sure anymore." Then I pointed to the picture and the Juicy Couture hat. "But this girl obviously isn't a Mart Girl. Most stores that carry expensive, trendy clothes like these can't afford to carry too many different sizes. So, yes, that leaves online shopping, so I'm betting that she's in the North Face data bank."

"Yeah, but we already know her old address, the address they must have shipped this jacket to."

"That's true, but we women are brand loyal. Once we find a product we like, one that looks good on us, we stick to it until something better comes along. In this price range, I don't know of any other company that's cornering the market on this type of product. And they sell lots of other things girls her age would like."

"So you think she's reordered since moving?"

"Young girls gotta have cool clothes. I'm willing to wager that your Diana has ordered some summer duds, and maybe even some back to school things for the fall."

"Okay, let's say she has. How does that help?"

"We just need to get her address from North Face."

"Do you plan to hack into their database?"

"No, silly. I just need to call and pretend to be her and to order something. They'll verify the shipping address as one of the very first things."

"They don't require a passcode?"

"Yeah, if you do it online; instead I'll just call."

I hopped up to get my laptop so I could go online and get the customer service number for ordering. "But first, I have to pick out something to buy."

I logged onto the website and selected two fairly expensive outfits. Then I found the 800 number and punched it into my cell. Moments later I was writing down Diana Jones' address in Providence, Rhode Island.

After disconnecting the phone I handed the paper to Connor with a big grin on my face, "It looks like she's going to

Brown in the fall."

He picked me up and spun me around while we whooped and hollered. Then he tripped and lost his balance, and we both fell onto the sofa still laughing. At that exact moment the door to the RV opened and Jared stepped in.

Chapter Twelve

"Get off of my wife!"

Connor, half on top of me, supporting himself by his arms, looked over his shoulder at the man who had just barged in—my husband. I cringed and felt a shiver of fear move along my spine when I saw the furious eyes of an enraged and insanely jealous man, the man I had finally managed to run away from, partly for this very reason.

Connor must have sensed the extreme seriousness of the situation for he gently eased himself up off of me and backed up two steps before turning to face Jared. On his way to standing up, he had taken a quick moment to meet my eyes and to convey a most puzzling look, but one that showed absolutely no fear at all. I wondered briefly if that could be because he had already challenged the dragons of terror in Iraq. I was to quickly learn that he had nothing to fear from this man, or most any man for that matter.

Jared advanced toward Connor, his fists clenched at his sides and anger undulating from him in waves. It was almost palatable, the fierceness that emanated from him and I was instantly up and trying to shield Connor from Jared's burgeoning wrath. As Jared continued to advance on Connor, Connor nudged me aside and not too gently either. I could feel his muscles had tensed so he'd had no choice. If there was going to be a confrontation, and apparently there was, Connor had already steeled himself to take on the battle.

I watched in horror as Jared reached out and grabbed Connor's throat. Then things happened so fast that I honestly couldn't say what happened next, other than hands flew and fists flailed and legs and elbows connected. It all happened in less than thirty seconds. Thirty seconds of hardly any sound at all, just a few grunts and one or two smacking sounds. I blinked, and then stared, my mouth agape. Jared was on the floor unconscious. Connor was standing over him, his hiking boot grinding into his chest.

"What do you want me to do with this *husband* of yours?"

I gulped. Connor appeared to be used to having the upper hand and seemed unlikely to relinquish control until this latest enemy was either vanquished or dispatched.

"Is he dead?"

"Do you want him to be?"

"Uh, no. This isn't Iraq, you can't just kill him."

"He attacked me, and yes, I can. Just say the word."

"Let's just get him out of here."

"What, so he can keep harassing you?"

"You don't need a murder trial right now. Think of Diana, or better yet, her father."

"So, what do you suggest?"

"He needs medical attention. We need to take him to a hospital."

"You're kidding, right? The man is out to get you, wants nothing better than to capture you and do you harm, and you want to just let him go, better yet, nurse his wounds?"

"I don't know what to do!" I wailed.

There was a loud moan and Jared's head flopped to the side. Connor kicked him under the jaw and he fell silent again.

"We don't have a lot of time here, make up your mind."

"Let's get him into his car, or whatever he came here in, and take him to the nearest emergency center or ranger station."

" Good idea. You follow in my Jeep, we'll dump him and leave."

The callousness in his voice unnerved me. "Why the sudden intense anger?"

"I didn't believe you before, now I do. This guy is scum. I'd rather break his neck and send him toppling down the mountain."

"We can't do that," I whispered, "and you know it. He's not someone who can just disappear. You heard the helicopters; there have to be plenty of people who know where he was heading. They had to have brought him here."

"So, we need some answers." He knelt down, pulled Jared up by his collar and slapped his face back and forth until Jared opened his eyes.

"How did you know she was here?" he hollered at Jared, whose head bobbed and swayed while he tried to keep it up, as if he was trying to make sure it didn't fall off his neck. His eyes were dazed and he did not appear to know where he was.

"Who?" he asked with a thick tongue.

"Her," he said, pointing up at me, "your wife."

Jared looked at me as if he had never seen me before, his eyebrows raised as he studied me with the most perplexed look on his face. "Do I know you?" he asked, just before his eyes crossed and his head fell onto his chest.

"He's out again. He definitely has a concussion and quite possibly amnesia, the best of all possible scenarios. Let's get him as far away from here as we can. But first, let's see if he has anything on him that'll tell us how he found you."

I watched as Connor emptied his pockets, pulling them inside out and displaying the contents on the carpet. I half expected to see some kind of high-tech tracking device, as that was how he had managed to find me before. But his pants pockets only yielded a set of keys to a rental car, his large ostentatious gold money clip with large bills folded under the clip, a folding card case with charge cards in it and a comb. Connor pulled a single folded sheet of notepaper from Jared's dress shirt pocket. Written in Jared's bold hand was a phone number.

"This mean anything to you?"

He held it up and I looked at it. Then I read the numbers out loud. They looked familiar but I couldn't place them.

"I think that's a Texas area code."

"Of course! That's Daniel and Julia's number. I just spoke with them a few days ago."

"From what phone?"

"My cell. But it's not one that has that GPS tracking feature."

"How do you know?"

"The clerk at the mini-mart where I bought it told me so. She didn't hesitate when I asked; she seemed like she knew what she was talking about."

"And you believed her?"

"Why wouldn't I?"

He just shook his head, "How long were you on the phone when you called Daniel? Over three minutes?"

"Oh yeah. I talked to Angelina for at least five."

"Well, there you have it. That's how he found you."

"Then why the helicopters?"

"That was probably just to get him close where he had a car waiting."

"So we can find the helicopters and get them to take him to a trauma center."

"Not likely. They'd have to be miles away in this terrain. They could be anywhere by now. C'mon, let's just get him someplace where he's somebody else's problem." He took off Jared's belt, tied it tightly around his hands and propped him up against the sofa. Then Connor turned and stooped in front of Jared, his back to him, his feet straddling Jared's legs. He reached back, positioned Jared's joined hands around his neck and began to stand with Jared's arms looped around his neck. Halfway up he bent and arched his back and settled Jared's body against his broad back. It was obvious that he'd done this many times before. It was then that I remembered that Connor had been a medic in the Army. Of course he'd done this often, but probably not in a situation such as this. "Get the door will ya? And grab his car keys."

"What about the rest of the stuff?"

"That's up to you."

I could have used the money, and I would certainly have enjoyed a shopping spree with the credit cards before the accountant or security caught on, but it just wouldn't have been right. I had run away from him and all he had to offer. It didn't feel right to take anything that belonged to him. I had cut those ties and I was now independent. I picked everything up and shoved it all back into his pockets as Connor dragged him toward the door.

"Help me get him into his car then follow in my Jeep. I've got a map that should point us toward the nearest medical center or hospital."

When we got Jared belted into the back seat of his rented Cadillac STS we discovered it was equipped with an in-dash GPS monitor. Connor verbalized his request. After finding out that the nearest hospital was over two hours away, he looked over at me. "We're going to plan two."

"What's that?"

"We get a reasonable distance away and I use the OnStar system to send for help for him, then we turn tail in the Jeep, hiako back here and regroup."

I nodded. It sounded like a good plan for us, and probably the best one for Jared; he'd get the help he needed a lot quicker that way.

I followed Connor for twenty-five minutes, five miles

past a ranger station. He pulled off into a deserted picnic area and I sat and watched as he pressed a button in the overhead console. Moments later Connor got out of the car, closed the door of the Cadillac using a torn piece of Jared's shirt, and walked back to where I sat in the Jeep, sweat poring out of me despite the air conditioning being set on high. I straddled the gearshift and slid into the passenger seat so he could drive. I was completely unnerved and didn't want to do anything but sit and shake.

"Well that ought to get somebody rushing here fairly quickly, I told OnStar assistance that I was having a heart attack."

"What about his bruises and his split lip?"

"A man can't have a heart attack after getting beat up?" he flashed a smile over at me as he belted himself in and turned around before pulling back onto the road, heading toward the campground.

"Speaking of which, how did you do that?" Clearly there was awe in my voice and he seemed pleased.

"Hand-to-hand combat. The Army teaches you how to defend yourself. I was a proficient student, in fact, I was an instructor for a while, until someone got my Irish up and I damned near killed him."

"Sounded like you wanted to do that this time."

"Oh yeah, I did. Not happy you stopped me either. He'll get better, and come lookin' again." His voice had changed; it had softened with a husky brogue. I sensed this was happening because he was upset and more unnerved than he cared to show.

"You okay?"

"Yeah, you?" he asked as he reached over, took my hand and squeezed it.

"I'm mad at myself for making such a stupid mistake with the cell phone."

"I don't believe you can buy a cell phone these days that doesn't have that capability." There was quiet for a few minutes as we both tried to sort out our thoughts.

"I'm sorry I didn't believe you," he whispered. "It just sounded like such a weird story."

"So I hope you appreciate my timely demonstration," I said with a chuckle.

"Hmph, now what?"

"Well, you go find Diana, there's no point in you hanging around and getting messed up in this. If Jared comes around, he might be able to describe you. It would be best if you got far, far away from here and Rhode Island sure fits that bill."

"Yeah, that it does. It's amazing that you found her like that. I would never have thought of it."

"Well, we girls like to look nice for the men in our lives, or the men we'd like to *have* in our lives."

"I feel badly about leaving you alone now."

"I'm not alone. I have Stumpy to keep me company."

He smiled and let out a long sigh. "Okay, I'll go. But first I'll help you straighten out the mess I made in your RV. I think we may have knocked over a few things and I'll catch a few more bugs for you, too."

"That would be greatly appreciated."

We heard a siren off in the distance and we both closed our eyes hard before blinking them back open.

"I hope he has amnesia for the rest of his life," Connor said. "That way at least he won't remember you and keep hunting you down."

"And I hope he doesn't ever remember you or what you did to him."

"Nothing permanent, if you don't include the head thing." We both laughed at the ludicrous statement.

"If he does remember, he'll be looking for two of us, so I'm glad you're getting out of here. When can you leave?"

"I'll drive to Portland and get a flight to the east coast. I just might leave tonight. I'm anxious to see Diana and find out if she still feels the same about me."

He pulled up in front of the path that led to my RV. "Do you think your neighbors saw me carry him?"

"No, they've been gone for a few days, took their car and went somewhere. But they sure can't say anything—what goes on with them is considerably weirder than what appeared to be two guys fighting over a woman."

"Yeah, you'll have to keep me posted on that."

"And you'll have to let me know what happens with you and Diana."

"I've got your e-mail, so I'll keep in touch."

We went into the RV together to clean the mess and to feed Stumpy. When we discovered that Stumpy's terrarium had been knocked over during the fight, I panicked. It was one thing to house and feed the lizard, it would be another to wake up with him crawling on top me.

Despite an hour of crawling on hands and knees we couldn't find him anywhere. I consigned myself to the fact that I would either run off the road one day when he ran up my leg while I was driving, or I would track him down by his tell-tale droppings that looked like an inch of pencil lead, with a white streak at the very tip. Fortunately I hadn't seen any in the RV yet, and as I was pretty obsessive about keeping my RV clean, I did not want to find any.

The place shipshape again, I hugged Connor good-bye, and told him I hoped to be introduced to his Diana one day. He promised to keep in touch and to let me know what happened when he found her on the other side of the continent. Then just before leaving he collected some ants for me. I could not believe I was bringing a container of ants into my house. How quickly one adapts, I thought, as I took them inside.

Chapter Thirteen

After Connor left I got the collapsible ladder out from under the RV, along with a bucket, sponge and extendable squeegee. I had intended to wash the RV in a day or two anyway, but the dust and leaf debris the helicopters had churned up made it absolutely necessary to do it now. When traveling I tried to clean the windshield fairly often so that the dead bugs wouldn't bake on but it was such a tiring job that I was never really up for it. Occasionally, I was lucky enough to find a truck stop that had a truck wash and then I would run the whole coach through.

As I was up on the ladder wiping away, I looked over at my neighbor's RV. There was something to be said for a sand-colored RV, even the windshield cover they had snapped on was camel-colored, so I doubted they'd even notice the grit until they got back on the road again.

I didn't know whether I should e-mail Brick or call him on my cell phone. Certainly I had to tell him about Jared. Trying to downplay the potential seriousness of my latest run-in with Jared, I opted for the former, and sat down with my computer in my lap to type a play-by-play for him.

Within an hour he replied, reminding me that he had told me about cell phones and how easily one could be traced. I knew that, as Brick himself had tracked me with one before. I just had no idea that what I considered to be a disposable, no-contract phone had the same kind of internal chip that allowed one to do that. Then he added a terse message about how quickly things could change, how different everything would be if Jared died. For a while, it was as if we were instant messaging each other as one message was sent and read and another appeared on the screen.

Brick: What happened to Connor? I don't suppose due to the circumstances, that you're going to tell me where he is now.

Jenny: We tracked down Diana and he's on his way east to find her.

Brick: East, I suppose that's all I'm going to get from you. You are clueless, you know that? What he's doing, what you HELPED him to do, is exactly what I fight against every single day—older men preying on teenagers. For God's sake Carrie, this is what I do! I go after the pedophiles—the predators!

Jenny: It's Jenny now, remember, you named me. And this isn't like that, they're in love.

Brick: That's what they ALL say. All the forty-something guys hanging out at the high school games. Do you think they're going to say they're horny bastards looking for nubile, young flesh?

Jenny: They're both adults now. Jenny is eighteen.

Brick: And that's the only reason I'm not arresting him and you for helping him find her.

Jenny: You having a bad day?

Brick: You're making it that way.

Jenny: Just because we're on the opposite side of the fence on this doesn't mean you have to be so angry with me.

```
Brick: Oh yes it does!
Jenny: Well, fine then. Goodnight!
```

I waited and waited for a reply, but I didn't get one. I grabbed a wine cooler from the fridge and made my way back to the bedroom. On the way back through the hallway, something caught my eye, something moving in the vicinity of the bathtub.

I saw something move through the wavy glass door that enclosed the tub and shower. It was dark and long. Putting my wine cooler on the counter by the sink, I slowly opened the shower door. It's designed to catch and hold fast, so it made a popping sound and caused a vibration I felt through my arm. Stumpy felt it too, and darted around the bottom of the tub. I had one option here if I was going to corral him, otherwise I'd be consigning him to free run of the house, and I really didn't think I wanted that. No, I was sure I didn't.

After several half-hearted tries where my hand jerked away at the last second, I had my hand over him. I could feel him twitching against my palm, Eewww. But actually, it wasn't so bad. His skin was dry, and although not smooth, not as lumpy as it looked. I managed to scoop him up off the floor of the tub and I held him in one palm while keeping the other hand ready in case he decided to dart off my fingers and become a lemming leaping over the cliff.

He was really kind of pretty, luminescent in the fluorescent light, his scales were multi-hued, mostly tan with a gray cast, with rows of vibrant blue and green speckles running down his back, converging to a single row and leading to the area of the missing tail. I ran a finger down his spine and cooed to him and watched as this horrible red thing under his chin grew and grew like a balloon ready to pop. It went down and then it blew up again. This continued for several minutes while I stood fascinated. Little did I know that he was proving himself to be all male.

Gingerly, I walked with him to the kitchen area where his makeshift terrarium was. I gently eased him down off my hand, onto the rock and sand bottom, filled his water bowl and introduced him to the ants. He was ravenous and I felt a bit guilty about covering him up with the top of the broiler pan so I could retrieve my wine cooler and slide into bed. But there was no way I was going to go outside and scout bugs for him. Tomorrow, I reasoned I would fashion a leash of some kind. That'll be a cute sight, me walking my lizard. I just had to chuckle. God, if Jared could see me now, he probably wouldn't even want me back.

It was a mistake to focus my thoughts in that direction, but now that I had, I was curious. I picked up my wine cooler, turned the TV to local news and got ready for bed. At eleven o'clock there was a news item on a Jared Jameson, who was found in his rental car, clearly having been in an altercation and having experienced what was first thought to have been a heart attack. Doctors confirmed that he had a concussion and that for the time being, his memory loss was so severe that he didn't know who he was, or why he was almost 3,000 miles away from his home. Anyone with information was to call the number running in a banner across the bottom of the screen.

So, he'd made it to the hospital in Klamath Falls; that was something. At least he was getting the best care, and with any luck, when and if his memory came back, the fact that I had once been his wife would be expunged from it.

I turned off the TV and snuggled against pillows propped against the headboard to read a few pages of my romance novel before nodding off. God I was tired, I thought as a big yawn took over and made a deep cavern of my mouth.

I read for a few minutes before I heard a loud commotion outside my bedroom window. Now what? I really didn't need any more aggravation today. I whipped up the blinds and glared out the window that faced the loop on my side of the village campground.

Outside there was an older man tugging on the arm of a

young woman. She was striking with her red hair and creamy white complexion and she was shouting, "No, I don't want to go in there! Please don't make me do this, please Daddy, don't! You can't make me, I won't do it!"

"You have no choice! And believe me, I know this isn't the worst thing you've ever done! Now stop it, and get in there!"

She looked up and saw me staring out the window as she squirmed and tried to get out of her father's firm grasp. She mouthed the word *Help* before he spun her around and forcefully pulled her toward the door of the RV.

Until that moment, I hadn't even realized that my neighbors were back. And up to their old tricks. What were they forcing this girl to do? What was her father forcing her to do? The first and only thought that came to mind was that they had to be shooting a porn movie in that luxury RV. The thought made me sick.

Well enough was enough. That girl didn't want to do whatever it was that was expected of her in that RV. I had to do something. I closed the blinds and ran for my phone. I hoped Brick was in a better mood, because his day wasn't over yet and there was still time for it to get a lot worse.

Chapter Fourteen

In less than an hour, pandemonium broke out in our little corner of paradise. There were cop cars, sheriff's vehicles, unmarked Fords, and over it all, a helicopter hovered until it found a place to land on a nearby road. Brick, and a few men from his team, had arrived from Carson City.

Ten minutes later, the luxury RV had been stormed and everyone was standing outside while officers searched for signs of any nefarious filming going on. Brick and I were in my kitchen and it was safe to say that his day had gotten a lot worse, except for the fact that we had actually begun a new day.

"Are you always going to be putting my job in jeopardy?" Brick lashed out at me.

"I'm sorry, I thought they were doing something wrong."

"Well, they weren't! They're just two teachers tutoring students. And they choose to do it in their RV because this is their summer vacation!"

"I said I'm sorry!"

"Sorry isn't good enough. Because of you, we've spent money bringing state and federal agents out here. You said you saw them taking clothes off a girl, and that she was screaming that she didn't want them to. You said both the man and the woman were holding her down, while another man stripped her. You led us to believe we had a child pornography case here. We dropped everything to get here."

"I thought that's what was happening. I really did. I can't tell you how sorry I am!"

Just before I had called Brick, in an effort to make sure I wasn't crying wolf, I had gone around to the other side of the neighbors' RV, and using a lawn chair I found there, I had peeked into a window that had a partially drawn shade. The girl's father and the woman *had* been trying to take off that girl's clothes. The other man had joined in when it appeared they weren't having any success with it.

Tears were streaming down my face now and I didn't know what to do. But I had to get out of there. I ran out the door and across the compound to the bathhouse. I had some major repair work to do on my face and hair. My mascara was smeared and my hair was half in, half out of the loose ponytail. I was miserable, and when I looked in the mirror while leaning on the sink, it was all I could do not to slump to the floor in a disheveled heap. I had really messed things up. Brick was furious and I would be lucky if the neighbors didn't press some kind of charges against me.

I heard a scuffle behind me, then a sniffing noise. I turned to see the cute little redhead huddled in the corner looking over at me. Her eyes were redder than mine and the tissue she held to her nose was shredding with her nervous fingers.

"It's you! You're the one I saw them abusing. You're the one who mouthed for me to help you. How did you get here?" I grabbed a hunk of paper toweling and went to kneel by her. I handed her fresh reserves to blot the run off. She was crying and sobbing big time now.

"I told them I was going to be sick. The policeman let me out and I ran. And I know he's out there, looking for me!"

"Who is *he*?"

"My father!"

"So it was your father helping them take your clothes off?" My eyes had popped wide and my stomach clenched from the disgusting thoughts that brought.

"Yes, I wouldn't cooperate. And he *had* spent a lot of money to get me here."

"Whoa, whoa. Are you saying your father brought you here so you could be in some kind of porn show?"

"What? No!" She swiped at her chin where tears had pooled, then she sniffed loudly. "I wasn't brought here to be in a porn flick!"

"I don't understand. What were they doing when I saw the three of them trying to get your shirt off?"

"They were trying to get the shirt!"

"Trying to get the shirt?" I clearly did not understand.

"Yes, they had to have it for that geeky, prissy girl."

I shook my head. Was this ever going to make sense? "The shirt? They had to have the shirt?"

"Yes. You have to wear the school uniform for the test. The shirt is part of the uniform; it's got the logo. They had the pants but they didn't have another shirt. You can't get in for the test if you don't meet the dress code."

This was getting harder and harder to navigate. "The test?"

"Yes! The test!" She was losing patience with me and I almost couldn't blame her. I had missed something here, something major.

"Okay, they needed your shirt, you didn't want them to take it, and they got it anyway. What did they do with it?"

"They gave it to her, the look-alike. The girl who was going to take the test for me."

Afraid I would sound senile, I asked anyway. "What test?"

"The entrance exam! The test to get into Stanford."

"Stanford in Palo Alto, California?"

"Is there another?" she asked sarcastically. I was losing her as an advocate, she was clearly distraught and I wasn't helping a bit.

"Okay sweetie, I think I have it now. These people you went to see, instead of coaching you to take the test, they brought someone in and made her look like you so she could take it for you?"

"Yes."

"And let me get this straight now . . . you were for it and then changed your mind?"

"I sort of wanted to go to Stanford. But I knew I wasn't good enough. I don't like school. I don't like to study. I just wanted to go to school there, you know, be one of the co-eds, go to parties, hang out with college kids, make a lot of friends."

"What changed your mind?"

"I found out I was pregnant the morning we left to come here."

"Ah ha. And I don't suppose you've told anyone."

"Nope."

"Any ideas what you want to do now?"

"I want to get married and have the baby."

"I take it this is not going to please your father."

"Oh no! He's going to kill me. He went to Stanford, my mother went to Stanford. And even with all their contributions, I can't get in if I don't pass that stupid test. But I don't want to go anymore. I never really did."

"Then you need to tell them that."

"Just like that, huh? Just go tell them. You don't know my parents, this is going to ruin them."

"I doubt that it will, but even so, it's better than ruining your life doing only what they want you to do. And with this new development, you're going to need their support more than ever."

"Support? They're going to disown me!"

"Kids always think their parents are worse than they are.

You have to give them a chance."

"I don't think so."

"What about the people here, they're breaking the law. What they're doing is not right. You need to tell someone, they have to be stopped."

"I don't care. And who would I tell?"

"Me." Brick walked into the bathroom and leaned on the wall.

"Who are you?" Visibly, I watched her shrink further into the corner.

Brick reached into his waistband and brought out his badge. He walked over, knelt before the cringing girl and let her read it.

She let out a heartfelt sigh. "I'm in big trouble, huh?" Then she started laughing, almost hysterically.

"Figures! The one time I stray with a boy, I get pregnant; the one time I stray from the straight and narrow, I get caught."

"There's a lesson there," Brick said as he helped her up, "don't stray."

"How much did you hear?" I asked Brick.

"All of it. I came running after you the minute you left." His eyes met mine and I could see he was trying to communicate his apology.

"So it wasn't all my imagination." I had to get one dig in. I just had to.

"No, I guess it wasn't." Being contrite didn't set well with Brick, I could see that. "I should stop doubting you. Although this is a far cry from a porn ring."

His hand on the girl's arm, the other on the small of my back, he led us from the bathhouse. "In fact, I'm not exactly sure if what your neighbors did was a crime."

"Oh, it has to be! They were cheating!" I said.

"No, technically, they weren't. However, they were paying others to commit fraud and to cheat. This is one for the D.A. to figure out; this is not where my field of expertise lies."

By the time we walked back to the campsite, a crowd had gathered. The girl's father was making wild hand gestures and it was quite apparent that he was not a happy camper. I noticed the girl trying to keep close to the side of the RV, where several officers of the law were congregating.

No less than six other agents were standing around, wondering just what the hell was going on. Brick tapped one on the shoulder and pointed to the girl while he gathered others behind my RV. I watched as he gestured, pointed, and then looked straight at me. Then he winked, and I knew everything was going to be all right. Except for the fluttering inside me that was making me all too aware of him as a man again.

Chapter Fifteen

It was a long time before everyone cleared out. The professor next door and his wife, both teachers as I had guessed, him at the college level, her at the high school level, had been arrested on charges of contributing to the delinquency of a minor, or some such nonsense that Brick said they'd have to define later. Their vehicle had been locked up and all the officers were disbanding. The girl and her father had an appointment with the judge, but for now were being sent home to deal with her other issues.

Brick, his hand around my waist, was whispering in my ear. "I am so sorry, I've been a real shit."

"Yeah, I know," I said as I looked up to smile at him.

"Well you're not going to like this either, but I have to go back on the chopper. But God if I didn't . . ." He leaned down and his lips kissed all along my neck, sending shivers down my spine and heat zinging through my veins.

"I could sneak around and siphon out the gas," I whispered into his hair.

"I don't doubt it, but we really have to get back. The rally starts tomorrow and I wouldn't want to miss running into ol' Snooks, of the two-color eyes. I have a good feeling about this rally, and we have lots of coverage, so I'm sure we're going to do well."

The "well" he was referring to, as I knew from previous conversations, was to find and arrest an assorted number of child predators, particularly the one who had his sister. The man with the odd colored eyes being the main target.

"It's an unfortunate side of RVing, but there is a disturbing element of society that took to the roads as soon it recognized that the camping atmosphere was ideal for pedophiles. It gave me a whole new job that I really wasn't looking for."

"I know, and I'm sorry about that. And I'm sorry about all this," I swept my hand around, indicating the RV next door and the different groups of men scattered about discussing procedure.

"Hey, you did good," he kissed my temple, "I'm sure the schools involved will be interested in how easily the system's been duped. Again, it seems we just can't stay ahead of the bad guys."

"That's okay, as long as you can catch up to them eventually. It seems there's a lot more of them than there are you good guys."

"Oh yeah, that's for sure. Hey, I gotta go. But you just don't know how much I want to stay, maybe show you how good a good guy I can be . . ." His lips were just below my ear now, I was melting and he knew it. Molten desire was surging through my blood creating frissons of heat everywhere, and I do mean everywhere. His arm tightened around my waist and he gave me a quick pat on my bottom. "I got plans for you babe, hang tight, and this time, try to stay out of trouble." A quick peck on the lips followed and off he went, his little entourage following behind him. They all piled into the cars and trucks lining the road and then he was gone again.

I don't think I have ever felt so alone in all my life. Brick was gone, Connor had left, the neighbors were gone, even Jared was out of the picture indefinitely. A few flies swarmed around my head and as I waved them away I thought of Stumpy. Damn, it was time to get some more bugs! This sure was a disgusting pet I had managed to acquire, I thought, as I trudged not too light-footed into the RV.

I looked around and felt closed in for the first time since running away. And as the song says, "I was so lonesome I could die."

I went online to find out more about my little critter, namely how to fill his pantry. The side-blotched lizard, first identified in Utah in 1852, sports small dark, bluish-black blotches on the sides just behind the front legs, hence the reason for the name. The spots are more distinctive in the male than in the female but as I didn't have two to compare, I was still clueless as to its sex. Until I read about the gular fold, a fold of skin covering the back portion of the throat, that funny red balloonish thing that had fascinated me earlier. Pumping it up and down was a very strange way to attract a female if you ask me, but apparently it was effective; the females lay two or three clutches of eggs per season containing two to twelve eggs that hatch in only two months.

As to what they feed on, the list was limitless: ants and their larvae, flies, mosquitoes, damselflies, dragonflies, beetles, bees, aphids, caterpillars, ticks, scorpions, spiders, and mites, and sometimes the males cannibalized their young. Wonderful, simply wonderful. I was tempted to just let the sucker loose to fend for itself when I read the next line. The side-blotched lizard usually lives in pairs.

Oh no! There was a wife and most assuredly babies, the ones daddy hadn't "et" yet. I fell off the bench laughing. I just couldn't imagine myself doing anything else as preposterous as crawling along the ground lifting rocks for the "bounty" they might be harboring.

Mostly ground dwellers, the lizards climb boulders, logs or rocky cairns for vantage points, to bask or claim their territory by doing "push-ups." Apparently this is where the tail comes in handy; they need it for quickly dashing after their quarry. Without it they are prey to larger lizards, snakes and birds. Oh the guilt.

They rarely wandered, home range sizes are .06-acre for the males, .02 for the females and .01 for the juveniles, so if he had a family it was close by. I wondered if his wife would still find him attractive, without his tail and ability to do "push-ups" like Stallone for her.

So okay, I had a dilemma, there was a decision to be made here. Was I going to let him go, look for his family, or continue to care for him until his tail grew back?

I could hardly let him go knowing he would most likely starve or be prey to a hungry hawk. If I found his family and he couldn't fend for them, wouldn't I then be obligated for all of them? The thought made me shutter. The females in most species are strong, I told myself, thinking of pioneers and lionesses. Momma lizard, if there even was one, and the little ones would just have to manage on their own. So . . . it looked like I was to become a bug hunter. Then it occurred to me, there were pet stores. I could buy bugs! Except here I was in the great American wilderness, and I hadn't seen anything resembling a pet store or bait shop. I heard the sounds of kids calling to each other. I looked out my bedroom window to the road . . . boys. What was that rhyme about puppy dog tails and snails? I reached for my wallet and headed out the door.

Chapter Sixteen

After breakfast I took a long nap in the hammock, I had lost a lot of sleep lately and I was tired. I awoke a few hours later when some men came to get the RV next door. I recognized the two men from the service station Connor and I had ducked into when we were evading the Abramsons. They gave me admiring glances as I watched them efficiently unhook everything and store the awning, lawn furniture, grill and carpeting before driving it off the lot. I guessed that the neighbors were either still in jail, or too distraught after being charged to deal with their RV. I felt a little guilty about that too. This was all my fault. Yet, they shouldn't have been doing what they were doing, clever little scam that it was. I wondered how long they had been doing it, how many students had been "helped" by their special brand of tutoring.

Gosh, who would have thunk it, scamming on the S.A.T.s and college entrance exams by using ringers. I could certainly see how there was money to be made; all those parents desperate to get their kids into the best schools, so they in turn could get the best jobs to ensure their futures. The ones I'd seen dragging their kids into that RV had certainly seemed desperate.

Then I thought of Jared in the hospital at Klamath Falls.

I was a petite inconsequential woman, how was it that I was affecting so many lives these days? I was beginning to feel old. I was wallowing, and I knew it for what it was, so I gave myself permission. I would go fix myself a drink, set the timer, and allow myself half an hour to sulk. Then I was going to cheer up and make some plans. A thought was niggling in the back of my mind that maybe it was time to move on.

I hadn't seen the deer I wanted to see, or gone fishing, or white water rafting. Hell, I could always come back, I reasoned. I *had* seen the Clarks Nutcracker that feeds exclusively on the seeds of the white bark pine and I had some amazing pictures to prove it. I went inside and fixed myself a vodka tonic before returning to the hammock.

I had tried to call the hospital earlier to check on Jared, but due to the H.I.P.P.A. laws they weren't able to tell me anything, especially as I wasn't willing to cough up the fact that I was his wife. But Brick had his connections and a few minutes later, he e-mailed me that there was no change in Jared's condition.

As I sat in the middle of the hammock, my leg cocked under me, looking out at the mountains, I wondered how it had come to this. My husband was in the hospital and I really wasn't all that concerned with his welfare. I was only concerned so far as it affected me. How had that happened?

I thought back through the years, alighting on the more memorable occasions, both good and bad. It was obvious that the bad memories far outweighed the good, just in my attitude. But I wondered how someone who had been so much in love could be so calloused as to whether the husband they had promised to love and cherish, died or was comatose for life. After thinking about it, it occurred to me that it was simple really. I had not only fallen out of love with Jared, I had come to detest him.

I tried to flip back in my mind to the exact moment when each of those events might have happened. For the falling out of love part, I saw me, dressed as a schoolgirl, doing things to pleasure my husband, not because I wanted to, but because I had to. How did men get these perversions, I asked myself as I sipped on the mind-numbing vodka. I knew I had made the drink twice as strong as I liked but there had been a reason, I needed to work through all this and some mind-numbing was definitely called for.

Was it because during those formidable years, those of early puberty, a young Jared was traumatically rejected by a girl in a pleated skirt, a white shirt with a Peter Pan collar and scuffed saddle oxfords with knee-highs? Was that girl being continually punished in his mind? For my sanity's sake, I hoped that in my youth I had never casually dismissed a young suitor in such a way as to pattern his life for sexual revenge.

Was it inbred? Had Jared's father enjoyed his mother's charms only if she pouted and preened in a tiny school uniform? Is that why she had felt so compelled to spend so much time in Europe away from her husband?

What had happened, when had it happened? The honeymoon had been normal, I supposed, yet I really hadn't had anything to compare it to since I was a virgin. Thinking back, I remembered the first time he had brought home a "costume." I had thought it was for a Halloween party but he said no, it was for a private party—ours. I was a French maid that night, complete with phrases I'd had to memorize, and Lord knows what I had been asking for at the time. He had been insatiable that night; I did remember that—and the fact that the servant's outfit found its way to a prominent section of my closet.

My pleasure, which had been important to Jared at one time, became inconsequential. Each new thing he brought home was to stimulate *him*, weave a fantasy in *his* head, or prolong *his* pleasure. My mind focused on correlating events, dates, times, holidays. It came to me then; it had been the third year of our marriage, about the time he wanted to make sure I was exclusive to him by fashioning odd jewelry for me to wear—things with his initials instead of mine. I thought of those damned earrings he had made me wear to the Country Club Christmas Party that year, three-inch dangles in solid gold, a "J" for Jared for each ear, my name had been Deborah at the time, so the "J" had been awkward, even though my last name was Jameson. It still meant I was his.

A horn honked off in the distance and then I heard the timer on the microwave beeping. My half hour of retrospection was over. What did it matter when it came to pass that I didn't love my husband anymore? I didn't, it was plain and simple. He'd caused me pain and anguish, humiliated me, and made me feel less of a woman than a bowery girl. He'd used my sexuality, making me play an innocent to feed his lusts, and he had never been satisfied. I was ecstatic to be free of him, and no, I really didn't care right now whether he lived or died. He had destroyed me that much. I was only just now coming back to the girl I had been.

I took my drink inside, debated about refilling it, but decided against it. It was time I made some plans for Stumpy and me. It was time to move on. I could come back some other time when I needed the isolation. Right now I needed some interaction with people, and I knew exactly the people I needed to see to feel better about myself. I was going to go visit Daniel and Julia, and their sweet daughter Angelina, and I was going to take her a puppy, a small white one that could sit in her lap, just as I'd promised.

But first I would take this opportunity to call my sister and my parents. With Jared in the state he was in, it would be safe to talk to them and to assure them that I was fine and happy with my new life.

An hour later I was exhausted from the emotions. Both my sister and my parents had wrung me dry with their concerns and worry. They had read about the reward, knew about Jared's accident, and were anxious for me to visit. Although my sister was not that far away, just one state over in Washington, I was not absolutely sure this wasn't some kind of ruse and that rushing to see them wasn't walking right into Jared's plan. I told them maybe in a few more months, I'd come too far to screw up now.

Just before hanging up with my mother, she mentioned that Sheila, Jared's assistant, had been leaving messages, urgent messages. My signature as his next of kin was desperately needed on some papers for the business to continue running, in order to pay the employees and handle the day-to-day bills that were piling up. That smacked of coerced subterfuge, as I could hardly believe there was no second in command, no one who had check writing privileges other than Jared, not Jared who was so organized and prepared. More than ever, I doubted his loss of memory. No one ran a multi-million dollar business without a back-up plan, without provisions for the business to continue in his absence, not as much as he traveled. But then again, Jared did not trust many people. He hadn't even trusted me.

Chapter Seventeen

That night I sat at my picnic table under the stars and began to organize my trip east. I had decided that it could be a long time before I got this far west again, so I wrote down the two places I really wanted to go to before heading southwest: a winery called 12 Ranch Wines that was fairly close and the Japanese Gardens in Portland.

I swatted at the mosquitoes that were especially vicious tonight. It was odd to look out at the horizon and see snow on the peaks and still have mosquitoes swarming around my ears. I had run out of repellent but was determined to enjoy my last night outdoors. I had actually tried to capture a few of the pesky things for Stumpy, but was not fast enough, even after letting them light on me. I managed to kill a few of them but I couldn't capture them and I had already learned that Stumpy had one peculiarity about his food—it had to be alive to find its way onto his tongue. So, now I had him on a leash so he could catch his own food, but apparently the collar I'd fashioned for him out of twist ties was so foreign to him that he could only sit there and blink. Here I had my own personal mosquito trap, but I couldn't get it to work.

The evening news hadn't mentioned Jared and due

to the special assignment Brick was on, he was going to be incommunicado for a few days. All in all, it was probably a good thing for me to get out of here. Just as that thought crossed my mind, I heard a twig snap.

My head jerked up as I trained my ears to where the sound had come from. The noise had come from behind the fallen tree on the opposite lot, not fifty feet away. I slowly gathered my notebook and my lizard and made my way backward toward the door of the RV.

"There's no point hiding from me," a man's voice growled, his tone was menacing, but I couldn't place it as one I was familiar with. "I got you dead to rights." A tall, lanky man in a khaki flight suit stood up and walked out from behind the foliage of the downed tree.

"Wh. . .Who are you?" I managed to squeak out.

"Let's just say I'm a friend of your husband's. He wants you home. I want the reward. It's a good deal for both of us." He was coming toward me, and I knew if I let him get much closer, he'd surely overpower me.

"Haven't you been watching TV?" I asked as I let Stumpy, still on the leash, slide down my leg to the ground. I was probably choking him, but I had no choice. I felt it when he landed on my foot and scurried off. I dropped the leash so he could get away. "He's in a coma, he has no idea who I am. I assure you that he doesn't want me anymore. And believe me, there's no way you'll get a reward from his trustees. They would rather I be out of the picture entirely, I'm sure."

"I'm one of the helicopter pilots he hired to bring him here. I know just how badly he wants you back. It's all he talked about on the way here from Salt Lake City. His Deb, his precious, little Deb. Actually he referred to you so many times as his naughty little Deb, that I believe he has some very special plans for your homecoming." He was close enough now that I could see the glint of his sardonic smile. He had overlapping teeth in the front, yellowed and stained by what I assumed was tobacco, judging by his noxious breath. His eyes were dark and fairly dancing with avarice and his thin lips quirked to the side in lewd grimace.

"Didn't you hear me? He's in a coma, not lucid!" I moved out from behind the table and acted like I was coming out into the open area, as if I wasn't afraid of this jerk who wanted to capture and sell me back to my husband. I could not believe this was happening to me again. When was I going to learn? I spotted the hammock and an idea formed.

"He'll be right as rain in a day or two, and ready for his Darlin' Deb. And I'll be able to cash in."

Sidestepping to the right, I was almost at the hammock.

"Don't think you're going to get away, 'cause you're not."

I reached up and grasped the hook holding the hammock to the tree trying to act nonchalant. As if taking down a hammock would be the only concern a girl would have when accosted by a man who wanted to take her against her will.

"What are you doing, leave that alone!"

"I'm just taking down my hammock, you don't want to leave these out at night, the dew is hard on the hemp fibers." I gathered one side of the hammock to my chest, and walked to the opposite tree and removed the second hook. Now I was ready, he only had to come close. "I'm going in now, you're welcome to sleep outside and we'll talk again in the morning." I threaded my fingers through the netting, and started toward the RV. I knew he'd come after me.

"Oh, no you're not. You're not going anywhere."

When he grabbed my shoulder and spun me back toward him, I leapt on him. Catching him unaware, I knocked him to the ground and rolled him into the netting. His flailing hands and thrashing feet only helped to secure him more. I saw one of the hooks glinting in the moonlight, and after wrapping it around him, inserted it into a belt loop on his pants. I got up and ran to one of the outside storage compartments and grabbed the rope I used for a clothesline and tied his hands and feet. All the while he was hollering and cussing me out. I finally pulled off one of his shoes and his sock, and stuffed the sock into his mouth. I pulled the netting up over the sock so he couldn't spit it out.

"There! I said as I got up off my knees and smacked my hands together. "That ought to keep ya for awhile. Now, if you don't mind, I'm going to find my lizard and get out of here."

I went into the RV and found a flashlight and began my search for Stumpy. I found him by following his leash; he was under a bush looking up at me as if to say, "You know you dropped me, don't you? That really wasn't very nice."

I picked him up and held him at eye level checking him out. "No worse for the wear. You know, you're starting to grow on me." I had to chuckle at that, for sure enough, there was no longer a wound per se, but a nub making a meager appearance. I took him inside and put him in his terrarium, using the broiler pan insert for a cover, held down by a votive in a marble base.

I looked out the window at the guy squirming on the ground, and gave a long, drawn out sigh. *Now what?*

Well if I'd learned anything about reward mongers, it was that where there was one, there were many. I knew it was time to leave. I set about getting packed up and ready to go. No way did I want to go down this mountain in the dark, but at first light, I was going to be ready to get out of here. I decided to take a quick shower, and then unhook all the connections tonight, so that in the morning all I'd have to do was crank up the engine and back out.

Half an hour later, I was good to go but really upset about having to leave my hammock behind. Then it came to me. I knew how I could get it back, and safely. I went into my medicine cabinet and took out two of my sleeping pills. Hell, the guy might really appreciate this; the mosquitoes had to be driving him crazy. I found a cup with a lid that had a sipper straw through it. I dropped in the pills, melted them with hot water and threw a few ice cubes in. Then I went outside, and with a grimace and very tentative fingers, I pulled out the sock. The cursing began in earnest the second it came out.

"You want some water?" I asked innocently, ignoring every vile thing he was saying. "I'm leaving in just a few minutes, so this is your last chance 'til morning when some kids riding bikes will probably find you. I'd drink up if I were you."

He gave me an ugly glare, but motioned with his jaw to bring the cup closer. I assisted him in getting it all down. Then I stood and dropped the sock and cup on top of him. "If Jared does come back to his own mind, you can tell him that his "naughty little Deb" is not interested in playing any games with him anymore. And that he should save his money and his time, and just find somebody new to play with."

I spun on my heel and went back to the RV to wait. I dozed for awhile and woke just as the first streak of light creased the sky. I ran outside and shook the man on the ground and when I didn't get a response of any kind, not a moan or a growl, I panicked. I felt for his pulse and was reassured that he was still alive and that he was just in his own temporary mini-comatose state from the drugs I'd given him. It was kind of weird that this was how I was handling my man problems lately, I thought, as my mind reverted to Brick and the time I'd dosed him with the same drug while we were having lunch at an Italian restaurant. Hey, he'd been trying to arrest me, I'd had no choice, I reminded myself.

Quickly I unhooked, unwrapped, and spun Mr. Vile Mouth out of the hammock, being none too gentle. Then, as I was walking away, I looked back. Hell, I might as well get my clothesline too, I thought, and went back to untie the knots at his wrists and ankles. I had a moment of guilt when I noticed that the foot I had removed the shoe and sock from was covered with bites and welts. Not having seen the other, I couldn't tell if it was swollen or not, but it looked like it could be.

I stowed the hammock and the clothesline and fired up the RV. Then I went back to the medicine cabinet, and back out to the man sprawled on the ground. I shoved a Benadryl capsule between his dry lips and disgusting teeth. The sipper cup on the ground still had a tiny bit of water in it, so I held his head up by the back of his neck and let it trickle into his mouth. He sputtered and coughed, but the pill went down. I thought about giving him two, but wasn't sure how it would react with the sleeping pills. I put his head back on the ground, straightened out his body so he was flat on his back, and just for grins, I crossed his hands over his chest. That's exactly how I left him when I backed out a few minutes later, after having damned near scalded my hands to clean them.

I whistled as I wound my way around the tight bends in the road, mindful of the trees and the overhanging branches. I was on the road again, and it sure felt good.

Chapter Eighteen

I really wanted to go to the Japanese garden I had read about online, but after looking at the Atlas, I just couldn't justify the additional time or expense. Portland was on the opposite end of the state, far north, whereas I was far south. I shook my head and promised myself that I'd get to see the ceremonial teahouse, and the elaborate gardens of raked sand some other time. Thoughts of bridges over ponds, cherry trees that had been praised by the Japanese Ambassador as the finest outside of Japan and an entire garden resembling a monastery, crowded my mind as I pulled onto Route 62 to head south to Bonanza, home of 12 Ranch Wine Winery. I was running out of Cabernet Sauvignon and I was anxious to try out the unfiltered wines made from grapes harvested in Oregon.

That was one legacy Jared had left me, one that I could live with—love of a good red. I was tempting fate by not calling to make an appointment, but I figured, hey, if no one was there, I'd boon dock and wait. It wasn't as if I was on a timetable. I loved that part of RVing, the part where you didn't wear a watch and only paid attention to the time when you either wanted to catch a sunrise or time an egg.

Two hours later I was talking to Ken and Connie Marston

about their wine making process, the harvest they were expecting and Oregon in general. I had already noticed that there was a lot of the Old West still hanging around out here. It seemed that "lost" ranches and mines were everywhere, apparently no longer lost. And the general trend was to dress between dressed-out cowboy and state-of-the-art hiker. I hardly fit in with my jeans and sloppy sweatshirt combos, but I didn't really care.

While loading up my RV with two cases of wine, I took the opportunity to show off Stumpy and ask about pet stores. I was told that I would find plenty near Redding, California where I planned to stop for the night. I had to figure out my route. I was anxious to see some of California, but not anxious to get tied up in traffic, as I was still not all that experienced driving my new rig, and of course, gas was a huge factor, so I certainly didn't want to waste it idling on some crowded highway.

The campground I was heading toward was just north of Redding, an area called Whiskeytown Shasta Trinity National Recreational Area. I couldn't wait, it sounded so cool, and I was so ready for a new place with new neighbors—law abiding, if possible this time, please Lord, I prayed.

I knew when I was getting close to Shasta Lake by all the camping signs. I usually tried to look for independent campgrounds when I could, so I could get more of the local flavor but I was ready for a night of no surprises, so I opted for the K.O.A. this time.

Chapter Nineteen

I was at the pool, enjoying the breeze and the peacefulness of the view when I heard the gate creak. The young woman I had seen hanging clothes next door came into the pool area with two young children in tow—a little boy and a little girl, both with just swim trunks on. She settled their things on some chairs a few feet from mine. The children, out of diapers, but not old enough for school, went right to the edge of the pool and jumped in. I sat up in alarm because neither looked old enough to be in the water by themselves. I had my legs over the side of my lounger, ready to spring into action.

The woman noticed my movements, and smiled with pride. "You don't need to mind them any, they can swim better than fish."

I watched the two of them cavorting in the water, diving down, surfacing with big grins, and swimming with great, effortless strokes from one side of the pool to the other, mindless of whether they were in the deep section or not.

"It's how I met their papas, swimming."

I looked over at her, she was beaming at the children, "Papas?" I questioned, encouraging her to continue.

"Weren't much older than them really when we moved

to Cottonwood Holler, 'bout a hundred miles south of here. Momma and Papa were always busy on the farm, but I found time to go to the pond every day. Jasper lived to the east, Calvin lived to the west and I was plum smack in the middle. We were all close to the same age and we became thick as thieves that first summer. Every year after, we became better and better friends. We did everything together, but we especially loved swimming in the pond.

"We would float on the surface enjoying the cool water on those hot, itchy days. Usually we just ran to the pond after school and stripped down to nothin' and dove in. When I was nine, Momma told me I had to wear a bathing suit. But I hated it; it was yellow with black polka dots and a ruffled skirt, so I rarely kept it on. Then one day, when I was fourteen and we were all floating around the pond, laughing at something that had happened at school, Calvin asked if he could feel my titties. I didn't see why not, so I let him. It felt good, real good, his hands running over my chest. Then Jasper wanted to feel them too, and it felt even better.

"So, everyday after school we floated in the pond and I let them run their hands over me. One day, Calvin was walking beside me while I was floatin', and looking up at the clouds as we often did. Then his head went under the water and he came up between my legs. He spread my legs wide and he touched me with his fingers. Jasper came to see what was going on, and the next thing I knew, Calvin was putting himself inside me, and he was shovin' and shovin' to keep himself there. I watched as his face went hard and he strained his neck like he was real angry with me, then he clamped his eyes shut and he hollered. Jasper pushed him out of the way and then he did the same thing.

"From then on, we rushed right home from school everyday, and one or the other, and sometimes both, got on top of me on the grass near the pond. They pushed themselves inside me and made me feel strange things going on in my body. When my butt got sore from the hard ground, they made a pillow of their clothes for me. I thought that was real sweet.

"Every day we did this and I really didn't think much of it, except that most times I liked the way Calvin did it best. Well, you can probably figure out what happened. Five months later, my belly started getting in the way of them lying on top of me. Momma figured it out first and then Papa told them one of them had to marry me.

"We didn't know whose baby it was going to be, and neither Calvin nor Jasper wanted to be done with me. They both said they loved me and wanted to marry me. Well that was a big problem. We'd all heard of a man having several wives, especially in Oregon and Utah, but even though this was California, we'd never heard of one woman having two husbands. But Calvin and Jasper wanted to try it anyway. Momma and Papa wouldn't hear of it though and called me awful names.

"So Calvin and Jasper packed their things and came and got me, and we went to the wine country so they could earn money harvestin' the grapes. That's what they do now, they get one paycheck and alternate days, 'cause nobody really cares who's doin' the work as long as it gets done. I got a license doing hair, and the men take care of the kids on the days they ain't workin'. So far's workin' out pretty good, 'cept now we gots two babies, and the funny thing is, I ain't for sure which is the father of this un either. Could even be the same one for both, how's a woman to know?"

How indeed? At the start of this tale, I had not expected anything so revealing, certainly nothing so outlandish. What, was I some kind of weirdo magnet? Where were Ma and Pa Kettle? So far, in my RVing adventures, I hadn't had a "normal" neighbor yet.

"So you all live as husband and wife with your two children?"

"Yup. They take their turns with me, just as they always have. It's Calvin tonight, Jasper's in the field today. Anyhow's, that's why my kids swim like minnows. We all been teachin' em.

But when Mandy here gets to be nine or ten, you can bet I'm goin' to make damn sure she keeps her swimsuit on."

I laughed out loud, I couldn't help it, I just had to. Then I looked over at the kids playing in the water and sobered. "What do they think? Do they both call Calvin and Jasper Daddy?"

"Yeah, they do. And I worry some 'cause this is . . . well, it's just not normal, I know. And they's gettin' older and pretty soon it ain' t going to be seemly to have their momma on the couch watchin' TV stark naked between two men."

I looked over at her, my eyes wide and my mouth agape. I just couldn't imagine the scene.

She chuckled, and reached over and slapped me companionably on the arm, "Somebody's going to have to give me up pretty soon!"

Then a moment later, after we'd sat in silence, I heard her mutter, "And I sure hope it's Jasper, as I really do like the way Calvin kisses."

I rolled my head, and closed my eyes. This had to be one of the most insane conversations I'd ever had. Yet, I almost hoped I could be there for the big moment, when this woman decided it was time to make the boys stop sharing their toys.

Chapter Twenty

I returned to my RV, took a nice hot shower, and settled in for the night. I had two chores ahead of me before I could even think of curling up in my easy chair and watching a movie on DVD: cleaning the windshield, and Stumpy's terrarium, both disgusting chores that I dreaded. One, because I had to drag out all manner of equipment, including a folding step ladder, and the other because it was just plain disgusting. Stumpy had no discretion whatsoever, and once you started shifting the improvised kitty litter around, the stench quickly became overwhelming. Luckily, they were both outdoor chores. Shaking my head as I gathered cleaning products together, I admonished myself for stupidly taking my shower first, instead of after.

I had just taken the terrarium outside and returned to get a shoe box for Stumpy to reside in temporarily, when my cell phone started vibrating and spinning around on the counter.

I picked it up and recognized Brick's cell phone number. "Oh, this can't be good," I said to no one in particular. He was still supposed to be undercover on a special assignment.

Tentatively, I whispered, "Hello?" For all I knew he could be in a closet or a car trunk somewhere.

"De . . .Ca . . .I'm just going to give you a number."

Lately he seemed to have a hard time remembering which name I was using, which I thought was odd, as the last one, Jenny, he'd chosen himself.

"I always wanted to be Agent 99, if that helps any," I said.

"That's funny, the number 69 often comes to mind when I think of you."

"Oh, so it's going to be that kind of call," I said in a put on sultry voice.

"Oh, I wish that could be true. Another episode of phone sex with you would be far more appealing than what I really called about."

"Oh yeah, and just what might that be?"

"The message just relayed to me, is that hubby has just been released and was picked up by a private ambulance. Destination unknown, but it was headed for the interstate, and was last seen taking the airport exit."

"Is he conscious?"

"I'm told he signed the release papers."

"So he could be lucid, his memory could be back."

"Maybe, maybe not. No one at the hospital is talking. Things sure have changed due to those new privacy laws. But nobody's scrambling around, so far as we can tell. And, uh, no one has come forth to bail a certain irate, insect-eaten helicopter pilot out of jail, who was found this morning on a certain empty campground site. You wouldn't happen to know anything about that now, would you?"

"Uh, I plead."

"You're just one disaster after another, aren't you?"

"Listen I didn't ask for him to show up, but I certainly wasn't about to let him truss me up and take me to Jared!"

"No, I daresay not. Any trussing up is going to be done by me. And lately, you've given me more than enough incentive to lash you to a . . . well, never mind. One thing for sure, you certainly know how to go about making enemies, I'll give you that. Glad you got away though. You okay?"

"Yeah. I'm fine." I couldn't tell him that the thought of him tying me up and, well . . . having his way, was flooding me with sensations.

"Where are you?"

"Hillbilly Heaven according to my new neighbor."

"What?"

"Never mind. I'm outside Redding, California. I'm on my way to pick up a puppy for Angelina. Then I'm going to take it to her—"

"Don't say where! In case this line isn't secure, just don't say where."

"Ooookay."

"I like the idea that you'll be with Daniel though, he can look out for you for awhile."

"I don't need anybody to look our for me!"

"I know, I know. You're Miss Independent now. How's the new rig?"

"Oh Brick, it's wonderful! I love it. It handles really well, even though it's huge!"

"I hope you'll be saying those exact same words to me soon." He said with a husky voice and then he chuckled and I smiled at the sound of it.

"Huge, huh? Are all men impressed with the size of their manhood?"

"Don't know. I rarely talk to other men about their uh . . . impressiveness."

It was my turn to laugh. I missed him. What I wouldn't have done to have him here with me right now.

"How's your case?"

"Got 'em! Bagged and tagged. I like it when they're easy like this."

"Any luck on the other matter?" He knew exactly what I was asking and I could almost hear him deflate from the question.

"No sign of him. No one's seen him, and we canvassed that whole place. He just wasn't there."

"I'm sorry."

"Yeah, me too."

"So what's next?"

"A big thick steak, a baked potato so loaded I won't be able to eat it all and a frosty mug of beer. Then I'm going to sleep for two days and start all over again."

Well, I gotta go, I left Stumpy under a bucket. No telling where he could be by now."

He laughed. "You are one amazing woman. See ya around." I heard the click as he shut his phone.

"Yeah, see ya around," I muttered, lonelier now than I was before he had called. I walked back to my bedroom and dumped a pair of shoes on the bed so I could use the plastic box I kept them in for Stumpy.

Chapter Twenty-one

I was just finishing my third DVD for the night when I heard voices raised in anger just outside my door. That's one of the weird things I had discovered while camping; any noise outside that was anywhere close, sounded like it was just outside my unit, a few feet away. Often, it was across the road, or a few campsites down.

I lifted the corner of my kitchen window shade and peered out into the darkness. My eye was drawn to a campfire that was glowing red with dying embers. The ménage a trios, that was my neighbors, was gathered around it, Jodi, dressed in a halter top and cut offs, was lounging in a chair next to Calvin. Calvin was gripping her hand between them while Jasper was pacing, pointing a finger at one or the other with each turn, and hissing and snarling between words that visibly snapped out and hit their mark. Jodi was cowering, and I could see she'd been crying. She was swiping at her eyes with the back of her hand and scrunching her nose up sniffing. I couldn't make out what Jasper was saying, as it was obvious he was trying to keep his voice down while still conveying his anger. But one phrase, said over and over finally came through. "Why me, why not him, huh?" The last time it was moaned with disbelief rather than venom. I watched as Jasper's shoulders shook and he sagged into a chair sobbing.

Oh dear, she was doing the Dear John thing. Why did she have to pick tonight of all nights? Why now, when I would have to be a party to it? But I couldn't stop watching, this was more entertaining than any of the three movies I'd watched.

Jodi stood up, sauntered over to Jasper and rubbed his shoulders. She bent to whisper something in his ear intermittently but it didn't help, he just sagged more. Finally, he sat up, hunched forward and put his hands on his knees. He was saying something to Calvin and Calvin was shaking his head vehemently back and forth. It was apparent that whatever Jasper had said clearly upset Calvin and he wanted no part of it. Calvin stood with his fist raised and Jasper jumped up to confront him but Jodi intervened, stepping between the two men. A hand on each man's chest, she rubbed Calvin's in a placating manner while she spoke in low tones. It was clear that she had stepped between these two before.

Then she dropped the hand that had been massaging Calvin's chest and ran her hand down Jasper's until she reached his belt buckle. With a practiced hand, she unclicked it and pulled him forward by his waistband. They walked hand-in-hand to the camper door, then she let him precede her while she looked back at Calvin and said in a soft voice, so soft I had to move closer to the window to hear, "You go take a walk now, it's something I just gotta do and you know that. If it were you, I'd have agreed to it, too. Jesus Cal, it's been seven years, what's one more time? Then it'll be over and it'll be just you and me. It's the way we want it, the way it's got to be. I gotta go do this with him now. You take a walk, a long one now and when you come back it'll be the way you want it to be. I promise."

I watched every feature on Calvin's face harden. His fists were clenched by his sides and his back was steeled, he wasn't taking this well. The camper door closed behind Jodi and as we both listened, him ten feet from the camper staring at the door, me behind cover of my kitchen blind, all but climbing into the sink to hear, we heard the sound of the lock being turned.

I was afraid to move. Calvin looked ready to explode and I certainly didn't want him to discover I'd been eavesdropping on a very private conversation. He stood staring for a long time. Then he ran both hands through his sandy hair, raking it into thick strands that stood, then fluttered into place when he dropped his hands to his sides. He was the most dejected man I had ever seen and I couldn't even see the front of him.

I could not imagine all the emotions that had to be going through him at this moment. Did he feel betrayed by Jasper, or by his wife? Was he thinking about what Jasper was doing with the woman who had just promised to be his, only his? After all they'd been through, even knowing Jasper'd had her countless times over the years, how was this affecting him *now*?

By his body language, I could tell that this was not ever going to be considered a banner day in his book. Yeah, so he'd won the woman, but at what cost? Was he going to lose his best friend who had been like a brother? And were his kids going to lose their uncle or father, as the case might be? Would he ever be able to forgive Jodi for her act of defiance, and her resolve to say good-bye in a fashion that clearly hadn't bothered him before, but now galled the hell out of him? I could imagine some of his thoughts, or at least the direction of them.

I watched as Calvin jammed his hands into his pockets and ambled off toward the road, kicking stones out of his way as he walked. When he got to the road, he turned and looked back at the camper. A more forlorn look I could not imagine and I wondered if I should go outside and try to comfort him. Then I chided myself for even thinking of becoming involved. I had my own Peyton Place to deal with and his troubles were small potatoes compared to mine! Hell, Jodi would have to turn tail and come after him with a butcher knife for his problems to come even close to being on par with mine! Still, he looked *so* unhappy.

I grabbed a sweatshirt and tossed it over my cami-pj top, took two min-bottles of wine out of the fridge, shoved my keys in the pockets of my lounging pants and shuffled into the sandals I had left by the door. I quietly left the RV, silently berating myself for being a busybody in the first place. If I just hadn't lifted that window shade . . .

Chapter Twenty-two

I caught up with him at the crossroads, just before the camp store. He was still kicking stones, but now they were being viciously chucked off to the side of the road as he was putting his whole heart into it. When he heard me approaching, he spun and for a moment I knew what it felt like to burst a bubble, to not be the person someone was expecting with their whole heart. His face went from elation to devastation in one second and I knew I had made a mistake venturing out to talk to him. In that second, I also decided that I wasn't going to tell him I'd overheard everything.

"Uh, hi Jenny. What are you doin' out here so late?"

"Actually, it's more early than late now, it's almost five. I couldn't sleep, thought I'd go find that owl that keeps waking me up."

He waited until I caught up with him, motioned me off the path and grabbed my elbow as I stumbled, and lead me into the woods. I was almost ready to panic when he dropped my elbow and pointed up into a tree that soared above the others. If it hadn't been for the eyes twinkling bright in the semi-dark, I never would have seen it as his feathers were the perfect blend to match the tree branch.

"There's the culprit, a common old barnyard coot, lookin' for mice and making the rest of us suffer for it."

I stared up at the owl, doing anything I could to avoid looking Calvin in the face. "How come you never see two together?"

"'Cause they're not stupid like humans."

I could have bit my tongue.

"Sorry, I'm feeling stupid tonight, and it hasn't even been a drinkin' night."

I was carrying the two mini-bottles by the neck down by my side; I lifted them and let them clink. "I can remedy that, care to join me?"

He looked at me, quirked his head to study my face and smiled. "Yeah, sure, why not? She's gettin' it on with another man, I can certainly drink with another woman. You know don't you?"

I passed him a bottle and opened mine. Then I took a big sip before answering and reversing my earlier decision to keep mum. This was just too juicy to pass up; I was living next to a mesmerizing soap opera and I was as avid as any fan. "I know you all were *trying* to keep quiet, but I was up and you were right outside my window."

"We were trying not to wake the kids. It's not good for them to see their parents fighting, so we usually take it outside when things get iffy."

"I take it they've been 'iffy' for quite some time."

He took a long swallow and looked over at me. "We were too young when we went off on our own, way too young. Everything was fun and games, and then . . ."

"And then?"

"And then they weren't." It was succinct and final, so I went back to sipping my wine.

He took a long swig, draining half the bottle at once. "I wasn't in love with her at first. It just kind of grew. I don't know how it was with Jasper, but there came a day when I didn't want him touching her, and it's been hell ever since."

"How long ago was that?"

"Couple years."

"So you should be ecstatic, after tonight he won't be touching her again."

"Yeah, after tonight," the words were delivered short and clipped. I was not helping his irritation, I might even have been adding to it.

"You'll have a real marriage now."

He turned to stare at me, eyes wide, jaw completely unhinged. "Yeeahh! And how's that going to go? I'll be the daddy to two kids and one on the way mind you, all or none of which may be mine. She's always had help at home, one or the other of us was always there, now it'll just be me, and she'll be on her own *a lot*. I'm going to have to buy him out of half of everything we own, so there goes the savings account, and I'm not even sure I'm the one she truly wants. What if she really loves him, but thinks the kids are mine. What if he's better in bed and she misses that? What if she finds out that one man doesn't do it for her and she starts lookin' for another?"

"She hasn't told you that she loves you?"

"Hell, no! All she's said is that one of us has to go and she told Jasper it had to be him. I mean, I do agree that it's better for the kids and all, and I really *do not* want him touchin' her anymore, but hell, he's touchin' her now ain't he? What kind of love is that?"

I took a deep breath. This was clearly out of my realm as confidant, comforter, and counselor.

"Nothing about your relationship has been typical. Things just don't fall into the usual slots, so maybe you should just take it one day at a time. Be cordial, leave the door open for family ties and see Jasper off the best way you can. Then see how it goes. No marriage comes with a guarantee. And they don't all start with love either. And those that do, don't always end with it."

"You been married?"

"Ummm, technically, I still am."

"What happened there? Seems like you got it all together, how come it ended?"

"He wasn't who I thought he was, either that, or he changed and became someone I didn't like anymore."

"You got kids?"

"No, and that makes it easier to step back and undo it all because there's no one else to think about except yourself. You don't have that option, and neither does Jasper or Jodi."

"Yeah."

We had walked the entire loop and were almost back to the road in front of our sites. He looked up and smiled over at me, "Thanks for the wine and the talk."

"You're welcome. I wish you the best, I really do—all of you. And about her loving you, have you told her that you love her?"

"Hmmm, not in so many words."

"Gentlemen usually wait for ladies, but in this case the lady rarely goes first, if my romance novels are anything to go by. I suspect her feelings for you are stronger than her feelings for Jasper, not that she might not have strong feelings for both of you, mind you."

"Why do you say that?"

"There must be a reason she chose you over Jasper. All other things being even, that's the only one I can come up with. Ask her."

He quirked a tiny smile over at me and then grinned broadly, "Okay, I will!"

We turned the last bend and there was Jasper, bag in hand loading it into the trunk of a taxi.

"Looks like it's up to you how this is going to end."

"Yeah, I get to be the noble one. While his handprints are all over my wife, I have to be the one to shake his hand."

"Remember, until just a few moments ago, by tacit agreement, she was his wife, too. You're very lucky he's giving her up without more of a fight because I'm sure he loves her every bit as much as you do. His heart is breaking and his whole life is changing. You can make it harder or you can make it easier, it's up to you." I walked off the path and took a diagonal across my site to get to the door of my RV.

Calvin stood with one hand in his pocket, the other dangling the wine bottle. Then he walked over and set it on the picnic table. Squaring his shoulders, he walked over to Jasper. He offered him his hand and then when Jasper hesitantly took it, Calvin pulled him close and held him tight. I saw him whisper a few words in his ear and then pat him on the back. From where I stood, both sets of eyes were misty with tears. I looked over at Jodi, standing in the door of the RV, one baby on her hip, the other holding her leg. She was crying too, and it just about broke my heart. *Who would have thought I would be so upset about a woman choosing between two men?*

I unlocked my RV and went inside. Dawn was coming and although I usually loved to see the sunrise, this time I kind of wanted the solitude of being in my camper all alone. I could hardly believe it, less than eight hours ago I was lonely, now I just needed to curl into myself and let go of other peoples' problems for a while. My heart hurt, and I just couldn't imagine how Jasper's was hurting now.

I walked down the hallway to my bedroom and jumped back two feet, banging my head on the wall when I saw a man in jeans and cowboy boots sleeping in my bed!

Chapter Twenty-three

His back was to me, but the noise of me bouncing off the wall woke him with a start. Before he was able to roll over, I recognized him by his ass. No one filled out a pair of jeans quite like Brick.

"Where the hell have you been?"

"How'd you get in?"

"Who cares? Get in this bed with me."

I walked over and sat on the side close to his hip. He smiled up at me and with a barely-there touch, tucked a strand of hair that had come loose from my ponytail behind my ear. "Hi beautiful. I sure have missed you." His thumb caressed my ear and then his hand went around my head, and he pulled me down for a kiss that involved only lips, soft, gentle lips that began a slow reacquainting process. "Mmmm, missed this, too."

A strong hand ran from my shoulder to my back, and before I knew it, I was on my back with Brick beside me doing wonderful things with his pelvis against my side. He slowly worked his way over my body until he was centered over me. His prodding manhood was engaged in a frontal assault, focused on the target between my legs. As he moved up and down sliding his erection into the notch between my thighs, I heard myself moan. My hands found their way around him and as my fingers stroked the thick hair at his nape, my hips lifted to accommodate his wanton thrusts. My blood warmed while my head grew light with a giddiness I hadn't felt in years. God, I was horny, really horny!

"Mmmm, you feel good," he murmured as his lips left mine to trail down my throat. I closed my eyes for a second, as if by doing so I could physically separate myself from what he was doing to my senses. It was crux time, did I want to do this, because if not, now was the time I needed to let him know. He had swollen to a thickness that was telling me, with each new thrust against me, that soon there would be no turning back. He was unbelievably hard.

Yes, a voice inside my head whispered, *yes*, I did want this. But only this, only his body entering mine. No humiliating costumes or toys, no role-playing, no acting like an innocent being degradingly ravished. Just us, Brick and I, skin to skin, exploring and pleasuring and savoring each other's response.

My hands ran down his back until I could cup his buttocks and pull him hard against me, causing my mons to rub along his enormously swollen and hard ridge. As if by its own volition, one of my hands released his ass, and grappled to get between us where it clamped onto him and squeezed. He gasped and air hissed between his teeth, as a long sigh fluttered against my neck.

"Are you protected?" he panted as his lips slid up my neck and captured my lips. A deep tongue-lashing kept me from answering as his hands went under me and gripped my ass checks tight. A few hard tugs had me thrusting to meet his erection and my legs lifting to climb his hips. I joined his frenzied tongue with mine and I felt the ridge of him press against my straining, swelling vulva. Arching off the bed, my legs circling his hips and using them for support, I met his steely shaft with my very aroused and delightfully engorged nubbin. It was all she wrote. I came with such strong contractions I knew he could feel them through both his jeans and my lounging pants. Mere seconds later, I felt him jerk, spasm, and then cuss.

It seemed that contraception of any kind would be unnecessary. Neither of us said anything, when a few moments later he lifted off of me and pulled the pocket door closed to give him privacy in the bathroom.

When he came back a few minutes later, I was falling in and out of a dreamy, relaxed sleep. He moved me over, shifted me so he could bring up the covers and climbed in behind me pulling me close. I don't know how I could tell, as I still had all my clothes on, but I knew that he was naked. I tucked my hands under my cheek as I lay on my side away from him, smiling. How sexy was that? He'd lost control when he'd felt me coming against him. *Sweet.*

"So where were you?" his gravely voice rose like a fog in the dark. I wasn't sure how long I'd been asleep, but even so, I knew what he was talking about.

I told him about Jasper, Calvin and Jodi, and how their mutual marriage had ended.

"You sure can pick 'em. I only get the novice tuba player next door, occasionally accompanied by a howling dog."

"You just don't have my knack for zeroing in on odd balls."

He kissed the back of my neck. "It takes one to know one."

"Are you saying I'm odd?"

"Oh no! Let's see, in less than three days you've befriended a pedophile, managed to have two professors arrested, given a man amnesia, caused another to be nearly bitten to death, adopted a tailless lizard, and been a confidant to a love triangle. That's not odd, not at all."

"Hmph. I'm going back to sleep. And Connor's not a pedophile."

"You do that. When you're asleep, it's the only time I can

get any rest." He nuzzled my ear and kissed my temple.

I smiled and spooned back against him, wiggling my butt into his pelvis. His "Mmmm," of approval was all I remember before nodding off again.

Chapter Twenty-four

I was awakened by the sound of the kids playing next door, some game that involved shouting and making noises like airplanes. I shifted and looked over my shoulder, verifying what my fanny was already telling me—there was no one in bed beside me. I took a moment to stretch before I put my feet over the side and realized my head felt funny. While I slept, or during the event that had immediately preceded it, my ponytail had slipped to the side and was weighing down one side of my head. I reached up and removed the elastic and then rubbed the spot against my scalp where it had tugged all night. I hated it when I did that and I was roughly digging into my scalp when I heard Brick's voice yelling close to the outside of my bedroom window, "Catch it! Catch it! C'mon, reach!"

I shook my head and stood looking down at myself. Well, I didn't need to dress to go see what was going on outside. I managed to wash my face and brush my teeth before my curiosity got the better of me.

As I passed through the kitchen I saw Brick had made coffee and even left a mug out for me. I filled the cup and went to see what he was up to.

He was throwing a balsa airplane, with a rubber band

wound tightly around it up into the air, and the kids next door were running to catch it while all three made airplane sounds— chugging and petering out sounds when they couldn't get to it in time and it crashed into the grass. Jodi was sitting at my picnic table looking fresh and lovely, a can of Pepsi in one hand and a donut in the other. I couldn't help but notice her eyes following Brick's movements instead of her kids'.

She looked up as I closed the door and the step retreated. I had forgotten to lock it in place again. I gave her a, "stupid me" smile, and re-opened the door to push the button on the side control panel. The step swung back out and locked in place.

"Hi," she called over in a soft, embarrassed voice. I'd caught her looking and she had to know I knew everything that went on last night between her and Jasper and Calvin. She must be thinking that I was thinking that she was insatiable. I was.

"Hi!" I called, putting more into it than I felt. I looked around but didn't see Calvin, so she supplied the explanation.

"Calvin went off to work today, even though it's Jasper's day to work. I guess everyday will be Calvin's day now." She sent me a sideways smile that was two parts chagrin, one part pleasure. She had what she wanted; now she just had to accept all the changes it would bring to her, the children, and to Calvin. Her eyes were puffy from what had obviously been a sleepless night and her lips were evidence that she'd most likely had a fair amount of make-up sex with Calvin after the break-up sex she'd had with Jasper. I couldn't help but mentally shake my head. The scrapes women managed to get themselves into.

Thoughts of Jared came to mind and I wondered if he was still in a state of amnesia, completely unmindful of the wife who was running away from him.

I watched Brick play with the kids, admiring his physique and ease of movement as he agilely caught errant throws, several times saving the doomed plane from splintering against rocks and trees. It was a quiet morning in the park as everyone in the immediate vicinity who'd been privy to the disruptions of the night—from both the owl and the lovers' quarrel—were taking the opportunity to sleep in.

I sipped my coffee and let my mind wander back to my bed and to the moment when Brick had given me such sweet innocent pleasure by simply pressing his body into mine. Apparently I'd pleasured him, too—when he hadn't exactly been ready for it. And I hadn't had to wear a tacky costume, nipple clips, or a schoolgirl uniform to do it, I thought with satisfaction.

A car door slamming on the gravel road a few sites away shook me out of my reverie. Brick must have tensed too because the kids stopped in their tracks and mirrored his movements. With hands poised in the air, all three had turned their bodies to the sound. The kids were probably anticipating one of their dads. Brick, his eyes focused on the black sedan, gave a slight nod to the man in dark sunglasses standing beside the car. It was obvious that he had been expecting his arrival.

He stooped, gathered the kids to him, whispered a few things in each one's ear, and placed the balsa airplane in the older child's upraised hands. Then he stood and his eyes met mine. I knew what it meant. He had to leave.

He walked over to where I sat and pulled me to my feet by my elbows, then he lead me over to the door of the RV and opened it for me.

Once inside, standing in the kitchen, he pulled me to him and placed his chin on top of my head. I hugged him around the waist as he softly rocked me back and forth. "I have to go. They need me to testify against a fifty-four-year old man who tried to abduct a thirteen-year-old girl he'd met on line, namely me. I'm glad I was able to make this detour though. It was wonderful seeing you. And I'm sorry about last night."

"Sorry for what?"

"Well, that wasn't exactly what I'd had in mind."

"It was nice. And perfect for where we are right now."

"You never did answer my question."

"What was that?"

"*Are* you protected, are you using birth control?"

"Uh, yeah, I'm on the pill, have been for years."

"Good to know," he whispered as he tilted my chin up and looked into my eyes. "Good to know." His face lowered and his lips covered mine as he lazily meshed his lips with mine. It wasn't a searing kiss as some of his others had been, and it wasn't particularly passionate, but it was thorough, soft and warm and full of promise. I knew he was lingering as long as he dared before separating. He chucked my chin, "I promise to do better next time. Believe it or not, I really do want to be inside you for the finale one of these days."

"I'll hold you to it," I whispered to his back as he went down the steps and out the door. I watched through the kitchen window as he strode across the lawn and met the man waiting at the car. Brick thrust his hand out and they shook perfunctorily, then Brick slid into the passenger seat as the other man, who obviously was another agent, got behind the wheel and drove off.

Chapter Twenty-five

As I cleaned up the mess from breakfast, I decided it was time to move on, again. I'd stayed a few days longer than originally planned and I was itching to get back on the road. Besides, I didn't really want to be here when Calvin got home this evening.

I didn't want to see Jodi sad, but then, I didn't want to see her happy either. Not right away at least, not when Jasper was out there somewhere looking for a job and a place to live, and being completely miserable. Jodi and Calvin needed to be alone without any outside interference so they could get things ironed out between them and make their new family work. The less people who knew about their previous situation the better, I reasoned.

I packed up before stowing the lines because I did not want to be talked out of this. I was ready to continue with my journey—destination Tucson, where I would pick up an adorable little puppy that I would soon deliver to Angelina in Austin.

As I predicted, as soon as it became evident that I was pulling out, Jodi came running out of her trailer. "Are you leaving?" she hollered, clear disappointment in her voice as she ran over to where I was crouched, my head bent under a "basement" door, my gloved hands coiling hoses.

"Yeah, I should be getting back on the road. I have to meet that lady in Arizona and get that dog before somebody else gets him."

"Well, I sure will miss you! You're been a real good friend."

I stood and looked at her and at the distress I saw in her eyes. I had just finished with the sewer hook ups, so I pulled off my disposable gloves and tossed them in the trash bag at my feet. I gripped her by the shoulders and forced her to look into my eyes.

"I know you're lonely now. You've been used to having someone around all the time, but you'll get used to it. It'll be fun, especially once the kids go off to school." There was no way this woman was going to pass the test to home school, of that I was certain. "Once you get the breakfast dishes put away and the laundry started, you can watch the talk shows and the game shows, sit at the pool without having to be distracted by the kids and go shopping. You'll see, it won't be so bad."

"How about you? Aren't you lonely? That hunky guy came out of nowhere and now he's gone."

"Yeah, he tends to do that. But no, I'm not lonely. I love seeing him, but I enjoy being by myself. I love my alone time. I get to do whatever I want—go wherever it pleases me. I eat what I want, I go to sleep when I want and I read what I want, which reminds me . . ." I ran into the RV and came out with a handful of romance novels I had finished reading.

"Here, when the kids take their nap, grab a candy bar or some chocolate ice cream and read a few chapters. Start with this one," I said as I sorted through them until I found *The Flame and the Flower,* by Kathleen Woodiwiss. "If this doesn't make the time fly and keep you from being lonely during the day, I don't know what will." I gave her a fierce hug and handed her a piece of paper with my cell phone number and e-mail address on it. "Here keep in touch, but please, please don't give this to anyone else."

"Oh, I won't," she said awed by the little strip of paper in her hand. "Thank you so much," she said as she gathered the books in her arms. "I'll get the kids and go to the camp store right now and get me a Snickers bar for when I get the kids down this afternoon. Thank you!"

I watched as she slowly walked back to her trailer, reading the back cover of the book I recommended. I could see her eyes widen just as she turned and went up the steps. I didn't know if Calvin would thank me or not, but I had a sneaking suspicion that I had just created a new romance book junkie.

I turned back to my chores of cleaning the lot and stowing equipment in the "basement." Then I went inside, pulled the slides in, went over my checklist and got behind the wheel. I had already secured everything in the house and placed the Road Whiz and NASCAR Atlas in a dashboard compartment. I was ready to continue south through California on Route 5, first through Sacramento, then Fresno and Bakersfield, before picking up Route 40 to head east toward Arizona. I had a lot of driving ahead of me but I was revitalized and rarin' to go. Brick's visit had been nice and I'd loved seeing him even for the very short time we'd had together, but the experience of meeting Jodi, Calvin, and Jasper had reminded me of how painful love could be. I knew I wasn't ready for that. I loved being independent and responsible for just me. And I loved the excitement of a new adventure every time I turned the key. I couldn't wait to see what was around the next bend. I pulled out slowly, careful and mindful of how many kids were playing outside on this beautiful, sunny, late spring day.

I stopped at the camp store to check out and was surprised that there was an envelope for me. An overnight package had been delivered just moments ago the lady said, surprised that I hadn't been expecting it. I turned it over in my hand and looked for the return address.

It had been sent from an address on Leesburg Pike in

Tyson's Corner, Virginia. The address looked vaguely familiar but I couldn't place it right away. It had been addressed to me as simply "Deborah a.k.a. Jenny, National RV Dolphin, License number NJR 72869."

My heart sped up and I held my breath as I pulled the tab that opened the flat envelope. I looked inside but couldn't see anything, then I turned it upside down and a small white piece of plastic fell into my palm. It took me a minute to figure out what it was, then as I turned it over in my hand I saw Jared's full name embossed in the center of it. I knew exactly what it was. It was Jared's hospital bracelet. He was letting me know he was out, he was lucid and he knew where I was, for the moment.

I dumped everything in the trashcan beside the counter, thanked the woman, and ran back to my RV. I was getting out of Dodge just in time!

Chapter Twenty-six

I can honestly say that I do not remember the first hundred miles south on Route 5. Automatically, I must have changed lanes when necessary, moved with traffic and braked when it was needed. The thought that Jared's memory was back, at least as far as I was concerned, was a real downer. I had hoped for a reprieve of at least a few months. Why couldn't the man stay comatose, I practically screamed at the windshield!

I had originally planned on stopping for a night in Sacramento but as I ended up going through that area after the dinner hour, I figured I'd keep going. Traffic wasn't likely to be any better than it was right now and it was quite manageable at the moment. I thought I'd better take advantage and push on. I don't usually like driving more than three hundred miles on any given day. It's hard on the eyes, and the back, and I worry that my full time and attention won't be there in a critical moment, should I need it. I was just nowhere near wanting to settle right now, especially at a pre-planned site. I sifted back in my mind. Had I told anyone I was heading to Sacramento specifically? Jodi knew I was going to Tucson and then on to Austin, but nothing more informative than that and they were some pretty daggone big cities to just hunt and peck and hope to find someone in. I was feeling safe, but not totally.

The clock on the dash showed it was after nine, and I needed to get gas anyway, so I pulled over at the next truck stop. Brick must have finished with his testifying by now, I reasoned. No courtroom I knew of was tending to cases this late, so I decided to call him and share the "good news."

His one-word answer when I told him about the hospital bracelet summed up his feelings and mine. He didn't often cuss, but I guess he felt this instance was worthy.

"Mmmhmm, the new I.D. and vehicle didn't last long. I wonder how he's finding all this stuff out so fast?" I whined.

There was silence on the line while Brick mulled things over. Then he bit out, "Satellite. It has to be through a satellite of some kind. But how? How's he doing it?" he was clearly as baffled as I was.

"I don't know. I know he's smart and up on the latest technology, but I can't fathom how he found me at the very first place I stopped in California."

"That's it!"

"What's it?"

"You stopped."

"Pardon?"

"Hold on, let me check something out."

I heard fingers tapping computer keys, exclamations, and then a long exasperated sigh. "What a clever, clever man."

"What did you figure out?"

"Before I tell you, let me see if I'm right. How do you decide where you're going to stop, which campgrounds you're going to use?"

"Uh, I don't know, close to the Interstate, by a fairly large city, in case I want to shop. Oh, and I like K.O.A.s and places listed with the Family Campground Association."

"And?"

"Umm, oh yeah, and I check to see if they're in the Good Sam Directory."

"Just as I figured."

"Just as you figured what?"

"Do you have one of those Good Sam stickers on the back of the Dolphin?"

"Uh, yeah."

"Great. Any others I should know about, discount or otherwise?"

I thought for a moment. "Yeah, Family Campground and Camping World, and it's not just about the discount you know, they rate places for quality."

"I know, I know, hold on, let me check something out." I heard him rifling through pages in a book, then he stopped and I heard, "Mmmhumph, mmmhumph."

"What already!"

"According to the 2008 Trailer Life Directory, there are five parks listed for Bakersfield, that is where you said you were heading right now, right?"

"Yes."

"Well, three belong to Good Sam's."

"So?"

"How hard is it to get on the phone and call all the parks in any given area, particularly when you have the unlimited staff to do it?"

"I'm not following."

"You're on the run. He figures which direction you're heading from where you were before, then he figures out how many miles you can go in any given time frame. He has his cronies call all the parks around major cities close to an interstate. Bingo! I mean he has the make, model, color, and license tag since he was just recently in it and one of his cohorts was trussed up on the ground right beside it all night."

"So you're saying he's calling around and the people who answer the phones are telling him whether I'm there or not? Why would they do that?"

"Well, it's damned easy to lie or sound official and it's

certainly not privileged information."

"So you really think that's what he's doing? Just calling around and asking?"

"Think about it. He's never come across you as you were arriving at one of those places, only after you've been there and are settled in. The first times, before in North Carolina, he had the G.P.S. bugs, then when you removed them and sent him on wild goose chases, he couldn't find you. But once he found you in Oregon, he had to know, I mean odds are that you were heading south. It was just a matter of time. But it is kind of odd that he alerted you with that envelope. It doesn't make sense for him to tip his hand if he's so all fired up to get you back in his clutches."

"Maybe someone else sent it."

"What was that address again?"

"I think it's the mailing address for his store at Tyson's Mall."

"Well then, it's him or someone who works for him."

"So what should I do?"

"First thing is to remove those stickers. Don't give anybody any more information than you have to. Second, change up and don't be so predictable."

"Predictable!'

"Yes, you're very predictable. Hell, I've only known you a few months, he knew you for six or seven years!"

"Don't get angry!"

"I'm not angry, just worried. Are you tired right now?"

"Getting there."

"Well get your gas, get back on the road, and wait until I call you back."

"Why, what are you doing?"

"It's what you're doing. You're going to bypass Bakersfield. I have a friend in Tehachapi, he's a State Trooper. I'm going to see if he can suggest a place for you to dry camp. You've got water and your holding tanks are empty, right?"

"Yeah."

"Good girl. Hang tight, I'll call you right back."

He clicked off and I did too, a frown creasing between my brows. Could he possibly be right? I was predictable? Geez, who wants to be called that?

After checking my tire pressure, I went into the convenience store part of the station to pay, then I put a hundred dollars into old Betsy. I took my time pulling into the lane heading back to the interstate, hoping Brick would call before I was back in the driving groove. He didn't. In fact, it was over an hour later before I heard back from him.

"Sorry, some jerk thought it was necessary to rob the Denny's I was in."

"Robbed? As in stick 'em up?"

"Oh, yeah."

"Gosh, are you all right?"

"I'm fine."

"Did you shoot him?"

He laughed and I could just see him, his head thrown back, his mouth curved in a generous smile, and his eyes closed in delight. It made *me* smile.

"No I didn't shoot him. Broke his nose though, bad break too, as I did it with my elbow."

"Wow. I'm impressed."

"Don't be. Just sucky timing."

"For him."

"Yeah, for me too, I was just about to get a pedophile I'd been tracking. He was hiding out in the girls bathroom."

"I gather he got away."

"Actually no, he got hit by a car. But there's nothing we can charge him with. The undercover cop hadn't even gone back to the restroom yet. Then with the robbery, we both blew our cover. So, I've been here for an hour and now I've got police and emergency crews all over the place. I'll be writing all this up until midnight. I got an address for you; it's for the Tehachapi

State Police Barracks. They're expecting you in an hour or so. Just pull onto the back lot and dry camp there. No one will bother you."

"Oh, okay, that's sounds . . . uh . . . good."

"And uh, hey, do me a big favor."

"Yeah sure, what?"

"Just stay in the damned RV. I got enough to worry about without thinking that some trooper in uniform is going to sweep you off your feet while I'm two states away."

I smiled, not only at his words, but also at his gruff voice.

"Yeah, okay."

"And tomorrow night, don't be predictable! Goodnight."

I said goodnight to a dead phone, as he had already disconnected.

An hour and forty minutes later, I rumbled onto the back lot behind the State Trooper Barracks and found they had left a whole section clear for me. I gratefully pulled into the slot, turned off the motor and flicked off the front lights. Moments later, I was curled up in a ball in my bed listening to the generator keeping me cool, savoring thoughts of Brick, who even in absentia, was keeping me safe.

Chapter Twenty-seven

When I woke up and started moving around, I noticed that a piece of paper had been stuck under the windshield. Facing me, in big bold letters were the words, "COFFEE AND DONUTS BY THE DOOR." And sure enough, when I opened the door, there was a big thermos of coffee and a bag of donuts sitting there, just waiting for my avid appreciation. I waved to no one in particular and took the bag and the thermos inside and had myself a sugarfest.

I had showered and dressed and was about to take the thermos back, when my phone rang. I didn't recognize the number and almost didn't answer it, but then it had never been all that easy for me to bypass my curiosity. So with a tentative, "Hello?" I listened for the reply.

"Jenny?"

"Uh, yeah?"

"It's Connor."

"Oh, Connor! So you're there?"

"Yup. I'm here. Not that it's doing me any good. I need your advice."

"Did you find her?"

"Oh yeah, you were spot on. She's here. She's taking

summer classes."

"Well, what's the problem?"

"Approaching her, that's the problem. Just how do I do this?"

"What do you mean, how do you do this? You go up to her and say, "Hi, honey, I'm so glad I finally found you.""

"She doesn't know me from Adam, for one thing. So that's liable to scare her off. And the two times I've seen her, she's had a gaggle of friends cloistered all around her."

"Well, it would help to have her alone for this monumental occasion."

"Yeah, that's what I thought, too." I could hear the exasperation in his voice. "I don't even know how to find her again and when I do, I don't want to appear as if I'm stalking her; but like it or not, it seems that's exactly what I'm doing. Good God, she's so damn beautiful she makes my eyes water from the staring."

"I don't suppose there's a way to get her alone in a classroom or dorm room?"

"Are you kidding, the security around here is pretty tight. You have to have a school I.D. to go anywhere on campus."

"Well that's easy, enroll and take a class, that'll give you access. Man, if you could find out her schedule, you could even get into one of her classes."

"How long has it been since you were in college? It doesn't work that way anymore. You have to apply and that could take months, especially to a school like this. And from the look of some of these classes emptying out, I don't think they can fit another student in anywhere."

"I suppose you've tried Admin?"

"Yeeeaah! No luck there, it's all about the student's privacy. Even with what I thought was a plausible story, I got nowhere."

"Just curious—what was your 'plausible' story?"

"Boyfriend home from the war. Hey! I looked the part."

"They didn't even offer to contact her for you?"

"They sent me to her advisor, who is nowhere to be found."

"You can go online to MySpace.com, and if she has an account, contact her that way."

"I tried, there's no account for her. I even got a student I ran into in the library to try Facebook here on campus. She's not set up there either. I guess she's got more important things to do right now, what with beginning classes and adjusting to a different routine. It's barely the second week of the summer session here."

"Hmmm."

"So, I'm hanging out at the bookstore, 'cause I figure everyone ends up here eventually. You register, you get your class assignments and then you get the books."

"Well that's not a bad idea."

"Except that this could take forever, plus security is bound to wonder what I'm doing here, all day, everyday."

"How about putting an ad in the school paper?"

"Oh that's a brilliant idea. And just what would it say, "Looking for elusive girlfriend named Diana, don't you think it's about time we met in person?"

"Got your point." We were both silent for a moment while an idea began to take shape.

"She's a freshman. Most freshmen can't wait to 'experience' college."

"What are you getting at?"

"Find out where a freshman who's underage has the best chance of getting beer and what bar is known to be lenient when it comes to checking I.D. at the door. Then Friday night, hang out until you either see her, or some of the friends she's been hanging out with. You buy the beer for a round or two and you just might hit pay dirt. If she's not there with them, maybe they'll tell you where she can be found."

"Uh, isn't that illegal, helping a minor get alcohol?"

"You got scruples now? Just a few days ago you wanted to murder somebody, remember?"

"That was different, these are kids."

"Somehow they're going to get the beer, with or without imparting the information you need."

"You got a point there."

"If I think of anything better, I'll call you, but that's the best suggestion I can come up with."

"Okay, I'll try it. I'll call you on Saturday and let you know what happened."

"And if I don't hear from you, am I to assume you got thrown in jail for aiding a minor?"

"Either that, or Diana and I have connected in a very meaningful way, if you get my drift."

"Connor, if you find her, don't you dare rush her! No matter how she reacts to you, you be the adult. Her father can still come gunning for you, you know. Remember your vows, yours and hers—vows of celibacy until marriage."

"Yes, mother. I'll be a perfect gentleman."

"Yeah, right."

"I'll be exactly what I have to be to get her to fall in love with me again. If I need to be slow and easy, then that's what I'll be. But I am on leave you know, I don't have a lot of time here."

"Well, that's a good plan. Take your cues from her and let things happen naturally. Who knows, you two may not have that 'chemical thing' going on and this'll all be for naught."

"Trust me, it won't be."

"How can you be so sure?"

"Some things you doubt, some things you don't. I can't explain it; I just know that she's the one for me. Call it kismet, fate, destiny, serendipity, karma, whatever. Diana was made with me in mind. I'll prove it to you with a wedding invitation."

I laughed at his boisterous blustering. "You do that! And

I'll drive from wherever I am to dance at your wedding."

"Well, keep your dancing shoes handy, I'm going to hold you to that. I'll get back to you . . . real soon."

"Good luck! I'll be waiting to hear how things go," I said as I disconnected. I had to smile at his brash confidence. For his sake, I hoped Diana had been honest with him. If she'd been stringing him along, he was going to take this rather badly.

I put the phone down and washed the thermos before taking it back to the state troopers who had been thoughtful enough to provide it.

I was greeted with genuine friendliness by a handful of smartly dressed and keenly interested troopers. I didn't know what Brick had told them so I didn't explain my stay; I merely thanked them for being so hospitable and asked for directions back to the interstate.

It was mid-morning now, so I wasn't able to leave without an armful of subs and potato chips, along with well wishes and an invitation to come back anytime. Twenty minutes later, I was pointed toward Tucson and a white Bichon puppy.

Mentally, I challenged myself to come up with the name Angelina would pick for her new little pouch. Her doll, Lula Belle, was her sidekick now but I had no doubt that Snowbell, Bluebell, Tinkerbelle, or Annabelle would be her number one priority for some time to come.

Chapter Twenty-eight

My general impression of California, as I wended my way southeast, was of sand dunes—huge hills of sand with little growth on the higher peaks and sparse scrub brush on the low lying rises. It was pretty desolate between cities but I didn't really mind; the route I'd mapped out was specifically chosen so I could avoid the Los Angeles area and its world-class traffic jams. Brick detouring me to Tehachapi had served to dump me in the middle of nowhere but I had lucked onto a multilane highway that skirted Edwards Air Force Base and led to the ever-popular town of Barstow where I had the choice of heading south to San Bernardino, or east into the Mojave Desert. My general game plan was Yuma, Tucson, Las Cruces and Austin. Beyond that, I didn't have a clue how the heck I was going to get there.

I was deciding between Route 40, and aiming for Needles, where I could pick up 95 leading south into Yuma, a mere two hundred miles later; or to brave 15 South, and barrel into San Bernardino and San Diego, before running parallel to the Mexican border on East 8, when my cell phone rang.

It was Carol, the owner of the kennel where I was to secure Angelina's puppy in a week's time. Carol's husband was a vet and he had determined that, although it was not unusual to separate puppies from their mother at eight weeks, he wanted this particular litter to have the full ten weeks of mother's milk. They were an exceptionally small brood, and had reacted with extreme lethargy after their last series of shots. I thought it comforting that they put their concern for the welfare of the pups before monetary issues but was chagrined at the delay. What was I going to do for two whole weeks? I pulled over at the first rest area and pulled out my trusty NASCAR atlas. It was no longer crucial I head for Needles *or* Yuma.

I flipped through the points of interest pages and caught a blurb on the editor's best picks section. In a state the size of California, I was surprised there were only four honorable mentions: Blue Canyon, the snowiest place in the U.S. with over twenty inches of snow annually; the safari tent cabins at Safari West in Santa Rosa, where you can wake up to see a giraffe at your window; Los Angeles County as the most populous U.S. county with over ten million people; and the valley below the sea—Death Valley. It was purported to be 282 feet below sea level at Badwater Basin, the lowest elevation in the Western Hemisphere—yet only fifteen miles away was the highest point, Telescope Peak in the Panamint Mountains. I read that the record high temperature was 134 degrees, but for some reason I didn't take that in at the time. At Baker, I swung onto 127 heading north toward Death Valley National Park.

When I stopped at Tecopa Hot Springs for gas and walked out the door and down the steps, I felt as if I had entered a sauna. Again, the thought didn't register: Death Valley—record heat—people died here . . . Instead, I marveled at how efficient my air conditioner was working. What a remarkable time we live in, I thought, as I opened the little door that housed the gas cap. Even when I jerked my hand back from the heat that seared my fingertips, I marveled at how far we'd come. The pioneers of 1849 never entered my mind, or the fact that it was late summer.

Following 127, I came upon Ash Meadows, a national

wildlife refuge managed by the U.S. Fish and Wildlife Service, about nine miles southeast of the entrance to the park. A sign mentioned the Pupfish of Devil's Hole, saying it was the only place in the world where they existed, along with lizards of all types and sizes. I was ready for a break and curious as to what a "Pupfish" was. I also thought I could learn something about the creature I had reluctantly adopted.

Turning onto the gravel road, I thought about Stumpy in his terrarium in the middle of the hallway. I had a moment of remorse. This was his kind of country, yet I dare not let him loose here. Without a tail, he just wasn't ready. I felt like the mother of a teenager, denying her daughter the joys of attending a dance. Until youngsters had the skills to survive on their own, they just had to stay at home.

I stopped at Kings Pool and Point of Rocks Spring Pool. Not knowing what to expect, I tentatively got out of the RV and stretched while I looked around. There were large rocky hills, barren except for some scrubby brush. I could see a scattering of trees off in the flat lands. As I mopped my brow with a bandana I'd threaded through a loop on my shorts, I walked up a path where I could hear a babbling sound. *Where was everyone?*

I found a creek flowing over rocks. It was a cute little creek with crystal clear water and it meandered lazily along the pathway. How was this in the middle of the desert? There were a few picnic tables strategically placed so people could enjoy the shade of the trees and the babbling brook. *Where were the people*, I thought again, as perspiration ran in rivulets down my back and between my breasts. My shorts felt tight and I could feel the waistband cinching and sticking to my skin. Everything was getting clammy. I wished I'd remembered to bring my water bottle but I sure was happy I'd left the air conditioning running for Stumpy—gosh it was hot!

A short ways up the path I came to a pool, which appeared to be the origin of the creek. Obviously spring-fed, it continued to bubble from the bottom with an endless supply of water. I saw tiny iridescent fish swimming in the water and when I tried to touch one, I found the water to be very warm, similar to the hot tub I'd had in my old life on my triple-tiered deck high on a hill in Virginia. Wow! What a long way I was from "home," I thought as I tried to catch a fish in my hand. This water had to be close to a hundred degrees. How were these little creatures enduring this heat? How could they survive the water temperature, which I guessed was just shy of boiling? Had the water been cooler, I might have been tempted to wade in—God I was hot. I could feel the heat coming off of me in waves.

Following the path, I ended up at a self-serve visitor's center where I learned that the Pupfish, that only existed here, were an endangered species. *Yeah, since nature was damned near nigh onto boiling them to death.* I wondered how much longer it would be before they were finally extinct. I took my bandana off the loop in my belt and ran it under the stream of water from the vintage water cooler I found over in a corner. I read on the wall that the Pupfish were being closely monitored and that great care was taken not to disturb the algae growing in the streams, as that was their only source of food and where they lay their eggs, hence the lovely iridescent, sapphire blue water.

There was a boardwalk next to the center that offered a lot of information about the habitat of the area. The water from Crystal Spring, the spring-fed pool at the origin of the creek, was over 1,000 years old! I read how it began as water from rains and snow in the northern Nevada Mountains that had seeped underground through sand and rock toward the earth's warm center. The heated water then bubbled up through fissures in the earth's crust and formed the natural spring. This particular one pushed out 2,600 galloons of 87-degree water a minute!

I marveled at the beauty here, the Caribbean-blue rock basin and the brilliant green algae that created a pond that looked like it belonged in another world. That, along with the tiny blue Pupfish, made me feel as if I'd been transported to the tropics. And damn, it was as hot as a summer day on a Nassau beach! I backtracked my way to the RV, stumbling and staggering as if sleepwalking. It was odd that I hadn't encountered anyone in this mini-paradise, I thought, as I saw my Dolphin looming in a haze ahead of me. The heat was distorting the shape of it, either that or I needed glasses.

Inside it was nice and cool but I had the odd feeling that the generator was straining more than it should have been. There were still no other vehicles in the parking lot. I decided to take a quick, cold shower to revive myself a little before I headed into the park. I tossed a handful of brochures I'd grabbed when leaving the center onto the counter, made sure Stumpy had water and food, and stripped off my clothes. They stuck like paste and I had to peel them off slowly to keep from pulling at my skin, which seemed puffy somehow.

I felt a lot better after my shower, but I was a bit miffed that I couldn't get the water cool enough. It was as if an outside source was heating it, despite the fact that I was directing it to be cold by repeatedly pulling the lever to the right.

I put on my most abbreviated shorts and a silky halter-top that felt cool against my heated skin, and after shutting down the generator, I slid behind the wheel. I noticed the engine didn't turn over right away but chalked that off to the fact that I'd had the generator running a long time.

At Death Valley Junction, I entered the park on Route 190 from the east. It had taken me all morning and part of the afternoon just to get here but I wasn't tired, so I plodded on. I was eager to see all the amazing sights I'd read about and to ooh and aah over God's unique sand and stone creations.

Driving further west into Death Valley, I came across Longstreet's Casino located right in the middle of nowhere. It was a rather big place, with a hotel, amusements and restaurants. Finally, cars and people! I no longer felt like an alien on the planet. I found a parking space by some buses and shut everything down. I could see some RVs in the distance in an area that was landscaped with ponds. It didn't feel as hot as it had, so I didn't bother with the generator this time. Hell, Stumpy was a lizard, wasn't he? Hot and dry was how they were supposed to like it.

I had lunch at the casino looking out at the Funeral Mountains while I watched the people walking by, wondering where they had all come from and where they would all go when the casino closed. After chitchatting with the waitress, I found out that the casino never closed and that they had a 50-lot RV campground. Hmmm . . . maybe a place to park the beast tonight, I thought. But after further investigating, I discovered that they were full up. Not surprising, I thought, this was the only place I'd seen that had shown any signs of life for miles.

Knowing I had to continue on, at least until I could find a place to pull in for the night, I left money on the table and walked out the front door of the casino. It was like a blast furnace and I smiled, must be why the area was called Furnace Creek. I got back in the RV and gave a cursory look over at Stumpy. He wasn't moving, so I tapped the glass and one eye winked open. Okay, still with me. I slid into the driver's seat and motored up.

I drove by areas where the mountains were blue, green, purple and tan. Following signs, I turned the corner and pulled onto Artist's Drive and admired the splashes of color that reminded me of an artist's palette. The roads were becoming narrower and I worried what was up ahead, so on a scenic overlook I placed a towel over a series of rocks—those things can get hot baking in the sun—and fanned out the brochures I'd collected to see about finding a campground for the night.

I didn't dare turn the RV off this time, as I'd discovered it took way too long to cool it down again, and although I was worried about the gas I was wasting, I was running out of clothing—practically everything I had in summer clothing was in a pile in my bedroom, damp from me being hot and sweaty.

The little booklet on top drew my attention, as it seemed like a general flier on Death Valley itself. According to the words printed there, Death Valley was named by some lucky or unlucky pioneers in 1849. The story is that a hundred covered wagons left the Midwest in the fall of 1849 led by a Mormon battalion captain named Jefferson Hunt. Supposedly, he was familiar with the Old Spanish Trail across the desert. In Utah they headed south to avoid the fate of the infamous Donner party two years earlier.

They met up with a party heading the other way and took their advice on a short cut that would bring them out in the Tulare Valley, near the California gold fields. Some decided to "Go for the gold," while the others decided to continue on the proven route with their knowledgcable wagon master. The group that diverted ran into the mountains three days later and half of them turned around to go the long way. Twenty-seven wagons began the journey into the "Jaws of Hell itself." Shortly after, the group split again, and this time thirty-four men joined Reverend John Wells Brier and his wife, Juliette, in their struggle to continue on this chosen, yet treacherous route.

Eventually, they were reduced to walking, burning their wagons, and roasting their oxen to survive. By Christmas they had reached Furnace Creek in the heat of the valley. *Ohmygod, that's where I was right now!* Many members of their party perished but the rest had no choice but to continue the struggle and keep going. Legend has it, that as they finally found their way out of the desert, they looked back and said, "Goodbye Death Valley," attaching the morbid, but legendary name. After their 134-day journey, the meager walking skeletons were welcomed by amazed vaqueros of the Del Valle's San Francisco Ranch. The original party reached Los Angeles seven weeks after the others took the "short cut," recounting the beauty of the landscape, rhapsodizing over the yellow, pink, and blue wild flowers tucked into mountains with fascinating shapes and colors.

Oh Lord, I now knew that I should have stopped to analyze the niggling twinges I'd had earlier in the day. What the hell had I been thinking? I flipped through the rest of the brochures and found three RV parks in the area. I stood and picked up my towels and just as I took my first step toward the

RV, I heard the engine sputter and die out.

I couldn't have run out of gas, could I? I'd just filled up this morning. Oh, this couldn't be good. I ran up the steps, and once inside, I was assailed by a hot, molten, metallic smell. What the heck was that? I went over to the cockpit, slid into my seat and looked at the dashboard that was lit up with red warning lights. It took me a moment to read them all and to realize what was happening. The intense heat wafting from the firewall made me very nervous. Apparently I'd overheated something but I still couldn't believe it. I reached for the ignition and tried to restart the engine. Nothing doing. I turned the key all the way back and all the lights went out. I sat there in the silence that up until then had not seemed quite so profound. And let me tell you, realizing that you're all alone in a desert named Death Valley, in a dinosaur of a vehicle that requires engine or generator power to function and having neither, is a daunting and scary thing. I now knew where all the people were, and just why they weren't here where I was . . . all alone . . . in the middle of nowhere . . . without a way out.

I ran for my cell phone and punched the call button when Brick's name came up on the directory listing. Nothing. No tone, no beeps, no sound. I had no service, no little black boxes lined up on the side. The mountains were blocking the signal. Holy Moly! What was I going to do?

I told myself not to panic, not to let my mind wander and run through bad scenarios. Stay lucid, think positive, make a plan . . .

If I could get the generator to work, I could live in the RV, dry dock so to speak, and wait until someone started looking for me. Yeah, but just when would that be? I wasn't accountable to a single soul. No one in the whole universe knew I was coming here—to the home of the twenty-mule team trains and borax mining towns, that were no longer in existence. I looked out the front window to the mountains beyond. All I saw was rocks and more rocks, and precious few other things in between. If it wasn't for the asphalt road I was parked on, I could have believed I was back in 1849, looking at the same barren landscape that rag-tag band of travelers had come upon.

Stop! Stop thinking such desolate, depressing thoughts, I told myself. Get a grip! I had plenty of water, didn't I? Yes, I was sure I did. I ran to the refrigerator and opened it. It was delightfully cool. I stood there and counted the water bottles on the bottom shelf, deliberately taking longer than I needed. Twenty 12-ounce bottles. Well, that would be okay for a few days, I reasoned. I grabbed one and closed the door to protect the food for as long as possible. I held it to my forehead, then between my breasts to enjoy the coolness on my overheated skin before chugging down a few mouthfuls. While leaning on the door and looking out, I slowly allowed my mind to scatter. I had no idea what to do next.

I opened my laptop and typed a desperate message to Brick; totally oblivious to the fact that there was no way I could send it. When I hit the send button I realized how stupid I'd been—of course I couldn't send an e-mail. It's not like there was Wi-fi here in the middle of absolutely nowhere.

I forced myself to zone out, to think of inconsequential things, to avoid the panic attack I was sure was brewing inside me. How nice that I had a comfortable bed, how freeing it was to look out my windows and as far as I could see, there was no pollution, no traffic, no noise, no rain, no people. Nothing but sunshine and shimmers of heat, rising from the pavement that unwound like a black snake ahead of me. Snake! O my Lord! The desert had snakes and lizards—no offense Stumpy—and Gila monsters, and my mind conjured up a hundred wild beasts roaming the prairie ahead of me, most probably not even of this hemisphere.

Off in the distance I saw the sun beginning to set, turning the whole area into a kaleidoscope of colors too beautiful to describe. My eyes took it in for a moment and I even smiled at the sight, but then I realized what it meant.

Come nighttime, there would be birds of prey, jackals and hyenas and all sorts of hungry, desperate critters clawing to get into my RV to get to me. I felt my heart speed up and my blood coursing quickly through my veins, pounding to the beat of an internal drum. I ran back to the bathroom and to my medicine cabinet and took out a small bottle. I downed a tiny white pill before I could talk myself out of it. The last thing I needed to do now was sleep, but I knew myself, I couldn't afford to let panic take over. I needed to get some rest and come to terms with my situation. It wasn't going to happen if I wigged out. I munched on a power bar while I locked up for the night, closing myself in against the night, sealing everything against any kind of predator, be it small or large.

I sat back against the pillows on my bed, my legs curled up under me, my eyes wide with apprehension, until I felt the slow mellow feeling take over.

When I woke the sun was just coming up over the hill behind me. The shades were drawn but I could feel the change in the temperature. During the night I must have become chilled because I was wrapped in my comforter. Now I was kicking it off and desperate to get it off my clammy body. It couldn't be much past six I thought, and already it was hot enough to be stifling. Groaning, I eased out of bed and made my way up front.

I opened the refrigerator and was surprised it was still cool inside, not cold, as it should have been, but not terrible. I decided I'd better use what food I could before it went bad and figure out what to do with the rest. I debated about taking a shower but just couldn't justify the waste of water. It could be water I would need for drinking. My skin felt gritty and I didn't like the way I looked when I walked past the mirror above the dinette. My hair was lank and my face, though shiny from perspiration, looked dry and it felt like it crackled between my brows when I grimaced at myself.

Get over it! This is no time for a beauty analysis. This is

a time to ensure you have a future, I told myself, not a time to primp and worry about your corpse. Whenever someone found me, I wanted them to know I was smart and resourceful, not vain. Still, a little moisturizer couldn't hurt, I mumbled out loud and went back to the bathroom where I reached for one of my Clinique jars.

While I was slathering a think layer of cream over my face, I heard a low droning sound. I stopped and cocked my head to listen harder. It grew louder, and louder. I ran to look out the window and saw the culprit. It was a plane, a little tiny plane! I unlocked the door and ran outside waving my arms. But it had already passed over and was flying away. Stupidly, I called after it, "Help! Come back! Don't leave!" Of course, it continued on, making little putt-putting sounds as if it too were having engine problems due to the heat.

I took a moment to look around and scope out the area. Nothing had changed since yesterday. Flat land, high hills, desolate empty road. Then I saw it—a glimmer of silver, just a flash really, far off in the distance. But as I continued to stare at the horizon where I'd seen it, it grew. I watched until it became recognizable as a car. I stepped out into the road, shaded my eyes and waited for it to approach. It was still very far away. It grew brighter and larger as it barreled down the road toward me. When I could see the chrome of the grill flashing in the early morning sun, I started waving and didn't stop until it slid to a stop ten feet in front of me. The windshield was dark, I couldn't see who was behind the wheel. I couldn't even see what kind of car it was from the angle I was at but my first thought was that it was a silver Lincoln, just like the one Jared had been driving, the kind he usually rented when he traveled. I hesitated in my waving just long enough to quantify my thoughts. Was being rescued by Jared, better than dying out here alone in the desert? I was grappling with that thought when the front door opened and a man in a chauffeur's uniform stepped out. He had a puzzled look on his wizened face and held onto the doorframe as if ready to rethink leaving the safe, cool confines of the car. Then the back door opened and another man stepped out behind him. This one was tall and it struck me as odd that he had just exited the car with a cowboy hat on. He must have said something to the driver, as the driver got back into the car and closed the door behind him while the cowboy sauntered over, his boots crunching on the side of the road.

"Problem, Miss?" he asked and I could hear the drawl of a western gentleman.

"Yes, I did something to my engine and I can't get a signal on my cell phone to call for help."

His hand slid into the front pocket of his trousers, incidentally moving his sport coat aside and flashing a big silver buckle that practically blinded me. His shoulders were so wide they would have blocked out the sun, only the sun was behind me, casting my shadow in front of me. I thought it hilarious that the shadow of my head appeared to be in the area of his crotch. I had the urge to laugh and wondered if I was becoming just a bit hysterical here. As he drew closer my eyes were drawn to his, shaded by the brim of his hat. I had to guess at their color but not their intensity. He was assessing me from top to bottom. He flashed an engaging smile and white teeth gleamed between a full mustache. He was handsome in a just-got-off-a-bronco kind of way, every bit the rancher who didn't have to do anything more than go to tractor dealers and haggle. He had a confident stance that said he knew he was a man women couldn't help dropping their jaws over.

"So you need a lift?"

Hmmm. Did I want to do that? No, I thought not. "Can you just make a call for me?"

"I kin try," he said as he pulled a cell phone from an inside jacket pocket. He flipped it open, looked down at it, and sighed. "Nope. Caint. I don't get a signal out here either. Maybe Carlton can." He turned and motioned for his driver, who instantly opened the door and ran out to see what was wanted of him. I watched as they spoke and the driver went back inside the car. A few seconds later he popped his head out of the window and shook it.

"It seems we're not much help in that department. Why don't you just ride into town with us and we'll find somebody to come out and take a look at your uh, situation. Is it just you, or are there others? The word others was given a slight inflection that to me implied significant others.

"It's just me and Stumpy."

"Stumpy?"

"My lizard."

"Your *lizard*?" Again that weird, hesitant inflection.

"Long story. But I just can't leave him."

"Well, by all means, bring him along." His hand went up and his fingers snapped and the driver popped out of the car again and came running up.

"Carlton, see if you can help . . ."

"Jenny. Jenny, uh . . . just Jenny."

"I'm Craig, Craig Johnson—this here is Carlton."

Carlton nodded at me and I smiled and shrugged my shoulders. "Well, okay . . . just give me a minute to get some things together." It was so hot that I could feel the heat making my tennis shoes sticky on the pavement. I won't be but a minute, I promise."

I grabbed my purse, some clothes, a few toiletries, my laptop, and the terrarium. Juggling everything, I made it out the door where both men waited to relieve me of my burdens. I locked the door and followed them to the car, which now I could see was actually a limo. The abrupt change from the scorching heat of the desert, to the chilly confines of the air-conditioned interior, caused me to shiver and break out in goose bumps. I was experiencing a forty-degree drop in temperature in a matter of only a few seconds, so my overheated skin became clammy before equalizing itself to the change.

I was settled in the back seat, with Stumpy in the terrarium on my lap, when I noticed an open briefcase on the seat facing me. It was full of money.

Craig saw my eyes go wide and reached over to shut the case. "Just came from the casino, just counting my winnings."

"Well, glad you had a good night."

"Seems like the morning has been the real jackpot."

I blushed and tried not to meet his eyes, but this was a man who commanded your attention and held it. "So, uh, you live around here?"

"I live in Texas, but I own property in Pahrump."

"Pahrump?"

"Yes, it's where we're headin' now."

Oh Lord, he was talking me to his home? That couldn't be good. "If you could just drop me off at a hotel that would be great."

"That works out well for both of us, as I own a hotel in Pahrump. Also, several restaurants and a mall."

He could not know that none of this impressed me—not one iota. "Well, then maybe you could arrange a discount for me. I'm afraid it could be a while before I can get back on the road. I think I burned something up in the engine."

He was sitting beside me on the seat and I felt him shift and face me, "Discount? Little lady, you will be my guest. I wouldn't hear of anything else. We'll get you settled in a nice room, then we'll go to the local RV dealership to see about getting someone to tow your vehicle. And it would honor me if you would allow me to take you to dinner tonight."

"Uh . . ." I really didn't have any other plans, now did I? "Well, sure. That would be great. Thank you."

"Wonderful, always nice to share a meal with such a pretty little lady. Now tell me, what's a fine looking woman like you doin' on her own in a big RV in the middle of the desert?"

I wasn't about to tell him the whole sordid story of my life, but I found I could skirt the major issues and not be lying by just saying I was in the process of getting divorced and that

I was taking some time to be off on my own. He told me about his life in Texas, where he was both a rancher and an oilman and I told him the story about how Stumpy came to be my traveling companion.

He was pleasant, sincere, and very polite. If I hadn't needed a shower so badly, and some food, I would have been disappointed when we pulled under the porte cochere of what appeared to be a fairly upscale hotel.

"Here we are, is two hours enough time for you to settle in before we go see about getting your rig towed?"

"Oh, two hours should be plenty of time."

"Good. I'll leave you in the hands of my manager then." He stepped out of the limo when Carlton opened the door and waved a bellman over. Within minutes Stumpy and I were ensconced in a beautiful suite and room service was on the phone awaiting my complimentary lunch order. As I read them my selections, I chanced to look into the mirror above the desk. I had a big smear of moisturizer across my forehead. I'd been applying it in my bathroom when I'd heard the plane and then saw the limo. What a sight I was.

I settled into a deep, frothy bubble bath with a glass of champagne in one hand and a huge chocolate covered strawberry in the other. I loved soaking in hot water and although my Dolphin had a tub, it was not one I could stretch out in, and to fill it this high would have had water running all over the place.

A woman could get used to this kind of treatment, I murmured to the reflection of myself in the wall-to-wall mirror. But with my very next thought, I admonished myself. Yeah, sure she could, and then she'd end up right back where she was. Men of power tended to want to exert it in some way. Sure, Craig seemed perfectly affable and sincere, but they all did during the first getting-to-know-you stage. I wondered how Craig manifested his power. Was he one to swagger and show off all his wealth all the time? To demean all his underlings to boost his own esteem? Would he be the type to "buy" a woman with all he could do for her and then discard her after she had done all she could do for him? I mentally slapped myself. It was all just speculation, because pure and simple, I wasn't interested. I was fairly well smitten with Brick. Lord, if he could see me now. I wasn't living the simple life of a woman on the road in her trusty rig now. And speaking of trusty rig, I thought, I'd better wash up and get dressed. It was time to see just what damage I had wrought to my beloved Dolphin.

Chapter twenty-nine

The mechanic was as kind and polite as he could be, but he had some awfully rude news to impart. I had indeed fried my engine. The word "seized" was used several times before I heard estimates that were in the thousands, many thousands—like six and seven thousand. He had shown me the evidence, taking me under the Dolphin and insisting I feel the extreme heat still coming off the undercarriage.

I plopped down on a bench, avoiding a long tear in the vinyl where the foam poked out. We were in the vintage waiting area and despite having grease from my fingertips to my elbows; I put my chin in my hands. This was not good news, but what choice did I have. This was my home. I had to fix it. I was a hermit crab with no shell.

I nodded dully at the mechanic who left us to talk things over while he handled another customer. Mentally, I tallied my budget against what was in my household debit account. I would have to find an ATM and get some of the reward money out to cover the repair.

Craig was leaning on the doorframe watching me, his arms crossed over his chest. I noticed that his hat, pushed up on his forehead, almost touched the top of the opening. From the deep creases at his knees, I could tell they were bent to accommodate the low doorway to the office. The dealership and repair facility had been modernized with the advent of the new casino but you could tell that the office was circa 1940 and had seen its heyday many years ago. My initial thought was that someone had decided to build around it, rather than clear out the accumulated clutter.

Craig's gaze met mine and he cocked an eyebrow as if to say, so what are you going to do? I hesitated before taking a deep breath and flashing a quick smile. It is what it is, I told myself. I did this out of ignorance and had learned a valuable lesson about thermal dynamics.

"Well, it's either trade it or fix it, and other than what I did to it, it's really a wonderful RV. It's the perfect size for me and I'm used to how everything works. It's fairly new so I think I would stand to lose a lot if I traded it in."

I looked up to get his opinion, to see if he had any advice for me and was surprised to see a solemn, far away look in his eyes. My eyes followed his and saw that he was staring out the window to the boulevard and beyond. His eyes weren't focused on any particular thing; it was as if he had gone inside himself to think this over. "So, what do you think I should do," I asked, jarring him back from wherever his thoughts had been.

"I'll pay for it."

"Oh no, you won't! I have the money to fix it. I just have to get to an ATM machine to get it."

"I'm happy to pay for it; it's nothing, less than a wager at the tables."

"I don't care. It's one thing to put me up at your hotel for a few days, but definitely another to shell out thousands of dollars to get me out of a jam. I will pay for it, and that's that. Thank you for your offer though, it's very generous."

"It comes with no strings."

"I wouldn't care if it did. I'm an independent woman now and I pay my own way. I am getting great pride from that. I don't think it's something you'd understand, but this is the first time I've been on my own in a long time and it's very important to me that I take care of myself."

He pushed away from the doorjamb and reached for my hand. "Okay then, let's tell them to get started." He took my hand and pulled me up from the cracked vinyl bench and I let him lead me into the shop where the mechanic waited for our decision.

"Two weeks! I can't wait that long! I have to be in Tucson next week."

"I'm sorry, ma'am, it's going to take at least that long to get all the parts and then four or five days to get the work done."

"Oh my," I whispered as I turned away from both men and stared at my Dolphin over on the lift. Somehow it looked smaller high up in the air.

Craig came to stand behind me. I could smell his aftershave, one I knew to be David Beckham's *Instinct*. He put his hands on my shoulders and gently turned me to face him. "It's okay, I can get you to Tucson. It's a small matter really. Don't fret over it. We can drive or we can take my plane."

Okay, so maybe I was a little impressed.

"You'd do that for me?"

"And more if you'd let me." The look in his eyes was one I'd seen before and it scared me. It was the look of a man interested and not just in my welfare.

I took a big breath and let it out, conscious of his hands still on my shoulders that were starting to caress and knead in little circles. "Well, those are nice options." I looked over at the mechanic and nodded, "Take good care of her, she's all I've got."

Craig's arms stole around my shoulders and he walked me out of the shop in a very proprietary manner. "Come, let's go back to the hotel and get ready for dinner. I want you to tell me what you think of my new chef—I just hired him away from

Harrah's."

I did not like the feeling that I was "under a man's wing again." Although his touch felt nice, it did not feel right, but I didn't know how to shake it off without seeming incredibly ungrateful for all he had done for me. And hell, I had to eat.

Chapter Thirty

We had a wonderful dinner in the hotel restaurant watching the sun set over the eighteenth green of the hotel's golf course. I was in a lovely slip of a dress—honestly it really wasn't much more than that—which had been sent up by the shop in the galleria at the hotel—courtesy of Mr. Craig Johnson, a.k.a. owner.

I hated taking his charity but the only clothes I had hastily grabbed were tank tops and shorts. I hadn't even remembered underwear, so I would have to rinse my one bra and my one pair of panties out each night.

Even though the meal was served in tappas style, I'd managed to stuff myself with the delicious specialties of Craig's new chef. And of course, each selection had to be celebrated with its own complimentary wine, so I was sloshing on the inside, and was decidedly mellow when Craig stood and pulled me onto the dance floor to dance with him.

I hadn't danced in ages but it was one of those slow numbers that all you really had to do was lean into someone and shuffle your feet in time to the music. Being in a man's arms, and then somehow being wrangled between his thighs, made me think of Brick and just how much I missed him. I sighed deeply, wishing with all my heart that he was the man holding me in his arms instead of Craig Johnson.

At the sound of my sigh, Craig stepped back and looked down at me. "Aren't you having a good time?"

"Oh yes, a wonderful time. I'm just . . . Well, I'm just remembering another time, another place." I suspected he thought I was referring to my husband and to happier times. He couldn't know I was pining for a man I'd met not all that long ago. Interesting how I had left a man after six years of marriage, determined never to be vulnerable to a man's attractions again, and here I was like a broken record echoing Brick's name over and over again in my melancholy mind.

Craig gathered me back into his arms and brought me close to his chest and for a moment I took advantage. I closed my eyes and pretended he was Brick. I wrapped my arms around him and laid my head on his shoulder as the musician crooned and swayed on stage. My lips close to his neck, my hips swaying with his, I was transported to a place where it was only the two of us. I imagined it was Brick cinching me tighter, Brick's hand stealing down my spine to press me against his arousal.

When the song ended, we reluctantly broke apart and I felt guilty as soon as I saw his all-knowing smile. I had unintentionally sent him the wrong message; he thought I was coming on to him, that I found him desirable. On the way back to the table I tried to think of a way to let him know I hadn't meant to send those signals to him.

As soon as we were seated, a waiter tapped me on the shoulder and handed me a folded note card. I looked up at him in surprise and said, "For me?"

"Yes, the gentleman said to give this to you."

"Gentleman? Where?"

"He left. He did not wish to wait for an answer."

I took the card and opened it, my eyes widening with each succeeding word.

You don't appear to be "stranded," "desperate," or

"dying from the heat." You don't look like you need rescuing. In fact, it looks like the only thing you and your cowboy need is a condom. Don't call me again.

"Oh, dear God." My hand went to my chest and for a moment I couldn't seem to get any air into my lungs.

"What is it?"

I couldn't think of a thing to say. My eyes, filled with tears, blinked hard and fast trying to keep the hot tears from running down my face but they did anyway. I pushed back my chair, nearly toppling it, and ran out of the restaurant. I scanned the lobby looking for Brick, then ran out the front door and stood under the portico trying to catch a glimpse of him. There was no sign of him; he hadn't wasted any time getting away from here. And I couldn't blame him. What he had to have seen would have been devastating if I'd come upon him in a similar circumstance.

I sobbed and swiped the back of my arm over my face, trying to stem the hot flow of tears. Brick . . . he'd been here, he'd found me. He'd come to be with me, and instead had seen me dancing with Craig. And by the dreamy look on my face, it must have seemed to him, as it would to anyone, that the man holding me in his arms captivated me. He had no way of knowing that the man whose arms I had longed to be in at that moment were his.

"There you are! What in Sam Hill is going on?" Craig took my shoulders and roughly turned me to face him. I know I must have looked a sight with my makeup streaked and my eyes and nose red from my tears.

How had this happened, I asked myself. Why was Brick even here? Then it dawned on me, there was only one way this could have happened and I had been the one who had unwittingly put everything in motion.

"Do you have WiFi here?" I asked in a dead voice.

"Yeah, sure, every hotel has it. You have to. People won't stay in a hotel that doesn't."

"I have to go to my room."

"Tell me what's going on first!"

"I can't," I sobbed. "I can't say it or it'll be true."

But all the way up to my room my mind screamed it: *He hates me, he thinks I used him, he believes I betrayed him, and he'll never understand. He'll never forgive me.*

As soon as I could manage to get the keycard to work, I bolted through the door and yanked my laptop from its case. I opened Outlook Express and clicked on the Sent Messages icon. My heart stopped in my chest, my worst fears were realized—I had lost Brick forever due to my own incredible stupidity.

Needing to know just how badly I had screwed things up, I opened the message that I had tried to send when I had been stranded—when it hadn't been able to be sent due to not having a connection. It had apparently gone into a queue, waiting until there was a connection, which occurred the moment I walked through the lobby door of the hotel yesterday. I forced myself to read the words I had written, the hysterical ones that had brought Brick here looking for me.

HELP! I broke down in the middle of Death Valley. There's nothing but dirt and rocks for as far as I can see. I am stranded. I think the engine is gone. I may have overheated something. My situation is pretty desperate, I'm afraid I'm going to die in this heat. I can't get a signal on my phone to call for help. As soon as you get this, please ask someone to come look for me. I'm near Furnace Creek on a turnoff not far from Artist's Drive. Jen

Well, that had done it. The panic in my words had brought him. And now look at the mess I'd made of things! I slammed the top down on the laptop and threw myself across the bed and cried until I heard someone knocking on the door. I lifted myself up and saw my reflection in the mirror. My face was puffy and red, my eyes barely slits and I had crushed the fine silk dress into folds so deeply creased that they would probably never iron out.

I couldn't face anyone this way.

"Go away!"

"If you don't open up, I'll use the master. I'm not kidding, Jenny, open this door!"

"Fine! Fine! Just wait a minute!"

I went into the bathroom and grabbed a washcloth and ran it under cold water before sopping it all over my face. I didn't bother to wring it out, which didn't help the dress any. As I turned to leave the bathroom, I saw Stumpy in his terrarium looking at me with blinking eyes. "I know, I know! I've ruined everything!" I said the words with venom, but not for him, for me.

Sobbing and wiping my face with the dripping washcloth, I opened the door to Craig.

"You're going to tell me what's going on and I'm not leaving here until you do!" He kicked the door shut behind him and I noticed that the force of his heel left a black mark on the door. The sound of it slamming shut echoed for what seemed like several minutes as I stared into his concerned face. He had the note in his hand. I hadn't even realized that I'd dropped it.

"Your husband leave you this?" he waved the note sending it flying across the room.

I slumped down on the bed then kicked my shoes off. Technically, they were his shoes. At least they were faring better than the dress.

"No, not my husband. My . . . I don't know what to call him . . . I guess you could say he was my boyfriend in a way. But he's certainly not that anymore."

I flopped back on the bed and tossed the wet washcloth over my face. "It's a long story," I mumbled through the cloth. I heard him walk across the room and felt it when his weight pressed into the mattress. My eyes popped open and I bit my lip. Great, now what?

Craig lifted a corner of the washcloth off one eye and I turned my head. He was lying on the bed beside me, his head propped on his elbow. "I got all night, and I like stories, as long as they're not tall tales."

I had to laugh at that. "Believe me, I couldn't dream up anything as crazy as our relationship."

"I'm listening."

For an hour I told my tale, while he and I both stared at the ornate ceiling. Then he picked up the phone and ordered coffee and brandy. As an afterthought, I heard him include chocolate truffles.

"You know, I never do meet the right kind of women. Most take my money, some take years off my body, but you take the cake, my dear."

"Why is that?"

"You took my heart."

"I didn't mean to."

"I know. So, now that we're both broken hearted, what do you suggest we do about it?" His crooked smile of irony broke my mood.

I smiled back at him and said, "I say we go get a dog!"

He ruffled my hair with the damp washcloth. "Deal. I'll call my pilot and tell him to be ready whenever you say."

"Give me a few days."

"Take as many as you want. You gonna be okay?"

"Yeah."

"You're welcome here as long as you want, you know that don't you?"

I nodded, fresh tears now brimming my eyes. Why hadn't I found a man like this the first time?

Room service knocked on the door and Craig let them in. He left when they left, grabbing a handful of truffles as he went by the tray. "I should take the lion's share because my heart's bigger than yours."

"Chocolate must have been invented for star-crossed lovers like us."

"Remind me to buy some stock in Hershey in the morning."

Chapter Thirty-one

As soon as Craig left I searched my large tote for my cell phone. I hadn't bothered to turn it on since leaving the RV as I hadn't been expecting any calls. I could have avoided this major fiasco, if I'd only bothered to check it. Brick had tried to call no less than ten times. All the voice mails were terse with worry, demanding, and often filled with profanity that I wasn't picking up. The last one informed me that he'd finally tracked down the RV at a repair shop in Pahrump and that he was on his way to the hotel where I was staying. That had been a few hours ago, a few very long and stressful hours.

Ignoring his admonition not to call, I pressed the redial button and listened to it ring, and ring, and ring.

By two the following afternoon it was apparent that he was never going to accept another call from me. The service to his cell phone was disconnected and the e-mails I had been sending all night were bouncing back as returned mail. He had pulled his accounts and was no longer available to me. I had no way to get in touch with him.

Brainstorming the following afternoon, I remembered he had a friend who was a State Trooper in Tehachapi. I called the station where I had dry camped less than a week ago and spoke to the sergeant on duty. He took my message and said he'd have someone call me back. When they did, it was only to tell me that Brick had no desire to talk to me and to stop trying to contact him.

I couldn't believe I had screwed up what had promised to be a romance on par with the Highlander's. In desperation, I grabbed the file on Brick's sister that was poking out of the sleeve in the laptop case I had thrown across the room last night. It had a picture of Brick in it and I wanted to see his face. I needed to trace his lips, look into his eyes and talk to him, if only to his photograph.

It was a picture of him and Jillie. He was holding her in his lap while she was opening a present. They both looked happy and smiled for the camera. I could see his twinkling eyes mirrored in hers. Even though she was his half-sister, you could tell she favored him. I brought the picture to my lips and kissed his smiling lips. It was obviously the only way I was going to be able to kiss him until I could get him to listen to me.

An idea popped into my head and began to bloom. One thought formed after another until my head jerked from the outlandish way my mind was working. If I found Jillie, Brick would have to talk to me. I could find Jillie by finding Snooks, the man who had her. Snooks had one very distinguishing characteristic—he had one brown eye and one blue eye; any eye doctor would have noted that. Most people saw an eye doctor yearly if they wore glasses or contacts, 78% of all adults did. Living in an RV and working as a vendor at RV rallies would necessitate joining certain clubs for membership discounts. Doctors often provided special discounts to club members in order to increase their business. I had an ingenious idea of how to find out the names of those patients. Despite the H.I.P.P.A. laws, I thought I had a good chance of tracking down the names of men with heterochromia iridium. I would do a state-to-state search beginning with Oregon where Brick had been focused. I was very excited.

I emptied the desk of all the stationary I could find and got to work. I worked six hours straight and came up with nothing. It turned out that researching this was a lot harder than I thought.

I did my research on heterochromia iridium and discovered that multicolored eyes are a fairly rare phenomena, occurring in only about one percent of the population. So . . . the U.S. being just a tad over 300 million, that left just 300,000 people. It seems to occur without prejudice to sex, taking out more than half for the female population that still left about 140,000. Factoring in age, I figured I could narrow my search down to a paltry 90,000 men afflicted with this condition. I definitely had my work cut out for me.

Jumping from one chat room to another, along with doing an impromptu online survey, I discovered that most full-time RVers preferred to have their eye examinations at either Wal-Mart or Costco. Wal-Mart had approximately 2,500 locations; Costco, for the most part, used independent optometrists, so that narrowed it down a lot.

Flipping through the file I came upon several flyers that had been nationally circulated at the time of Jillie's disappearance. There was even a poster that had been used for television bulletins. I sat back in my chair and stared at Jillie's picture, begging her image to talk to me, to give me some kind of clue where to go next.

What I got was a perverse train of thought that began with: because of the large circulation Brick could have easily achieved with these fliers, and the news stations that would have eagerly jumped in to help, surely this man had to have considered going into hiding by at least camouflaging one eye, if not both. Maybe this man was wearing colored contacts. Nearly everyone wore disposables these days. Followed by: you had to have annual checkups to get prescriptions written, and as a fulltime RVer you would want a place that was convenient, inexpensive, and a chain of some sort so you could get your prescription renewed wherever you happened to be at the time that yours ran out. I had come full circle back to Wal-Mart.

I opened the directory for the Wal-Mart webpage under the heading of Oregon, and I began to systematically call Wal-Mart Vision Centers. My story was that I had found an engraved gold contact lens case with their business card tucked into a slot in the lid. The owner's name was etched into the case, but it read simply "Snooks." On the back of the card "heterochromia iridum" was written in big block letters, presumably by a doctor's hand, so I had to assume he had this eye condition, whatever it was. The reason I was trying to track this person down? There was also a valuable ring and a locket inside the case. Invariably, the harried receptionist slowed down and checked with her colleagues, often the doctors themselves. I left my number, sounding genuinely concerned about getting the case and the jewelry back to its rightful owner. I didn't expect any return calls; I just expected to systematically cross off every eye care center that a reasonable and thrifty RVing-type person might go to. If "Snooks" wore contacts or glasses or had eye exams, I was fairly confident a Wal-Mart store in the West serviced him. It was a shame I couldn't access some kind of database and do this with a few clicks of a mouse. Instead, I resigned myself to cold calling. I figured I could make thirty calls a day, and possibly knock off one or two states in a week's time, if I didn't go absolutely insane.

I treated it like a full-time job, getting up early, starting the calls by nine, and taking coffee breaks and lunch breaks before winding down at five. Carol had called and said the puppies were doing better and that mine could be picked up in a few days so I told Craig while we were having dinner. Craig and I had agreed his pilot would take us to Tucson in five days, so I didn't have any time for days off or for sick days. I also didn't have much time to be broken hearted or engulfed in grief—until the whistle blew and I was off duty.

From five o'clock to seven, I filled the time by checking

in with my sister and my parents and encouraging Connor in his search for his Julia. With only two possible days of the week where he might run into her again, waiting from one weekend to the next was sheer torture for him, as he knew time was running out—he was almost halfway through his stateside leave. He had only four more weeks to go.

At seven, Craig collected me and we went to dinner and to either a show or the casino, where I stood behind him and watched him bet thousands on a single roll of the dice. Afterward, he would take me back to the hotel and kiss me goodnight on the cheek. I noticed that each time he got closer to my lips.

He asked me once what it was I did all day, as I didn't appear to be sunning by the pool. I told him I was working on a book and he sniggered. Yes, I know, I told him; everyone is working on a book. He gave me an indulgent smile and nodded. After that he didn't ask any more questions. I wasn't lying when I said I was working on a book, because I was. The book in question just happened to be the online Oregon phone directory.

I called every other day just to see how the work on my Dolphin was coming along and was told maybe tomorrow about four times.

It was Thursday afternoon and I felt as if I was back in the grind at my old stock-brokering job, the job I'd had when I met Jared. I remembered things from that period, things like yesterday, Wednesday, had been hump day, and that tomorrow, Friday, was casual dress day. This whole week I had stayed in my P.J.'s until it was time to get ready for dinner with Craig. I smiled and wondered how much more casual I could get than a cropped cami and tap pants. The receptionist at a Wal-Mart in Pendleton, Oregon, who had automatically put me on hold when she picked up, finally came back on the line.

"Sorry to keep you holding so long, a little boy came in with his eyelid superglued shut."

"Ugh!"

"Yeah, but you'd be surprised how often it happens. He'll be fine though, Doc's with him now. How can I help you?"

I no longer had to even think about my spiel it was so practiced. "I found a gold contact case with your card in it. The only identifying thing is the monogrammed lid and your card inside. I was wondering if you might be able to tell me if you have a patient named Snooks. It also looks like he might have two different colored eyes by the doctor's little note on the card."

"Snooks? I know Snooks. He's not a patient here as far as I know though. In fact, I haven't even seen him for about two years. He and his wife used to go to my church."

Well you can imagine, I damned near fell off the edge of the bed where I was polishing my big toe. Polish went everywhere, ruining the lovely intarsia spread. I couldn't believe my ears.

"You know Snooks?"

"Well, like I said, I haven't seen him in almost two years. He used to sing in the choir. His wife helped out in the nursery—she taught my little boy Bible stories."

"Do you know where they are now? Do you know his real name?"

"I don't know where they are, they always traveled a lot. But I know his name was Robert and hers was Ellen, the little girl was Annie."

"They do have a little girl because there's a picture of a little girl in this little gold locket I found." I was improvising as I went along. My heart was pounding so hard I was surprised that it wasn't drowning out our conversation.

"Yeah, she was a few years older than my son, she used to play with him. Cute little thing, but shy, you never saw a kid so shy."

"This must be their case, the girl in the photo is very young, too. Do you remember their last name by any chance?"

"I'm pretty sure it was Burns."

"Robert Burns?" I asked not bothering to hide my cynicism.

"Yeah, that's why I remember it. Funny, huh? Only I think they spelled it B-Y-R-N-E-S. Hey I've gotta go, I've got another call coming in."

"Wait! What's your name?"

"Liz Preston-Hardin, now I really have to go."

I sat there shaking, the phone in one hand, the nail polish brush in the other, still dripping pink polish on both the rug and the comforter in steady, even plops.

Holy shit! I found him! My heart could not have been beating faster. I felt like I had run a marathon and now that the adrenaline rush was over, I was crashing. I could not get rid of the shaky feeling that was inside me, getting ready to burst out, until I realized exactly what it was that was getting ready to burst out. I ran to the bathroom and got there just in time. The ball of nerves knotted in my stomach from the moment she had said "Snooks? I know Snooks," had churned until the inevitable happened.

I took a quick shower because now I was clammy all over. I had gone from being overheated just before that last call, to filled with an emotion so strong it overwhelmed my system. I felt as if the blood running in my veins had been turned to the consistency of syrup and I heard each loud pump of my heart in my ears. At the same time I was shaky and spasmodic, as if I'd been on a caffeine high. I was now wiping my face with the towel and pacing naked around the room as I went over every word of our conversation. Afraid I would forget something, I managed to write everything down, but the scratchy handwriting didn't look at all like my own.

Calmer now, having doused my head and abraded the life back into my skin with the towel, I reached for the flier I had been staring at just a few days ago. A young Jillie stared back at me and I imagined I saw her smile.

"Jillie, are you Annie now? Have I really stumbled onto

something that could lead your brother to you? How could I have possibly been that lucky?"

I looked at the number on the flier and went over to the bed to get my phone. Now to get him to talk to me, and believe me, I thought. Surely he doesn't hate me enough to think I could get him all hepped up and send him on a wild goose chase.

The phone was picked up on the second ring and a man who sounded tired and bored asked me one question after another. With each answer lending more credence to the call, I was finally able to ask some of my own.

"Can't you just get Brick Tyler on the phone? Just have him call me; this is his sister we're talking about. He's an agent for the North Carolina State Bureau of Investigation, I'm sure you must have his number."

"I can't do that. I have to take everything down and have my supervisor review it before the information gets forwarded to *anyone*. Less than five percent of these calls yield any results. We have to be very careful not to get the families' hopes up."

"You tell your supervisor to call Brick Tyler. Because if you don't, he may never see his sister again!"

"Are you threatening me?"

"No! I'm just telling you we don't have time to screw around on this. Now I know you're recording this. Just get him on the phone and let him listen to what I've told you!"

I hung up with such force that the loud snap of the phone cover closing reverberated against the smooth stucco walls. I stood there listening to my heavy breathing and then sat on the bed and forced my head between my thighs. When I felt light-headed from this, I flopped back on the bed and immediately felt the scrape of dried polish on my bare back. Idly, I was wondering if nail polish remover would take it off without causing the dark colors of the fabric to bleed when my cell phone rang. I didn't recognize the number.

"Hello?"

"This had better not be some kind of trick."

"You know, I've just about had it with your attitude. If you could possibly think that I would stoop so low, I don't have anything more to say to you. For Jillie's sake, have another agent call me." Instead of slamming the cover shut this time, I pressed the red, end call button. The slick pretty pink nail reminded me that I hadn't finished my matching pedicure.

I walked over to the nightstand and dialed room service and ordered a bottle of their mid-priced cabernet and a bottle of nail polish remover from the sundry shop in the lobby. My cell phone started ringing but I ignored it until I had finished my call, making sure they knew not to chill the wine. For some ungodly reason, they often chilled reds out here. Ugh!

Then I strolled slowly back to my phone that was vibrating and repeating the Hallelujah Chorus over and over again.

"Yes?"

"I'm sorry."

"That's better."

"So what's this about Jillie? How did all this come about?"

"First you have to listen to me about the other thing, our little miscommunication."

"I knew this was a trick!" I knew I had to hurry or be cut off.

"No! No trick! Jillie was my motivation. I knew you'd talk to me if I found her, so I made it my job to find her."

"So you've found her?"

"Didn't you hear the tape of my conversation?"

"No, it's on a loop, they didn't want to waste time finding it and called me instead."

"I have not been double-timing you."

"I don't care about that. Tell me about Jillie."

"Jillie's waited four years, she can wait ten minutes more."

I briefly told him what had happened from the moment I broke down at Furnace Creek, until I had retched a few moments ago. It wasn't a pretty thing to relate but I had to tell him everything to give as much credence to this unbelievable tale as I possibly could. I finished by telling him that, although I still loved him, I was so shaken over our trust issues that I didn't think it would work out for us in the long run, so as far as I was concerned, our relationship was over anyway. I told him that by refusing to take my calls he had made my life hell for almost a week and that I was dearly tired of living in hell.

"Jenny, don't do this. Don't shut me out right now. You can't know how I felt when I saw you there in that man's arms, looking for all the world that you'd found a haven you would never, ever want to leave."

"That's exactly what I was thinking, only the man I was with, at least in my mind, was you. But I can't do this right now. I'm exhausted and still shaky inside, plus I have nail polish all over the place."

"What?"

"I was polishing my toenails when I was talking to Liz, it went everywhere. It doesn't matter . . . I can't talk now. I just wanted you to know I hadn't done anything wrong, nothing I'm ashamed of at least. I gotta go, room service is at the door."

"Jenny—!"

I hung up on him again and this time I threw the phone at the headboard. I heard something crack, but at that moment, I really didn't care if I'd broken it or not. I was almost to the door before I realized that I was naked. I detoured to the bathroom to grab the waffle knit robe that the hotel provided from the back of the bathroom door.

I took both bottles from the man at the door, and once back inside, I opened the most damaging first, the one that would prevent me from being ready for dinner on time.

Two hours later when Craig knocked on the door, I was snockered, but good. I had managed to dress, but not in any way that I would want to be seen in public. The door shut behind Craig and then he slowly removed his sport coat and took great care folding it before tossing it haphazardly on the back of an armchair.

Room service was dispatched again and we settled in for a night of long chats between gruesome movies. Around two in the morning Craig pressed a series of buttons and a porn flick came on. With an upward quirk of an eyebrow he turned to me and half smiled, "Interested?"

It was the most blatant come on I'd ever had, so I had to laugh.

"I'm serious."

I sobered. "I'm sorry, I know you are. It's just such an unusual approach."

"You're a very unusual woman."

"And all I yearn for is a quiet home life with a few kids, a dog, and maybe even a lizard thrown in for good luck." It was an odd thing to hear amid the heavy breathing and sultry music in the background.

"It can all be arranged, just say the word," he said in a husky voice.

"And what word might that be?"

"Mine. Say you'll be mine."

"I already did that once and it did not work out well at all, and I loved him."

"That was the problem. Love mucks things up."

I picked up my wine glass and raised it in salute. "You got that right. Love sucksalup."

He took the glass from my hand and put it on the coffee table in front of us, then hit the power button on the remote and all was quiet, except for the hum of the air conditioner. He stood and took my hand. I hesitated for a moment.

"I'm not going to ravish you, at least not when you're like this. Get some sleep, it's Tucson for us tomorrow." He picked up the wine bottle that was still half full; I remembered it as being one of three room service had sent up. "Unless you want to spend the whole plane ride in the head, I'd better take this with me. Get some sleep, we need to be at the airport by ten." He turned me toward the bed, then spanked my butt.

I knew I was fortunate that Craig was an honorable man; a lot of men wouldn't leave a woman in the state I was in without taking a few liberties. I counted myself lucky when I heard the door close behind him that he had only smacked my rump. My rump in Pahrump. That struck me as hilarious and I laughed myself silly, rolling back and forth on the bed.

Chapter Thirty-two

I woke up with sweat making my nightgown stick to my skin like a latex glove. My back felt as if there was a plaster cast on it and I was scared, suddenly very, very scared. I groped for the lamp on the nightstand and clicked the switch on the cord and the room filled with a stark white light that stung my eyes. Pinpoints of light lasered into my eyeballs and I had to close my lids against the sudden brightness. I squinted and slowly opened one eye so I could assure myself there was no imminent danger, no slasher at the foot of the bed.

Blindly, I scrunched my pillow up behind me until I was sitting up against the headboard. I drew a shaky breath and peeled the nightgown off and tossed it to the floor. Just about that time the A/C kicked in and caused me to jump. I held my hand over my eyes massaging them lightly, trying to forget the dream that had woke me.

But it was too vivid, as I'd actually been there at one time in my life; it wasn't the kind of dream concocted of imagination. It was the fact that I had participated that instantly brought shame and an inner terror that caused me to shrink in fear. I was bent over Jared's knees and his hand was coming down with a force that propelled me forward, but his grip on the back of my neck wouldn't let me slide off and escape. He favored a ping-pong-paddle as it had a "nice waffly pattern" that he liked to see imprinted on my bottom. He made me sit bare-assed on his naked thighs so he could feel the ridges while his fingers made me wet before taking me from the rear. I was not overly plump there and without sufficient cushioning I often felt the blows clear to my bones. At first it hadn't been so awfully bad as he smacked me until he became fully aroused, and that first time it had only required three paddlings. But as time went on it took more contact of the paddle to my burning, crimson bottom to satisfy him—thirty-two one time, enough that I couldn't sit or wipe myself without crying out for days, which I also think gave him pleasure.

Craig's off-hand, friendly smack to my butt last night must have triggered this nightmare I thought, despite the fact that I'd had so much to drink that it really shouldn't have even registered. It had, nevertheless, festered in my mind until . . . I looked at the clock . . . 3:23 a.m.

I shifted my weight to one hip and rubbed my bottom just to be sure I had been in the throes of a nightmare, as everything had seemed so real. It was smooth and cool, not inflamed or tender to the touch. More than ever I hated that man! How dare he haunt me and instill these awful feelings of dread and shame! I had left all that behind! When would I be free of him? I put my hand over my face and cried. Yesterday had been a truly lousy day and I could not wait until the sun came up so a new one could begin.

Then I remembered that Craig was flying me to Tucson in the morning to get Angelina's puppy and my heart lifted. It was the one bright thing in my life right now, seeing her face when she got her new puppy. I threw off the covers and jumped out of bed, idly aware that my rump was not sore as I'd halfway expected. I wondered if everyone dreamed as vividly as I did or if that was just one of my wonderful "talents."

I felt so good after a long, cool shower that I picked up

the phone and called room service. It was only four and I almost hung up when I realized it, but a calm, sweet-voiced woman answered, "Yes, Miss Jenny, what can I get for you?"

I wondered if all Craig's guests got this type of service or if he had instructed everyone to go the limit for me. I ordered a breakfast that would fill a moose and took a whole hour to systematically devour it all. Then I dressed in cuffed jeans and a shell sweater with a cardigan to match, as I had no idea what the temperature on the plane would be. I fed Stumpy from the stash I'd been collecting with help from the staff and let him out for a run around the bedroom. His tail was mostly grown in now and he seemed pretty responsive. When he winked at me as I put him back in his terrarium, I couldn't help smiling. We were a team and he didn't require anything from me but bugs. He wouldn't break my heart or give me nightmares, and he wouldn't play dead as I suspected Jared was doing so he could entice me out in the open, so he could hurt me again. There was something to be said for a pet that asked so little. I was almost dreading the day when I would have to set him free.

Chapter Thirty-three

The puppies were so adorable that I almost bought two. But then I thought about my life and how uncertain it was right now and realized the last thing I needed was another pet, especially one who would require me to buy carpet cleaner by the case. Craig watched as I held each one, offering advice and reminding me that if I wanted one for myself that he would buy it for me. I was so tempted, but honestly, I could barely take care of myself.

The little girl puppy that found my hair so enticing quickly became my favorite and after an hour of vacillating, I chose her. I gave the breeder a wad of cash, listened to the care instructions, and cuddled the little fluff of hair to my chest as we walked back to Craig's rented Town Car. "Angelina is going to be thrilled with this precious little thing," I said, as I cooed to it and kissed its tiny wet nose.

"Are you sure you don't want one of your own?"

"Thank you, but no. Stumpy's just my speed for now, low maintenance, and until he gets his tail all the way back, easy to keep up with."

"If you change your mind, we can come back."

"I won't. It's not time for me to give up any of my

newfound freedom yet. There will always be cute puppies."

He smiled over at me and tousled my hair. "You are making so many decisions lately that I wish would go the other way."

"I'm sorry. I just have so much I have to think about now. And wow, a puppy. Hell, the next week of traveling with just this one is probably going to exhaust me."

"Your wardrobe at least." He nodded with his chin to the area of my chest where the puppy lay curled above my breasts. I didn't have to look down; I felt the warm trickle soaking into my bra and sweater.

I gave a sigh of resignation as I lifted the puppy and put her on the ground at my feet."

"I think you're going to have to work on your timing, that's hardly going to do any good now."

The puppy began biting my toes and licking the straps of my sandal. She'd had a two-minute nap and relieved herself quite unabashedly and was now ready to play. After a few minutes, I scooped her up and tucked her into the carrier we had bought on the way here. After a quick ride back to the airport we were in the air and on our way back to Pahrump, where my RV was ready and waiting. While in the plane I made use of the pilot's glass cleaner to minimize the damage to my sweater. I actually only managed to make it uniformly wet.

At the dealership, the mechanic tried to convince me that he had finagled the manufacturer into paying for the new engine but he just couldn't carry the lie off. I knew that Craig had arranged to pay the repair bill before we arrived to pick up my Dolphin. I wagged my finger at him and tried to write him a check but he wouldn't hear of it. Finally he did accept the check, but I knew that he'd never cash it, so it was an effort in futility.

I listened to a lecture about overheating and asked a few questions that had been on my mind since owning the Dolphin, mostly those concerned with the operation and connection of the TV and DVD player and the generator. Then it was time to go back to the hotel to collect Stumpy and all the rest of my things.

I tried to get Craig to let me pay for my accommodations, and refusing that, at least the damage to the bedspread and carpet from the nail polish I'd spilled. The remover had worked in some places but had made big washed out blobs in others.

"In case you haven't had it drilled into you enough, I've a mind to keep you and take care of you and all these piddly expenses you manage to accrue for all time. And by the way, just how does one person eat $78 worth of breakfast?"

I hung my head in shame, allowing the puppy to burrow under my chin. "I was very hungry and I started very early, and I just kept eating until the sun came over the mountain. Everything on the menu sounded so good that I couldn't decide, I think I ordered a little of everything."

He chuckled and ran his finger playfully down the slope of my nose. He stepped back and slowly looked me up and down, as if trying to figure out where I'd put it all. In my tight jeans and pee-dampened sweater, it might've shown except for the fact that it was the first decent meal I'd had for days.

"I'll get a bellman to help you, I can't watch you go. You are by far the best thing I ever picked up in the desert. If you ever need me, you know I'm only a phone call away." He leaned down, scratched the puppy under her chin and kissed me by my ear. "I mean it. Anything."

I watched him walk into the hotel lobby, impossibly tall, confident to the point of cocky, and chivalrous as all get out as he opened the door for a middle-aged woman dragging a suitcase behind her. Effortlessly, with just one hand, he picked the huge bag up and carried it inside for her.

I sighed. If Brick had not come along first, Craig would've been an enticing appetizer on the man menu. That was for damned sure.

I gave "Sweetie," as in *Hey Sweetie, stop peeing on my shirts*, a nice long walk, and yes, I cleaned up after her. Then

I loaded up my Dolphin for the trip to Texas. My little Vespa, which I'd used to get around while the RV was being repaired, went on first, then I checked the tires and made sure all the basement doors were locked.

In the pile of stuff the bellhop had brought through the lobby and deposited on the curb were some interesting additions to the pile I'd left in my room that morning. Among them was a huge basket of fruit, many Styrofoam containers of food from the restaurant, a bag of kibble with a bow and a beribboned jar of what appeared to be fireflies, along with a huge bouquet of flowers. I could just envision Craig handing over a twenty-dollar bill to one of his young male guests and asking him to catch fireflies for him last night. I didn't usually opt for fireflies for Stumpy, as I'd read they had a ridiculously short life to begin with and I hated to be the one to make it even shorter, but I was not about to let them go so I could look under rocks at my campsite tonight. The fireflies would do nicely. Craig was the most thoughtful man I'd ever known.

I'd never traveled with any flowers before and was unsure where to put them while I was driving. I ended up floating them in an inch of water in the bathtub so they wouldn't die and anchoring them in place by taping the cellophane wrapper to the shower wall.

I was so happy to get my home back! After everything was in and I'd gone over the checklist, I sat on the sofa for a minute to just look around. I loved this RV; it felt more like home than the insanely expensive house I'd shared with Jared for the last six years.

It was cute and everything had its place—some little nook or cranny was reserved for each item, in a very practical and commonsensical way. Even the bathtub, small as it was, served a dual purpose now. It had everything I needed. I could not wait until tonight when I could pull the RV into a campsite, fill the bathtub with a nice aromatic bubble bath and settle into it with a glass of wine and my book. That was if I could find a place that had hook ups. There would be too much gray water draining from the tub for the holding tank if I couldn't. I am not very good at conserving water. I had never been one to fill the sink to do dishes. I'd always run the water continuously, washing each plate, cup, saucer or spoon and then rinsing each item before putting it in the sink drain before retrieving another. RVing had quickly changed that style of dishwashing. I now filled a dishpan and let things pile up before washing the dishes, and then when I was done, I found some shrub or flower that looked a little droopy instead of pouring it down the drain. In many ways RVing was a "green" lifestyle. Conservation and recycling was very important to this way of life. I was more than just okay with that.

I stood up and walked back to check on the puppy one more time before pulling out. She was already whimpering in her carrier so I thought the further I could distance myself from that the better, so she was stuck in my bedroom, tucked between the bed and the wall so the carrier couldn't slide. It would be darker back there too, and I was hopeful that she'd sleep some. It didn't sound likely though.

"Hey Sweetie, you be a good girl and pretty soon you're going to have a whole new family to take care of you. You'll have a nice big yard and a sweet little girl who probably won't let you out of her sight for a week. She's just going to adore you!" I stroked her nose through the wire mesh door of the cage. "Now be good! No more whining please!" Stumpy was in his terrarium that was jammed in on the other side of the bed so it couldn't slide around either. He looked fairly content, slumbering on a flat rock. I raised the window blind on his side as I knew he loved basking in the sun.

On the way back up front I noticed that the entryway had accumulated its usual collection of grass cuttings and odd specks of dirt. No matter how careful I was, I was always tracking in dirt, which was the one thing about RVing I would change if I could. Despite mats outside on the ground, two treads on the outdoor steps, and three carpeted interior steps, along with a mat at the top in the main living area, the carpet always looked like it needed to be vacuumed. I shook my head, resigned as always to the situation. I looked at the clock on the microwave, it was 2:30 in the afternoon. I'd better get going, I told myself, or I'd never make my first stop before the sun went down, which was usually my goal. Backing in and hooking up at a campsite in the dark when you were by yourself was not all that easy.

Settling into the driver's seat I had to smile at myself in the rearview mirror. Even though my RV had its foibles, it was mine, and I loved it. So what that I had to remember to turn off the A/C if I wanted to use the microwave, the convection oven, the toaster, or the blow dryer? My RV worked with 35 amps, so I was constantly blowing a fuse if I forgot. The A/C could draw 20—26 on its own and the microwave or toaster an easy 12. So what if I had to grill most meals outside to conserve propane? So what if I had to take G.I. showers or run out of hot water while washing my hair or shaving? So what if I had to unclog the bathroom sink every few weeks by pulling the drain apart and cleaning it as it didn't have a big enough drop or I didn't use enough water to push all the gunk through the trap? So what if things shifted in the refrigerator while I was driving and I wasn't always careful when opening it? Buying an RV and taking to the road had still been one of the best decisions I'd ever made in my life.

I adjusted my seat and the mirrors and belted up. Oh, it was going to feel so good to be on the road again. "Sweetie . . . quiet back there! Go to sleep! Stumpy make her shut up!"

Chapter Thirty-four

By the time I had driven a hundred miles, I was ready to take that dog back to the kennel in Tucson. I didn't know if I would make it to the campground I had selected from the Internet to be my first stopping place on my way to Austin. At the next rest area, I pulled over to walk *The Dog*. I was no longer calling her Sweetie, I was thinking Yappy might be more suitable. I fed her and walked her again before forcing her arched rump back into her carrier. She did not want to go back in the carrier. I could hardly blame her. I wrapped a tiny travel alarm I had bought just for this purpose in a hand towel and put it in the carrier beside her and patted her on the head. She seemed mollified for the time being.

Stumpy got the opened jar of fireflies placed on the bottom of his terrarium along with fresh water. I was getting rather good at doing this quickly as the first few times I'd done this maneuver, I'd ended up chasing mosquitoes and crickets around the RV for a long time before capturing them. The mosquitoes I'd had to squash, and although I considered them to be fresh kill, Stumpy had turned up his nose at their inanimate bodies. The cricket didn't have a chance though, that long tongue made quick work of him. I ran some cold water in a washcloth and held it to my face for a minute to revive me, then mopped at my shirt, again wet from holding *The Dog*. When would I learn not to cuddle her up under my chin?

Two hours later I pulled into Blake Ranch RV Park, twelve miles east of Kingman, Arizona. They supported Sam's Club guests, and although Brick had warned me not to be predictable by using Club parks over and over again, I registered and found a nice, wide, pull-in lot. I'd wanted to make it to Flagstaff, but only made it to just past Kingman. I just couldn't stand the noise the dog was making anymore, whimpering as if her heart were broken. I had to keep telling myself that this was normal for a puppy, that I really wasn't hurting her. I had no doubt that the first night away from mom and siblings would prove to be daunting indeed. As soon as I turned the engine off she stopped whining and resumed yapping. She had been quiet for a few minutes here and there during the last hour, but now it seemed she was up and wanted some attention. I could hear her thumping against the door of the carrier and rattling it. It was a relief to close the door behind me while I did the hook ups. Poor Stumpy, I wondered if he had ears and what he thought of the constant yip, yip, yip.

After settling in and playing with the puppy on my bed while I munched on some cheese and crackers, I took that much earned soak in my bathtub. The wine had mellowed me and I was even back to calling the dog Sweetie again. I was taking my laptop out and setting it up so I could check my e-mail, when I noticed it was suddenly very quiet, too quiet. I went looking for Sweetie. She had her nose right up against Stumpy's with only the glass of the terrarium separating them, her plume of a tail was wagging furiously back and forth fanning the air. It was so comical I had to laugh out loud. I picked up Sweetie and held her with one hand while I walked back to the front of the bus. When I felt her peeing down my shirt front again I almost dropped her. She got a bath, I got a quick hosing off with the showerhead, and after one final walk that yielded nothing, I put her to bed for the night. Then I brought Stumpy's terrarium out to the living area and closed the connecting door to drown out the puppy's frantic pleas.

I was delighted when I made the Internet connection so easily and waited while my mail downloaded. I was thrilled that I had a message from Connor, two from Daniel, and several from Brick. I guess we were no longer incommunicado. I was curious to learn if they had found Jillie yet so I opened his first.

Brick: I met with the receptionist you talked to in Oregon. She was very helpful but initially quite upset that she had fallen for your little ruse. The only thing she could add to what you had already learned was that a year before joining her church, the Byrnes had lost a young daughter to asthma. She said they were very protective of Jillie, whom they called Annie, which was why one parent was always in the children's daycare area during church services. She has no idea where they went. One week they were in church and the next week and all the others thereafter, they were not. She remembers them well because they kept to themselves a lot and the man's eyes fascinated her as she'd never seen the anomaly before. We cannot seem to find him anywhere. He must be on the road. We have six teams of agents working on this now so it's only a matter of time before we track him down. Thanks to you we at least have a name—we're checking all the credit bureaus, banks and credit card companies and all the D.M.V.s around the country for licenses or registrations. I know that it won't be long until we find Jillie. I feel very confident about that now. I owe you a great debt and a huge apology. Please see past my unfounded spate of jealousy, I know that I should have been more trusting. It was just that you were right there in front of me looking so content in the arms of another man. I admit that I completely lost it. And I was too stubborn to listen when you tried to explain. We have had a roller coaster of a relationship from the very beginning, it's time for an upswing now don't you think?

His next e-mail message asked for my location and asked me to please turn my cell phone back on. I had used so many minutes calling the eye centers that I had no time left on it. I had to remember to buy more minutes at the next convenience store that sold them. I didn't answer Brick despite knowing that he'd probably get the receipt that said I'd opened his messages. I had feelings that were too close to the surface and still needed more time.

Daniel was inquiring about my progress and trying to pinpoint my arrival. The other message was from Angelina telling me she was building her puppy a dog house, with her dad's help of course, and did I think her new puppy would like it painted green or blue?

Connor had the best news of all. He had found Diana. She had finally come to the bar he'd been hanging out at and after making eyes at her across the room he'd finally built up the courage to ask her to dance. I read every word with eyes agog.

Connor: I looked her right in the eyes and asked her to dance. When she simply nodded I reached for her hand to take her to the dance floor. You would have thought our hands had contacted through an electric fence. When I held her in my arms on the dance floor and she swayed to the music with her thighs against mine, I thought I'd found heaven for sure. I can't describe how wonderful it felt to hold her and look down into her smiling face.

Then the strangest thing happened. She said, "I knew you'd find me. I just knew it." There on the dance floor, right in front of the

```
DJ who was playing a song by the Decemberists,
I held her face between my hands and we had our
first kiss. If I ever wondered whether this was
real love or not, our first kiss settled the
matter—for both of us. We had the most amazing
night. We sat on the steps of her dorm until
the stars starting dimming their lights. We're
going to get married before I'm called back,
and we'd like you to be our combined maid of
honor and best man. Yup, we're tying the knot
legally, but not officially. Diana will stay here
while I serve out my final tour and when I get
back we'll tell her parents. Anyway, that's the
plan. Any chance you can head to the east coast
to witness our wedded bliss? Love, Connor.
```

Oh my, oh my. I hadn't expected things to go quite this well, and certainly not this quickly. I was thrilled for them and anxious to meet the girl who had stolen this wonderful man's heart. But could I go all the way east? Was I up to a cross-country RV trip so soon after heading west from the east?

I thought about it for quite a long time and then it occurred to me that I wouldn't necessarily have to take the RV east. I could park it in a campground and fly to Rhode Island and then fly back. It was perfect really, except that I would have to use my old I.D. and fly as Debbie Jameson, as I knew that in order to fly, you had to have a picture I.D. Since there'd been no sign of Jared, I figured he was still incapacitated with his memory loss. It wouldn't be a problem to be out in the open, I reasoned. The issue of the hospital bracelet that had been mailed to me was a little disconcerting, as I had no idea who had sent it, but I didn't dwell on it, since nothing had come of it. I hurriedly replied, asking for the specifics so I could plan my trip. I brought him up to date on Brick, Jillie, and our little fall out. In previous e-mails I had already told him about my overheating problem and the Good Samaritan I had found in Craig. With any luck I could visit

Angelina, drop off Sweetie, park my RV, and fly out of Austin or Dallas, and make it in time to give the new couple my blessing. I loved a good romance and this one was the stuff dreams were made of.

I finally went back to Brick's e-mail and told him how encouraged I was by the progress his team was making and that as soon as I could, I'd buy some minutes for my phone and turn it back on. I was still raw from some of the things he had said to me, so I didn't do more than answer his questions. I didn't tell him that I had Angelina's dog and that I was making plans to join Connor in Rhode Island. Connor had always been a sore spot with him anyway. They were like two dogs peeing, marking their territory, but Brick was too hardheaded to see that Connor had belonged to another bitch long before I'd even met him. Now, the thing with Craig I could understand, I was partially at fault with that one, but I still wasn't ready to pretend that things were all patched up between us. And I'd be damned if I was going to apologize for anything.

I swallowed my last sip of wine, dropped the glass in the soapy washbasin to wash in the morning, and began to make my way back to the bedroom. I stopped to say goodnight to Stumpy and realized that his tail looked completely normal now. Soon, I could let him loose without any pangs of guilt. It saddened me to think of him leaving me and getting back into his world, but he had a life to lead, and so did I. Besides, I had definitely not planned on our relationship being a permanent one at the onset. My mind flashed back to the night Connor had shamed me into adopting this little lizard and becoming his caretaker until he was back to normal. I had to smile remembering Connor's words, "First you give him a name, that honors him and makes him yours. Then you touch him to show you care. And then you feed him."

Somehow I just knew that he and Diana were going to make it. Despite beginning their marriage on the sly, I knew he had what it took to woo her parents over. He was smart and ambitious and with his Army training he would go places. He'd settle into a good career and be a good provider. They would have their Happily Ever After and I would have a good friendship with them, much as I did with Daniel, Julia, and Angelina, my extended RV family. I thought about Calvin, Jasper, Jodi and their children, and wondered how they were all doing. I had to smile; my circle of friends was shaping up to be every bit as weird as family.

I stroked Stumpy along the curve of his back, whispered good night and went to the back to hopefully get some sleep, despite *Demon dog* whining in the kennel.

Chapter Thirty-five

I don't know how it happened, but when I woke, there was a soft puff of fur burrowed into my neck. I blinked my eyes open and looked into two little black eyes and pulled back just in time to see a little red tongue and tiny teeth make a grab for my nose.

"What the hell? How did you get here?"

I scooped her up and held her over my head and away from my nightshirt, a long, soft t-shirt that I did not want christened. "How much did I have to drink last night?" I asked out loud. "Or better yet, how long did you whine and howl? You think you're smart, getting me to take you out of your kennel and putting you in my bed, don't you?"

Her tail wagged and her tongue lolled. She certainly was cute. "Well, it's outside for you, and right now before I have to wash my sheets." I held her with one hand while I felt the sheets. "Hmm, it's a miracle that they're dry. But I'm not putting you down, or anywhere near my chest until you've had your walk."

I quickly got her outside and praised her lavishly when she squatted and piddled and then I walked her for ten minutes more hoping for the serious stuff. She wasn't back in the RV five minutes before she'd selected a special spot for that little number, namely two. I fed the critters and myself, walked over to the bathhouse and showered and then broke camp so I could get back on the road. As delightful as Sweetie was, I was anxious to hand her off. I was afraid I might do something irreversible with regard to her training that would cause Angelina hardship down the road. I really knew next to nothing about puppies. Come to think of it, I'd known exactly nothing when I'd found myself saddled with a lizard, and I hadn't done too badly in the mommy department there.

After going over the infernal checklist, I lumbered out of the campground, careful to avoid the overhanging branches that always seemed to need trimming in these places. I had spoken to a woman in the bathhouse who had told me that at their last campground her husband had to get his saw out and take off a few branches before they could even pull their rig into their site. Of course, he had managed to fall out of the tree, and now she was waiting on him hand and foot while his back healed. I could see myself doing a lot of things, but shimmying up a tree with a saw blade between my teeth was not one of them. This RVing was definitely an easier adventure with a partner. Checking the lights, for instance—you're supposed to check your turn signals and brake lights before starting out for every trip. How does someone on their own do that, you ask? You pay a little kid to stand behind the bus where you can see him in the TV monitor and he waves his hands each time you put on a signal or step on the brakes. So, naturally this is not an item that gets checked each and every time I start out, especially if I head out early.

I got back on Route 40 and continued east. At Flagstaff I turned south and picked up Route 17. At Phoenix, I found a rest stop and walked the dog, which I had discovered did not whine or protest quite so much if I sat her carrier on the passenger seat so she could see me through the wire grid of the door. I strapped the seat belt around the carrier so it wouldn't shift and occasionally fed her tiny treats through the slots while keeping up an almost constant banter. Often, I discovered she was fast asleep and here I was still rattling on in an effort to amuse and entertain her.

After our walk I fixed my lunch and admired the scenery from a picnic table. A few people stopped to pet the puppy and several times another pet was brought alongside to sniff her butt. I did not like this part of the socialization. I felt that my sweet, innocent, little girl puppy was above wagging her tail and allowing the nasal inspection there, but apparently she was not. She pranced and let all manner of canines circle around her, as if knowing she had the exact smell that would entice. I watched as my *Sweetie* became downright trampy from the attention. The little bitch would be easy pickings when she came in heat, I thought. I thanked God that I would not have to be around for all that. That was Daniel's problem, his and Julia's.

I dragged Sweetie away from all her admirers and got back in the RV. I drove through Phoenix and Tucson, where Craig and I had flown to get the puppy, and picked up Route 10. At Las Cruces, New Mexico, I decided to call it a day and pulled over to find a campground. I found what appeared to be a lovely campground right off of I-10, at Exit 140. I say, "Appeared to be lovely" because I had noticed that sometimes what was depicted on websites wasn't always what you found. But in this case, Hacienda RV resort lived up to its name. From the high stucco arches of the motel to the pristine pool, it was first class. The only thing I could fault, if I could fault anything, was that the pull-in lots seemed bereft of trees. The trees that were there appeared to have been planted in a pattern, and each site had been allowed only two. But that was fine with me, as I didn't plan on being outside of the RV very much at this resort. This campground was one for my book, the book I kept on campsites that I wanted to return to if I was ever in the area again.

The view of the mountains was spectacular and I enjoyed walking Sweetie far longer than her tiny legs could manage and ended up having to carry her back. I took Stumpy out for a run and as I watched him scurrying around, darting under bushes and using every rock for a better vantage point, I realized that his tail was back, good as new, whipping back and forth as he ran and even shuddering as if delighted when he settled onto a steamy rock. I looked around the area trying to see things from his perspective. It was a wonderful place with a great climate.

Now I have great disgust for people who abandon their pets while on vacation, burdening complete strangers with their care, but this was different. Stumpy couldn't live in a terrarium forever, and I couldn't even begin to keep him as well fed in the bug department, as I'm sure he would like. And the plan had always been to let him lose when he could fend for himself. I looked over at him as he basked in the late evening sun. His name was no longer appropriate; he was a beautiful specimen of a side-splotched lizard with a long pointy tail that flicked back and forth sinuously. His skin was reflecting the sun and he was iridescent with bold blues and greens. Some lovely woman lizard would find him quite irresistible, I'm sure. And then as I watched, amazed as he did that red throat blowing up thing that he often did, he ran forward a few paces and did it again. I felt a twinge of sadness, my lizard wanted to mate; he wanted to have sex with a female gekkonidae. That was one thing I could not provide for him. I felt an overwhelming sadness when I realized that it was time to set him free, time to let him get back to what he'd been doing when I'd stepped on him and severed him from his tail.

I thought about leaving him right then and there, but I just wasn't ready to let him go yet. He'd been an ideal pet. I walked over to pick him up so we could go back to the RV and to Sweetie who was probably bellowing at the top of her lungs and disturbing every RV on our block when I saw something flash out of the corner of my eye. Holding perfectly still, I moved only my eyes to try to track it. I was deathly afraid of snakes, but I wasn't about to turn tail and run without my lizard. Then I saw her, a tiny version of Stumpy, not nearly as colorful, but most definitely a close imitation. She was more brown than green and her skin didn't sparkle in the sun, but I knew instantly that she was a she from the way she was blinking. It was almost coy the way she was holding her head and blinking. I looked back to Stumpy wondering if he'd even noticed her. Oh, he'd noticed her all right. He was painstakingly making his way off the rock so as to not show his hand. Once on the ground, he did that thing he does that looks like he's doing pushups, then he made a beeline for her and before I could blink, he was on top of her, riding her. I felt as if I should turn away and give them some privacy but I was fascinated. I stood rooted for several minutes as he pumped his body against hers, causing them both to flatten and then puff, flatten then puff. He was obviously in no hurry whatsoever as it appeared he was taking breaks between bouts. Then he stopped and stared at me dead on, eyes full wide as if to say, "Do you mind?" I shrugged, wiped at a tear, and walked away.

Back at the RV I cried as I cleaned out Stumpy's terrarium, then cuddled Sweetie in my arms as I sat crossed-legged on the sofa watching the local news.

It was as if there'd been a death or something. I was unbelievably sad for someone who had been so reluctant to take on the care of half a lizard so I had to smile despite my own melancholy. Stumpy was back in action and he appeared to be quite the ladies' man. He was going to do just fine back in the wild, and really from the beauty all around me, I supposed I couldn't have picked a better place.

After dinner I put on my bathing suit and took a dip in the pool that adjoined the motel. I played a water game with some kids, tossing around a little foam ball called a water bomb. We took turns soaking each other by trying to make it splat just before it got to them. I became pretty proficient at making it skip and then splat right in front of their faces just as they caught it. We had a lot of fun and I was soon approached by one of the dads who was sitting on the edge of the pool.

"You're great with kids."

"Not always," I said with a chuckle, thinking of the many times Angelina had tried my patience.

"You have any of your own?"

"No, that hasn't happened for me yet. Maybe one day."

"You here by yourself?" I was always leery of answering that kind of question in the affirmative around strangers. "No, my Sweetie's back in the RV resting."

"Oh." He'd clearly been expecting a different answer, but I left it at that. I wasn't really in the mood to chitchat right now and I really didn't want to encourage a man who had four sons. I wondered if his wife had left because she couldn't cope, or if somehow he'd lost her. A woman in an electric wheel chair came out from the bathhouse and rode over to where we were both sitting.

She was attractive with long brown hair and looked to be in her mid-thirties, but even with the towel draped over her, I could tell that she had no legs. "C'mon kids, time to get ready for bed. Randy, you didn't clean up after dinner and I thought I told you to get the laundry started." She looked over at me and glared. "I hope you're not looking at my husband with any ideas in your head. He's got chores to do."

"Charlotte!"

"What, I know you want her, you want every pretty girl. And if you hadn't run into that truck, I'd still be pretty like she is."

"Charlotte . . ."

"Don't Charlotte me, just get those kids out of the pool and ready for bed. I'm exhausted." She pushed a button and the wheel chair spun around then the steady drone of the motor reverberated around the pool area as she let herself out the gate and rode down the road toward the long rows of RVs.

As he stood he muttered, "How can she be exhausted, she doesn't do anything all day but harangue everybody. I'm sorry she was so rude to you."

I didn't say anything; I didn't know what to say. I hadn't

a clue.

"She used to be sweet, she didn't use to be this bitter. I can take it, but I worry about them," he pointed at the group of boys on the other side, who were drying themselves off and wrapping their small, lean bodies in big colorful towels.

"Well it's nice that you're spending time with them and treating them to a vacation."

"Vacation? This is no vacation. We're full-timers. I work the RV rallies, she home schools the kids. There's a big rally coming here in the fall, a Good Sam's Jamboree in Red Rock Park."

"Really?"

"Yeah, the Fall Jamboree. I gotta do some ground work for it, then come back for the event."

"Hey you wouldn't happen to know a man who goes by the name of Snooks, though his real name is Robert Byrnes. He works the rallies and full-times with his family, too."

"No, doesn't sound familiar, but there's a ton of people working these things. There's a big group of us who work the shows. I can ask around if you like."

"That would be great! I have a pen and paper in my beach bag, I'll write my phone number down for you. My name is Jenny by the way."

"No, don't write it down, she'll think I'm planning on havin' an affair with you. She thinks I want every woman I talk to. Just tell me the number, I'm real good with memorizing numbers."

I gave him my number and told him I was so sorry for what he was going through but that I was glad he was so concerned for his kids.

"I have to be, I'm the one that did that to her and she will never let me forget it."

"It sounds like you could use some counseling for the whole family."

"Jenny, I could use a lot of things, but counseling ain't

one. If I could find a woman who would take me and my four kids, I'd leave her to her bitter life because every day is more poisonous than the last."

"She needs help, too."

"She just wants me to pay for running into the back of that truck and coming out whole while she lost her legs."

"Have you ever apologized for your part in it?"

He turned and looked at me as if I was daft. "Apologize? I didn't do it on purpose!"

"Well of course not, but that doesn't matter. I suppose I'd still want the apology even if it wasn't intentional."

There was a long silence while he stared into the water. Then he said, "You would?"

"Yes. And then I'd need you to tell me all the time how pretty I still was, and that you were still attracted to me."

"But I'm not."

"Because she has no legs?"

"No, because she's so ugly about everything now. I tried to make love to her after the accident, but she won't have it. I finally gave up. I suppose that's why she thinks I'm out gettin' it somewhere's else."

"How long ago was the accident?"

"Two years last week."

"Well you can't keep going on like this, it's not good for the kids for one thing."

"And it's not good for me either. I plain and simply do not want to be around her anymore."

"Try bringing her some flowers and apologizing, maybe even a little gift,"

"Like what?"

"I don't know, a necklace, a ring, some little token. Something that says I still love you."

"That's just it, I'm not sure that I do anymore."

I stood up and looked over at the boys who were waiting for their dad at the gate. "I wish I could help."

"You already have. You don't know how lonely I am for someone to talk to."

"Talk to her, accept some of the blame, and find a way to show her that you could still desire her if she wasn't so . . . well you know."

"Yeah, I know. Well, thanks, I'll think about everything you said. It's nice to get another woman's perspective, you've said some things that make a lot of sense. And I'll call you if I find anyone who knows this Snooks guy. Why do you want him by the way?"

"He's got something that belongs to a friend of mine."

"Ohhh. I see, well I won't tip your hand then."

"Thanks. Good luck to you and the kids, and Charlotte, too."

On the walk back to the RV I thought about Charlotte, how young she was, and how hard her life must be, adjusting to being in a wheelchair and taking care of four young boys. Then I thought of Stumpy and smiled. Wouldn't it be wonderful if people could grow back appendages as easily as he had? I knew there would come a day when medical science would figure out how to do that but I didn't think it would be in time to help Charlotte. I sincerely hoped Randy would be able to break through to her and put their lives back together. Gosh, the interesting people you meet on the road, I thought as I put my key in the door and opened it.

Sweetie and two little piles were waiting for me. I muttered as I cleaned up the mess. "Pretty soon this is going to be Angelina's little disgusting chore," I said as I picked her up and showed her where the piddle pad was, on the floor by the sink. "Not once have you made it on the pad, what's the matter, don't you like the color blue?"

I took her out one more time, although I'm not sure why I bothered, before locking up and heading back to my bedroom to watch TV. It was quiet except for the hoot, hoot, hoot of an owl. I wondered what Brick was doing right now, as I idly stroked

Sweetie's fur and flipped through a magazine.

An ad for Jared's chain stores came on the television and I looked up to watch it. I recognized it as being an older one. He had been a very handsome man and still was. I wondered how he would have coped with a trophy wife who had lost her legs. Surely that would have cured his obsession for me.

The RV magazine had some beautiful pictures of Quebec and Nova Scotia and it occurred to me that after I saw Connor happily married that I had no agenda. I could go back to the RV that I was going to park in Texas, and then head north to see Canada.

Hmmm . . . I would need my passport for that and I had foolishly left it behind in the safe at my house—along with my birth certificate, and without that, no chance to get another passport. I could apply for a new birth certificate but that would take a long time and be very difficult without a permanent address to have it sent. My mind started processing things. I soon decided that if I could verify that Jared was still suffering from memory loss, that I might just risk a foray back into my house to get my papers before heading to Rhode Island to see Connor married. It would be easy to fly into Dulles, rent a car, and run in and out of the house to get those two things. I wished I knew if it had been Jared who had sent me his torn hospital bracelet. If it had been him, then he remembered me, and this just might not be the best idea.

I picked up Sweetie, held her nose-to-nose and whispered, "We're going to see Angelina tomorrow! She is going to be so delighted with you!"

Chapter Thirty-six

I was up at the crack of dawn, or as my sister used to say when we were kids, *the crap of dawn*, anxious to get on the road so I could present Angelina with her gift. I was always conscious of "quiet time," at the RV parks so I took my time and made as little noise as possible. I made sure I had everything done, so that when I turned the engine over, I was in gear and off of the site within a minute or so. Not everyone was as considerate as I was, but most RVers were.

Soon I was back on I-10, which would take me down into Texas and all the way over to Austin. By my calculations, I had about six hundred miles to go so it was iffy if I'd make it today but I was sure going to give it my best shot. Four hundred miles in a day was my typical limit but I hated the idea that I would be so close without making the effort to drive on. I was sure Angelina would hate that idea too!

I popped a book-on-CD into the player and settled in to listen to *The People of the Book*, while I admired all that the Lone Star State had to offer. It was a little odd listening to the voice of an Aussie and passing mile after mile of flat, dusty countryside dotted with scrubby brush. I could almost transport myself into the story I was listening to and envision myself in the Outback.

The really good thing was that between cities the speed limit was 80 mph, but I was not quite comfortable at such high speeds, even though the Dolphin never balked at maintaining them. I did want to make up some time but I didn't want to be unsafe about it. I'd come too far to run myself off the road and do myself and my Dolphin in.

When I stopped for gas just outside Fort Stockton, I added 800 minutes to my Tracphone and then, before I pulled back onto the highway, I punched in the new phone number Brick had given me. He'd told me that he'd been so angry with me before, that he'd smashed his phone to pieces with his fist the night he had seen me dancing with Craig. He answered on the second ring but in such a hushed voice that I wasn't sure it was him at first.

"We're staking out a booth at the Family Motor Coach Rally. We got a tip, so I can't talk now, I'll have to call you back."

"Okay, I'll keep my phone on and wait for your call."

"You're a doll. Drive safe." And then he was gone.

We really needed to spend time talking and resolving some issues that had clouded the waters around our fledgling relationship, and to catch up on us. I missed him, but I was still a teensy, tiny bit mad and hurt that he hadn't trusted me more and had readily assumed the worst, just because I was hanging all over this really handsome guy, with a dreamy I'm-in-Heaven look in my eye.

A few hours later I pulled off into a rest area. After walking Sweetie and feeding us both, I fell back on the sofa for a quick nap. Sweetie was curled behind my knees, her head resting on my thigh, when I heard my phone ringing. I really didn't want to move her, as she seemed so perfectly comfortable and quiet for a change but if that was Brick calling, I did not want to miss his call. He could have some very good news to impart.

Gently lifting Sweetie, I reached over to the console and

picked up my phone. The caller ID screen had the typical Private Number message that usually meant Brick was calling.

"Hi!"

"Hey Beautiful. Where are you now?"

"Somewhere in Texas. This state never seems to end." I heard his knowing chuckle and smiled from the sheer pleasure of the sound.

"It's big, no doubt about it. But really, where are ya?"

"Before I stopped to rest I had just passed a sign for Fort Lancaster State Historical Park. I think it's about fifteen miles ahead."

"So you're at the rest stop just west of the Fort on I-10?"

"Yup. I'm here, in my Dolphin, just me and Angelina's dog."

"Where's Stumpy?"

"I let him go in New Mexico." I smirked to myself because it sort of sounded like a refrain for a country song.

"Oh, honey, I'm so sorry. But you did the right thing you know."

"I know."

"Well hold tight, I'll be there in a few minutes."

"How, what . . .?"

"Just sit tight." I looked at my phone and saw that we were no longer connected. What was that all about, I thought, as I went back to the bedroom area to wash my face, brush my teeth, put on some lip gloss and redo my ponytail. Visions of State Trooper cars, sirens blasting down the highway ramp and into the rest area parking lot, came into my head. He'd done this before, so I wasn't all that awed by his resourcefulness, until I heard the sound of a helicopter over head. I mutely shook my head, as I went from window to window trying to gage where it was.

The sound got louder and louder, and soon the question was answered. It was landing in a field to the right of the main building, in a parking lot reserved for overflow. I wasn't surprised when just minutes later, there was a knock on my door. Before I could answer it, Brick barged in, tossed a bouquet of flowers on the counter by the sink that was at the top of the stairs, and made a beeline for me.

I was surprised when I was grabbed, lifted off my feet, forced backward and then tackled onto the sofa. Brick's hands cupped my face and bone jangling kisses rained all over my face. "Whoa. Whoa. Whoa!" I managed to utter between frantic kisses.

"No. No. No!" he returned, and then his hands were all over me as if taking inventory. "God, I've missed you. You just don't know how much."

I felt as if I did, as I had missed him everywhere but in my dreams.

Then his hands started to slow, alternately taking long leisurely strokes up and down my arms and caressing the side of my face. I thought it curious that I could still hear the whap, whap, whap of the copter blades, the length of two football fields away. Instantly my mind interpreted what that meant and I let out a long sigh. They weren't dropping him off. He wouldn't be staying. They were enroute somewhere and he'd made them detour. As if to verify this, he muttered against my neck between skin tingling, nipping kisses, "I can't stay, but God I want to. You're driving me crazy, you're all I can think about."

I managed to squirm up and lean back on my elbows, "What about Robert Byrnes?"

"Oh yeah, he's definitely on my mind. But when I think of seeing you, I don't think of smashing your face in."

"Making any headway?"

"Do you have any idea how common the name Byrnes is, and that everyone who has a son thinks it's quaint to name him Robert?"

"So you haven't found him?"

"We've found fourteen Robert Brynes, two who are

actually vendors at RV shows, but so far, not the one who has Jillie. We're on our way to Wyoming to check out two more and to find a teenager who left home to meet a man she met on the Internet who said he's a back-up singer for Coldplay."

"What's he really?"

"A fifty-five-year-old bank teller from Laramie."

"Why do these girls keep falling for that kind of stuff?"

"Rock stars are what dreams are made of, and at this age, teenage girls spend all their time dreaming and fantasizing about boys. They think they're smart, that no one can fool them, and they're afraid to tell anyone or ask advice because they don't think anyone will understand how they're feeling. How quickly they become committed to these perverts indicates a severe lack of attention at home. So these kids are usually loners, with parents who aren't always there for them."

"Well I am so glad they have you in their corner."

"And I am so glad I had a chance to see you. I am so sorry I can't stay and make love to you until we're both exhausted but you do know that I want to fuck you silly, don't you?" He took my hand and wedged it between our bodies.

"Hard to deny with the evidence at hand."

He chuckled and gingerly pried my hand away. "Your hands, your lips, you don't know how much I dream about them and what I want you to do with them."

"Well next time, plan on staying a little longer and I may take requests."

He flexed his arms and levered himself up. "Believe me, it's harder than you know, leaving you right now. Give Angelina a hug for me. Where's this mutt you're giving her?" He got up and adjusted his trousers while I went to get Sweetie who had been cowering in the corner by the refrigerator ever since Brick had rushed in and manhandled me.

I picked her up and stroked her, "Some watch dog you are. He could have molested me."

"Would've, could've, should've," Brick muttered against

the back of my neck as he reached over to scratch the puppy's ears. "He's cute."

"She."

"Okay, she's cute."

"Yeah. I can't wait to see Angelina's face."

As soon as I said that, I regretted it. We both were thinking the same thing . . . Jillie. Wouldn't it be wonderful to see Jillie's face? I turned and looked into Brick's eyes.

"It's just a matter of time," I whispered.

"I know." He kissed my hair, my ear and then turned to kiss me full on the mouth. "She's going to love you just as much as I do."

I had no time to absorb that statement or its significance. At that exact moment, the pitch of the copter blades thumping over in the field changed and was now being accompanied by a shrill whine. We both knew what it meant. He quickly kissed my forehead, ran down the steps and out the door, and across the field to the waiting chopper.

A crowd had gathered outside my RV to see what all the commotion was about and I wasn't too fond of crowds lately. I secured everything in the RV and cranked the engine. I now had another bouquet of flowers in my makeshift holder over the bathtub. I had just thrown Craig's arrangement out this morning so I was pleased to have a replacement, especially as this one was from Brick.

Pulling back onto the highway, I watched the helicopter rise high in the sky and then move out in a diagonal line, heading north. I wondered when I'd see him again and said another prayer for little Jillie and the teenager Brick was on his way to find. A warm feeling came over me as I allowed his words to repeat in my head, *She's going to love you just as much as I do.* It was an intensely warm feeling that caused me to shiver with delight.

Chapter Thirty-seven

It was just past one when I pulled in front of Daniel and Julia's house. They lived in a nice suburban house, in a small community that only allowed RVs on the property for loading and unloading purposes, the day of, or the day after a trip. But Daniel had insisted that I come here and spend the first night in their driveway before he took me to a local campground where he had made reservations for me.

Everything was quiet and dark as I looked at the low ranch-style rambler with the wide white planking and cornflower blue shutters. The house whispered Julia's soft touches: the ruffled curtains blowing behind a partially opened window, flower pots on both sides of the generous steps leading up to the porch, colorful butterfly bushes beneath the porch railings, and a beribboned eucalyptus wreath in the center of the front door, the door that was opening as I stared at it.

I watched as a little girl in pink pajamas with dark bouncy curls came running down the front lawn toward the RV. Angelina, her smile as bright as the moon shining above, came running to the door of the RV. I unlocked it just as she knocked and it flew open. She was in my arms, hugging me around my neck for all I was worth and babbling something that sounded like, "didn't think you'd ever get here, ever, ever, ever." She felt soft and warm from her bed. Visions of her nose to the glass while she waited for me to arrive, swam inside my head as she breathlessly told me she had "waited and waited," but then fell asleep. "My ears woke up when I heard you coming up the street. I could hear the Dolphin! It's louder than a car. I am so glad you're finally here! I've missed you so much!" Her arms around my neck were tight and it didn't seem that she planned on letting go anytime soon, so I picked her up in my arms and held her to my chest while I watched Daniel and Julia cinching their robes and stumbling out the door of the house.

They both had a glazed look in their eyes, and Julia's long hair was tousled and arrayed around her face. It occurred to me that I might not have woken them up, but that I had interrupted something else in progress. With Angelina still in my arms, I hugged them both and apologized for the late hour.

"We're just glad you're here, doesn't matter when," Daniel mumbled as he ran his hand through his hair. Yes, this was a man who could have used just a few more minutes. The rosy blush of Julia's fair skin confirmed it, that, and the whisker burns on her pale throat. I watched as they linked hands and he brought her hand to his lips—their eyes communicating a secret promise.

"Carrie, Um, I keep forgetting . . . Jenny, it's wonderful to see you again. Come into the house. I'll fix some coffee," Julia said.

"Forget the coffee, I'll bring in some wine. Got some great stuff I loaded up on in Oregon."

"Even better," she looked at Angelina clutched tightly in my arms and smiled, "Angie, where are your slippers?" Her little feet, wet with dew, were swinging at my hips. "You're getting wet grass all over Jenny."

"Oops! I was in a hurry and forgot them." Her tiny hand covered her mouth and she looked like the little imp I knew she was.

Julia leaned over and brushed the grass cuttings off the little feet. It was such a tender ministration that I knew instantly that mother and daughter had completely re-bonded, despite the years that they'd been apart.

All of a sudden Angelina began bouncing on my hip and furiously patting her hands on my cheeks. "Where's my puppy? Where's my puppy? Where is she?"

We were all in the cramped area that served as a foyer, so I backed up with her in my arms and plopped her down on the sofa. "She's in her carrier in the bedroom, but she hasn't been walked for a while, so before you two meet I'd better get her leash. You go outside with your mom and dad and I'll bring her out."

She was off my lap and in the bedroom before I could blink. I could hear cooing and giggling sounds coming from the bedroom and then Angelina, the carrier between both hands, came down the hall. She was walking on her tiptoes, holding the carrier gingerly in both hands and peeking inside. "She's sooo cute!"

I opened the gate and took Sweetie into my arms, attached the leash and led her down the stairs. She promptly did her business, and I gave Angelina her snack so she could reward her. Then she was whisked into Angelina's arms and held to her chest while she kissed Sweetie on the nose and let her lick her face all over. A strange look came over Angelina's face and we all watched, as a dark splotch grew large on her pink p.j. top, just under the puppy's bottom. She had been christened the exact way the puppy had christened me so many times.

"That means she likes you, she doesn't do that to just anybody!" I said with a chuckle, and watched, as Angelina's look of uncertainty became a huge grin.

The sound of Angelina's laughter filled the front yard and echoed off the RV while the three of us linked arms and watched her play with her puppy in the grass.

"Thank you. You just don't know how much she's been

looking forward to this," Julia said.

"I can imagine, and no thanks are necessary. She's a sweet girl and she deserves to be this happy always."

Daniel squeezed my shoulders and leaned over to kiss me on the cheek. "You're responsible for at least three people being ecstatically happy. Now get that bottle you were talking about and let's go inside."

"You have to work tomorrow, remember," Julia said with one eyebrow raised.

"Always the mother, even to me. I'll just have one glass and then you and I have some unfinished business to take care of. And don't worry, I'll get up in the morning, too," he said with a grin. The double entendre was too obvious, I burst out laughing.

I watched as Julia blushed crimson and turned to hide her face in Daniel's shoulder. His robe gaped and I saw he was bare-chested underneath. All that bronzed skin and curling hair made me think of Brick and of all the things we were missing out on right now. I was happy for Daniel and Julia, truly I was, but a little melancholy for myself. I wanted what they had.

Chapter Thirty-eight

True to his word, Daniel had one glass of wine after helping me carry a few things from the RV into the guestroom. Julia finished her wine, and after helping Angelina settle the puppy into the laundry room for the night, she asked me if I'd like to tuck Angelina in, as she'd already done it once tonight and it hadn't worked well at all.

I jumped up, anxious to say goodnight and to get away from the zinging heat I felt when Daniel and Julia looked at each other with those bedroom eyes. It was time we all turned in and got some sleep. Yeah, like they were going to bed to sleep. I shouldn't have been jealous, but I was. Not that I wanted Daniel, oh no, but I was coming to realize that I wanted a little bit of the life Julia had.

The puppy kept us all awake for forty-five minutes, then finally stopped whining and settled in. It was almost three o'clock before I nodded off.

The next morning I woke to the delicious smell of bacon frying and fresh brewed coffee. After a quick touch up in the hallway bathroom, I headed to the kitchen to find Julia making pancakes for Angelina. Sweetie was in her arms, dressed in doll clothes, licking syrup from Angelina's fingers. I made a mental note to let her know that too much syrup or candy wouldn't be good for the dog.

"Hi," I mumbled, as I staggered to a stool at the counter.

"Hi!" Angelina said and went into a long tirade on all the things Sweetie had been doing so far this morning.

"You thought of a name for her yet?" I asked, as I took the glass of orange juice Julia handed me. She looked perky and fresh and I knew the reason.

"Yup. Cutie Pie!"

"That's cute." Then I had to laugh, "Get it, Cute for short?"

Julia gave me a wry smile. "Funny. How many pancakes would you like?"

"They're shaped like cats. Mom tried dogs but they looked like bunnies. She's good with cats, though."

"I'll have two cats and a bunny," I said and tousled Angelina's soft curls.

"Daniel at work?" I asked.

"Yeah, he had to go in early but he'll be home early. He said to wait for him and he'll help you get set up over at the campground. It's real nice over there, we checked it out. I think you'll like it."

"I'm sure I will. So, tell me all about your new life here in Texas."

All morning long we talked about everything under the sun, and it was a hot sun we were under today. I got the grand tour of their cute little rambler, was entertained while I did some laundry, showed Angelina how to take care of Cutie Pie, and learned all about the area and their new friends. Daniel had a job as a heating and air conditioning technician and was making enough money so that Julia could stay home with Angelina. When Angelina ran into her room to get something, Julia leaned over and whispered that there was a little one on the way but that they didn't want to tell Angelina until she was fairly far along. I hugged her and cried with her.

"I owe my new life all to you, you know. He wouldn't ever have come looking for me if you hadn't threatened his custody of her."

"I'm so glad things worked out the way they did, because for a while there, I thought I'd made Angelina a homeless orphan."

"Daniel says you're the only person he would have trusted with her and he knew it right from the very beginning. You must have touched something in him."

"I just think he was ready to make some changes. He couldn't have gone on like that forever and I think he knew that. It wasn't the best thing for Angelina being on the road like that with no friends or family." We heard a loud wail of protest from Cutie Pie.

" . . . or dog," Julia added.

We both went to see what Angelina was up to and found her trying to tie a bonnet under Cutie Pie's chin. There was a bit of snarling going on and I had to intervene. "Let's let Cutie Pie go au naturale while we take her to the park at the end of the block and let your Mom get a nap. She looks very tired. I think your new puppy kept her awake last night."

"I think it was an old dog named Daniel to be truthful," she said and we both laughed at Angelina's forthright comment. She leaned close to me and whispered in my ear, "He takes her to the bedroom all the time but I don't think he lets her sleep. There must be something wrong with the wall in there, I hear them beating on it all the time." I just about lost it.

When we got back from the park Daniel was waiting to help me get set up at the RV campground a few miles away. He had a big grin on his face and I accused him of "working on the wall" again. Julia blushed and pulled him aside to explain, then he blushed. It was a sight to see.

Angelina wanted to come with us, so while Julia stayed home to fix dinner, we headed out, Angelina and Cutie Pie with me in the RV and Daniel in his company pick-up truck.

The campground Daniel had picked out was a wonderful place—my site, well treed and landscaped, was unbelievably pristine, not a weed or stone out of place. Daniel was familiar with all the idiosyncrasies of RVing and together we efficiently did the hook ups in record time. We had only one mishap. That was when I was walking Cutie Pie on the leash as Daniel was hooking up all the connections and hoses. He asked me to hand him the water filter that was on the ground and just as I was standing back up with it, Cutie Pie's nose detected a delightful aroma at the septic connection which she just had to investigate at that exact moment. She pulled me off balance; I tripped over the sewer hose, scraped my leg on the way down, twisted my ankle, and hit my ear on the side of the compartment door of the RV. I actually saw stars, lots of them. I recovered everything but my dignity and the ankle needed babying for a little while. Angelina, who had been squatting trying to get a caterpillar to climb up on a twig at the time, could not stop laughing and recreated the whole scenario for Julia when we got back.

Julia's nursing instincts kicked in and I was relegated to the couch with frozen peas wrapped in a towel around my ankle. Angelina slid in beside me, her head on my arm, and together we watched Dora the Explorer with Cutie Pie asleep on the sofa bolster beside me while Daniel helped Julia get dinner to the table.

I stayed with them off and on for three days until I got sick of the domestic bliss all around me, heartsick that is. They were so happy, all of them, and being with them like this just kept reaffirming what I was missing, and had been missing all during my marriage—a loving, adoring family. They were a unit, each caring for the other, completely unselfish and eager to make the other's happiness their goal. Angelina, the glue that had brought Daniel and Julia back together, was the light of their lives, and I knew that when the new baby came along, their joy would double.

On the fourth day I told them all about Connor and Diana,

and said I had to get back on the road. I had chosen a storage facility that would store the Dolphin inside a large warehouse while I flew to the east coast to witness Connor's marriage. They all begged me to stay longer, especially Angelina and I couldn't get away without promising to see them when I came back for the Dolphin. I finally got Daniel to take me back to my RV, where I drank myself into a stupor because I hadn't been lucky enough to find the wonderful life they were living. At least not yet.

Chapter Thirty-nine

I left the Dolphin at the U-Store-It Storage facility in Austin and took a cab to the airport. I had gone online at Daniel's and had booked a flight from Austin to Providence, Rhode Island, deciding that the detour to Virginia was just too chancy. I was afraid Jared would be home or learn that I was there before I could get in and out. I decided I would work within the system and try to get a duplicate passport since mine was still valid.

It felt strange getting on a plane as I hadn't been on one in years, not since the last time I'd flown west for my aunt's funeral and to visit my sister and parents in Washington State. Gosh! How long ago was that, I wondered, and was disgusted with myself when I realized it had been almost three years. I promised myself I would find a way to RV back that way for Thanksgiving or Christmas.

The woman I sat next to on the plane would not stop talking, so I finally had to feign sleepiness even though I wasn't at all tired. I created a fantasy about Brick in my mind and ended up squirming all over the place and getting annoyed looks from my seatmate.

My connecting flight was delayed and I remembered what it was about flying that I hadn't liked—the surprises, usually bad. I sat in the Charlotte airport for two hours before being notified that my flight had been cancelled. I would have to spend the night at the airport hotel.

As I was walking toward the exit, I noticed the flight board and saw that there was a flight leaving to Dulles in less than an hour. I rationalized that it was a sign that I could get away with sneaking into my old house to get my passport and birth certificate, which I had stupidly left in the safe when I had left so many months ago.

I went to the counter, changed my ticket and went back through security. Three hours later, I was in a rental car on my way to the house I had lived in with Jared during our six-year marriage.

Driving down the access road to the beltway, I marveled at how everything looked the same, but then again, it hadn't been all that long since I'd been here. Taking the winding road up the hill to where our mansion sat behind gates and down a long drive, I grew nervous. Sweat pooled between my breasts and I had to keep wiping my upper lip. I boosted the air conditioner in the car to the maximum setting so that I was sweating and freezing at the same time.

What if he'd changed the keys, the access codes for the gates and alarms? What if he was home? On an impulse, I got my cell phone out and called the local store where Jared's executive offices were. It was a number I'd dialed so often that I knew I'd never forget it. When I disguised my voice and asked for him, I was told that he was at a meeting at the Silver Spring store and that he wasn't expected back for several hours. I smiled and pulled away from the curb, where I had been parked at the bottom of the hill leading into our exclusive development.

The gates were open, but that wasn't unusual as we'd hardly ever closed them, and when we did it was only at night. I could see no signs of life. There were no cars parked on the cement apron on the side of the house and all four garage doors were down. I pulled around and parked in front of the last one, the spot that used to be mine, where I had parked my Mercedes, the car I had sold for the cash I needed to leave Jared.

I had no key or garage remote, but I remembered the combination that worked with the keypad beside each door. Taking a deep breath, I turned off the car and stepped out. It was eerily quiet, almost too quiet, I thought. Where were the birds that used to keep me company with their chatter high up in the trees? Where were the squirrels that would swing from one branch to another and steal onto the decks on every level to eat the blooms off my hibiscus plants? I tiptoed as if that would keep anyone from hearing me approach. When I got to the keypad, I punched in the four-digit code and held my breath when I pressed the # key, afraid it wouldn't work, that the sequence had been changed. The whirring and rising of the garage door in front of my rental car jolted me. I was going to be able to get in. A part of me hesitated. Did I really want to go in there? Did I really want to take this chance?

I stepped into the immaculate garage and looked to the left to see what vehicles were in the other bays. Jared's antique Porsche squatted there at the end, homage to the man's obsessions with rare things. No other vehicles were in the garage, no one was here.

I tiptoed across the cement floor and across the cushioned rubberized section in front of the workbenches and toolboxes before reaching the connecting door to the house. There was no sound save for my harsh breathing and the tiny echo of my heels tapping as I went from the rubberized section to the Versacover cement flooring again.

I reached for the door handle and gave it a tentative turn. It turned easily and opened when I pushed in. A small voice said this is too easy, but I didn't listen.

The garage opened to a mudroom and from there to a long hallway that took you by the indoor pool and then upstairs to the kitchen. The safe was in Jared's study, one floor above that. The house was so quiet and eerie and I wondered at that.

We had staff—maids, landscapers, and an occasional cook. Were they all off today, as they had been the day I had left? Had he fired them all, holding them responsible for my leaving?

I walked into my old kitchen and looked around, marveling at how big it was. It had never seemed all that big before. But then, I was now living in a bus whose total square footage was not even the size of the master bathroom in this house. I ran my fingers over the smooth, cool granite countertop as I made my way to the main living area and the grand staircase. The sun shown through the high windows of the first landing, leading me up the carpeted steps to the main living level where the bedrooms, guestrooms, billiard room and study were. The hallway was daytime dark, as the house on the backside was away from the sun, but still, it was easy to make out the familiar pictures on the wall and the golden threads in the draperies at the end of the hallway. The fragrance from the arrangement of flowers Jared insisted be freshened everyday wafted over to where I stood looking into the first room, my old sitting room. A nostalgic feeling came over me when I saw my old sewing machine and stitching looms, like shadows of stick men leaning against the walls. It looked like nothing had been touched. The Four Seasons cross-stitch I had been working on forever was still in its stretcher bars waiting for someone to come along and finish it. I smiled to myself; well, it sure wouldn't be me. Those are the kinds of things I had done to stay busy and to keep from growing restless. When you were a full-time RVer, you didn't have time for too many pastoral pastimes—you go, go, go, as there are always fun places to go and interesting people to meet.

I backed into the hallway and took a quick peek at the master bedroom door. This room had memories, too many to have flooding back right now, so I walked by with my hand beside my face. Next was the study and my target, the safe. The door, usually closed, was ajar but as it was so quiet I didn't give it much thought.

I crept into the room and walked over to the desk. I sidled around looking at all the expensive statuettes and art pieces Jared had accumulated over the years. The Remingtons, in niches in the walls, were his favorites and an impressive manly collection indeed.

I pushed his oversized chair under the desk so I could get to the painting on the back wall that hid the safe. My hand reached out to the corner of the frame that housed an antique hunt country painting we had bought while we were in Middleburg, celebrating our first anniversary. I gave it the slight tug that was needed to swing it away from the wall. The safe was digital and my hands were anything but sure fingered as I punched in the code—our wedding date forward and backward. The safe clicked open and a second later the door behind me clicked shut.

A chill that I likened to ice water flooding my veins made me gasp. I spun around to see Jared leaning against the polished cherry door, his hands crossed over his chest and a smug expression on his face. He was in business attire but I knew he hadn't been anywhere near the Silver Spring store. I had been set up. How had he known?

"I'm glad to learn that you still remember the date we were married because you seem to have forgotten where you live. Where *we* live. I'm afraid I'm going to have to remind you where it is that you belong." He took a step toward me, and I ran to the other side of the room.

"You're not getting away this time. You will never get away from me again!" His voice, barely a whisper, was low and harsh and it brought me to my knees.

How had I been so stupid? He'd set a trap and I'd walked right into it.

Chapter Forty

I tried to make it to the door even though I knew I had no chance at all. He was bigger, faster, closer. But I couldn't just stand there trembling and let him come get me.

I only managed to make the game more fun for him. He easily overtook me when I ran by the sofa, capturing me and quickly securing both of my wrists behind me. He knew I would fight and that I wouldn't be nice about it. I kicked and tried to pull away, using every bit of strength that I had. He took great pleasure in my pitiful, futile attempt. I had forgotten how big he was, how regularly he worked out and how cruel and bruising he could be. He forced me back to the area behind the desk and started pulling things out of the safe.

"What was it you wanted in here?" he said as if mocking me.

He rifled through wads of money with his thumb so I could hear the riffling sound, "Was it cash? Have you run out of money, my dear?" He put the money aside and dumped out a large portfolio, "Stocks, bonds, insurance papers? No?" he said eyeing me with a feigned look of puzzlement. He was taunting me, much as a cat with a mouse's tail under his claw would.

He drew out several large folders and let the contents fall

onto his desk. I saw my passport and my birth certificate flutter to the desk and inadvertently sighed.

"Ahhh . . . was it this?" He picked up my passport and waved it in front of my face. "Was this why you came back?" The game was over; I could see his rage building now.

"How did you know?"

"I didn't, you just told me."

"How did you even know I was coming here?"

"You were on speaker phone when you called the store, my assistant recognized the signal for your voice."

"I disguised it."

"I have it programmed to your unique pattern, you would not have been able to disguise it."

"Why would you do that?" I was frustrated and frantic, so I screamed it as I tried to get my hands out of his grasp. He tightened his hold and I could feel the pressure sending shooting pains up my arms.

"I think you can see why I would do that."

"But you're supposed to be at the Silver Spring Store."

"I would have been if you hadn't gotten on that plane in Austin using your real name. And I'm sorry your flight was cancelled in Charlotte, I was expecting you sooner."

"How can you . . . How did you . . . Who . . .?"

He chuckled. "I pay someone to constantly check these things."

"But I wasn't going to come here. I was going to Rhode Island!"

"No you weren't. I wouldn't have let you. If you hadn't gotten on the plane going to Dulles, you would have been snatched coming out of the Charlotte Airport. You just made things easier for me flying here. I've known where you were every minute since you walked into the Austin Airport. What's in Rhode Island by the way?"

"None of your business!"

"Oh, I'll find out. You'll eventually tell me."

"No, I won't!"

He lifted an eyebrow as if saying, *Now, now, you know that I'll get it out of you.*

"Did you really lose your memory or were you faking it, and why did you send that hospital bracelet?" I stomped my foot in anger at myself. I knew better! Why hadn't I listened to myself?

"That was a mistake on my part. I wanted you to know that you hadn't killed the part of me that remembered you and all that you were to me. In retrospect, I should have held that tidbit closer to my chest. Letting you know that my memory had returned was an error on my part. But it didn't affect the outcome, you're here now."

"Because I'm stupid," I gritted out, and again, I tried to pull away. His grip was unyielding.

"But still as lovely as ever and attracting attention everywhere you go it seems. So how many men have you slept with since you left me?" I watched the color bloom in his face and saw a vein by his temple pulse and wondered what he'd say if I lied and said ten. But I wasn't quite *that* stupid. His thinking two was bad enough and I was sure he'd make me pay for it.

"I never figured you for an easy lay, but then again I never figured you'd run out on me either. Well, no more." He released one hand and shoved the other behind my back, twisting it and forcing it so high that I felt pain shoot through my shoulder. Holding me in front of him, he wedged me between him and the desk. I could feel how hard and tense his whole body was and I could feel his excitement at having won the hunt and captured the prize. He picked up the passport and the envelope with my birth certificate in it and tossed them back in the safe. Then he opened the large custom jewelry case that was on the desk amid all the paper clutter. It contained all the jewelry he'd given me over the years. He fingered a few pieces while I watched him. His voice was wistful as he picked up each piece and reminded me of the special occasion when he had given it to me.

"I truly wish I hadn't left the Gateway to Paradise in a display case in the San Diego store. But, no bother," he said with a wave of his hand, "I'll just design another. And this time, I will see it installed in your labial lips. But first, let's get you more comfortable, let me show you your new quarters. I suppose it's too much to ask that you undress yourself for me?"

"You are a sick, sick man and I am not going to stay here so you can abuse me again."

"Oh, I think that you are." He opened the top desk drawer and pulled out a gun.

"You're going to shoot me?" I know my eyes were wide with shock. I never expected that Jared would have a gun, or that he would actually threaten me with one.

"Well, not in the conventional way," he said as he tipped the gun and looked at the long shiny barrel. "As it appears you're not going to strip for me, it's highly unlikely that you're going to sit still for the uh, deforestation of your pubic region. Unless of course, you've kept up on your depilatory regimen, in which case I would be extremely pleased, as you know how I like you smooth and prepubescent in that arena. This is a tranquilizer gun, it will assure that you do my bidding, quietly and with little fuss."

"No! Don't do this! Don't!" I screamed as I slammed back against him and broke away. I ran for the door. Halfway there I heard a small pop and then I felt a stinging sensation in my upper thigh. I did make it to the door but no further. On my knees, I hung onto the doorknob until my hands became numb and slipped off.

"No," I whispered, "Please, no." Jared was kneeling beside me now, gathering me into his arms.

"Shhh, I'm not going to hurt you, at least not yet. But I am going to make you my naughty little girl again. You've made me wait so long to be with you. You will certainly have to be punished, but first let me make you more comfortable." I felt him unbuttoning my blouse. I willed my hands to stop him but they wouldn't move.

My eyes and my ears were the last parts of my body to succumb so I had to listen to his soft voice cajoling me, as if I was a little girl, while my eyes looked into his lust-filled face and he whispered what he planned to do to me.

The next thing I knew, I was on a soft leather sofa in the video room Jared had on the basement level, next to his wine cellar.

I looked around but he wasn't there. I could hardly escape though; I was tied hand and foot, naked under a satin sheet. It was cold, so cold that I could feel the tips of my breasts tightly puckered and hard, painfully so due to the chill. Jared had always liked it cold down here so I had rarely come down to this level of the house.

I looked around and saw there had been many changes made to this room. It no longer looked like a viewing room, a place to watch old movies on a big screen, although the plasma TV was still there hanging on the wall in the center of the room. I was off to the side and around me was a variety of workout equipment. I could make out a pommel horse, parallel bars and a balance beam.

When had Jared taken up gymnastics, I thought as my head reeled. It was so heavy I had to lay it back on the sofa bolster. My eyes tried to focus on the series of pulleys and chains hanging from the ceiling. All around the room were ropes, cushioned pads, and mattresses. What the hell were they for? A shelf over in the corner contained bottles, jars, and tubes; one tube I recognized as K.Y. Jelly, a large jar on the top shelf appeared to be Vaseline and one of the bottles was baby oil, another—almond-scented massage oil. A feeling of dread came over me as I realized what Jared intended to use these things for.

In fear, I rubbed my legs together and quickly discovered tenderness at the top of my thighs. I had been waxed, and none too gently judging from the soreness of the touch of just my inner thighs overlapping to that sensitive region.

I heard someone coming down the steps and into the hallway. The door opened and I saw Jared stroll in. He was dressed as usual in an impeccable business suit.

"Hi, honey, I'm home," he called out, trying to sound jovial, but sounding sinister instead.

"Untie me you filthy bastard! How dare you molest me like this! I am not going to be your wife anymore; I'm going to divorce you! I want you to let me go this minute!"

"I don't think so, sweetheart. And after what you've put me through the last few months, I don't really care what you want anymore." He came over and sat beside me and lightly ran his fingers over my cheek. I jerked away.

"You know, a lot of women would be happy to have the life you had. You didn't have to work; you could buy all the clothes and doodads you wanted and you had one of the most premier cars manufactured in the world, until you sneakily sold it, *and* I was always surprising you with expensive, designer jewelry. All you had to do was satisfy me sexually. How hard was that? Most women would find pleasure in that chore. I'm a handsome man and very innovative in the bedroom arts. But not you, you had to run away from all this." His hand waved in the air indicating the house above us. "You had to humiliate me. Then you let other men have you. So now it's high time you were punished." He stood up and took the sheet with him. I instantly felt the chill of the room and bemoaned my traitorous nipples.

His bold eyes caressed me and I could see passion ignite in his eyes. "You are still the loveliest woman I have ever seen." He reached his hand down to caress my breast and I shrank back against the sofa. That enraged him. The caress instantly became a painful squeeze, followed by a brutal pinch to my nipple. With my nipple between his thumb and knuckle, he pinched so hard that I felt pinpoints shoot out behind my eyes. I screamed from the pain and then I kept screaming, hoping someone would hear me, though I knew the house was too isolated for that.

"An expression of your extreme discomfort is allowed but I'm not listening to you scream like a banshee unless I'm causing you to!" He reached into his pocket, took out a handkerchief and wadded it up. "Scream like that again and this gets stuffed in your mouth!"

He went over to a low table and picked up the TV remote, pointed it at the large screen and I watched as the screen filled with images. "I thought you might like to see what I've been doing since you were gone, what I've *had* to do to be pleasured since you weren't around."

I watched, horrified, as a middle-aged man bent a small child over a chair and pulled her plaid uniform skirt to her waist. While she pleaded for the man to stop, he tore her panties and unzipped his pants. I couldn't watch anymore and averted my face, using all my strength to turn my body into the back of the sofa. I was sobbing with all my heart now, as all I could envision in my mind was Angelina in that very same position while a perverted old man pawed at her and slaked his evil lust inside her tiny little body.

Unfortunately, I didn't realize that my pitiful sobs and keening noises were turning Jared on until it was too late. I soon found myself jerked up off the sofa and folded almost in half against the end of it, while Jared acted out his own sick fantasy, pretending that I was that little, helpless girl. I could sense him focusing his heavy-lidded eyes on the perverted scene above us while he continuously plunged into me, stopping only to renew generous handfuls of lubricant where our bodies met. I was sure this was for his benefit and comfort and not at all for mine.

I managed to keep the bile from choking me, as his hand on the back of my neck forced my head upside down. He jerked suddenly, followed by a full body shudder and then he groaned his pleasure. His disgusting mission accomplished, I thought he would leave me alone then, but he didn't.

From my skewed vantage point, I saw him cross the room

and carefully select a ping-pong paddle from a varied assortment of paddles. I tried to scream, but the sound got caught and came out as a wretched sob. My throat was dry from all the heavy breathing and gasping and now I was even hiccupping. I was terrified, as I knew what was coming; he'd played this horrible game with me before. I'd just had a nightmare about it the other night.

This time his eyes, as he approached, told me that things would be different. He tapped the paddle against his hand as if hefting it, testing it for the task at hand. That he was looking forward to meting out this punishment was obvious—his leering smile and the crude way he groped me while repositioning me made it evident that he would derive great pleasure in doling out my penance. I cringed inside because I knew, without a doubt, that in order for him to be sated this time, I would truly have to suffer—tonight there would be no faking it.

"Fifty really good smacks should do it, make you understand how truly bad you've been. You've been a very naughty girl, you know."

"No," I whimpered, "please no." Then I bit my lip, because I knew that's what he wanted me to do. If I cried, if I pleaded, that would be the icing on the cake, it would please him to no end.

The first few whacks were painful and brought the cries I was sure he was salivating for. I could just picture the gleam in his eyes and the desire building in him. After ten I was less sensitive, so he hit me harder. After twenty I was writhing, frantic with rising terror and on fire with a deep burning pain. At thirty I thought he was going to kill me, that this was the way I was going to die—turned upside down with my backside as red as a baboon's. At forty, my mind shut down and I was in another zone—watching from someplace outside my body as Jared wound up to deliver near lethal blows. By forty-five I had passed out. I never knew if he'd made it to the prescribed fifty.

Chapter Forty-one

When I woke, Jared was holding my shoulders, speaking softly and trying to get me to drink some broth. "There, there, it's over. And if you're a good girl, we won't have to do that again."

I knew I had to keep my strength up until I could figure a way out of this, so I didn't resist. I drank the broth, but I refused the chunks of chicken. I knew that I wouldn't be able to eat anything solid for quite some time, as I wouldn't be able to stand the pain of eliminating it, and so did he. It was a punishment on top of a punishment; there was no end to how demonic he could be.

"It seems I can no longer trust you to stay here and be home for me when I return from work, so I'm going to have to tie you up. You'll have enough chain to get to the bathroom but not enough to get to the door or window. I have to go to work now to make the Gateway for you, so you'll be on your own for a few hours. Feel free to use the TV, there's other videos in the cabinet, some very good porn, so help yourself."

"Jared, don't do this. Let me go."

"Never. That will never happen. You are mine and I won't ever give you up." He placed a kiss at my temple and then ran his hand down my side. He bent and closed his mouth over my nipple and he suckled it. I closed my eyes and swallowed hard trying to keep the broth from coming back up.

"Clothes, can I have my clothes?"

"No, no clothes. I prefer you like this. But here, I brought some ointment for you. Roll over so I can put it on you." I didn't help him but he easily managed to get me on my stomach on his own. He took generous dabs of salve and smoothed it over my cheeks. It was hard to believe from his gentle, caring caresses that this was the same man who had made me need the salve in the first place. He acted as if someone else had done this to me and now he was here caring for me, trying to make me believe that I was the most precious thing in his world.

When he was finished, he stood up and wiped his hand on a towel and then he drew a line of kisses down my spine, ending with a long, lingering one on each hot cheek. I cringed inside but tried not to show it, as he didn't do well when I showed any sign of rejection. While I was recovering from his ministrations, he took the opportunity to attach a thick chain to my ankle. "I'll be back this afternoon with a nice surprise," he whispered in my ear and then he was gone.

I tried to sit up but was unable to tolerate the pain, so I stayed where I was and tried to figure a way out. I finally eased myself off the sofa, thankful it was buttery soft and conformed so easily to the awkward bend of my body. I gingerly walked around. It was very slow moving as each step sent shooting pains up my thighs to my buttocks. Jared had been right; I could make it to the bathroom but nowhere near the door or window. I looked around for a phone, but of course, there was none. I wished I was one of those secret agent types who could reach into the wall, know exactly which wire took care of what and either place a call with only a stripped wire or alert the alarm company that there was an intruder so someone would come investigate. Alas, I had no 007 skills. My only skill was repeatedly getting myself into hot water. I found the sheet that had been discarded, wrapped it around my body and went back to the sofa. I stretched out on my tummy and tried to fall asleep. I was dreading Jared's "surprise," so it was no wonder that I slept fitfully.

Chapter Forty-two

I heard him the second he returned. He was galloping down the steps and even though I couldn't see him, his gait sounded jaunty, as if he was somehow pleased about something.

I didn't bother to move or acknowledge him when he came into the room. My nose twitched and my tummy grumbled from the smell of the food he had brought. He was tempting me with solids again.

"Dinnertime. I brought you some spaghetti, one of your favorites," he said as he placed a big bag on a card table and drew up a chair. "Oh, I don't imagine you're quite ready for the chair yet. Maybe you'd be more comfortable eating on the sofa." He brought the table over and forced me to eat. I didn't say a word.

"I have a great start on the Gateway, I secured all the stones this afternoon. With luck I should be able to install it by tomorrow or the next day."

"Whoopee," I deadpanned.

"Hey, it's really going to be a thing of beauty. Wait 'til you see."

"Most women can't view themselves in that area."

"Oh, yeah, well . . . I'll get you a mirror."

"Why are you so set on this? No one's going to see it but you. I imagine healing will take forever, if one manages to heal without getting an infection down there to begin with; it will be nothing but pain for the woman and I can't believe it will give pleasure to the man. So why are you spending so much money and effort on labial piercings? Surely, there isn't a huge market for this type of thing."

"You'd be surprised. I have advance orders for the Gateway. I was offered $60,000 for the one that's on display in San Diego, of course, it has two perfect, yellow, one-carat diamonds and two very rare sapphires. And for your information, sales of nipple clips and wires, as well as belly button rings, have tripled in just the last six months. I think the Gateway will be a big seller for the high-end market, but I haven't installed it on anyone yet. I've been waiting for you. You will be the first to be adorned with my Rainbow Gateway."

"I don't want to be adorned."

"As I said before, what you want no longer matters to me."

I stopped talking and refused to eat anything else. He stared at me in anger. Then after a few moments, he reached over and pulled the sheet that had been tucked under my armpits down to my waist, exposing my breasts to his heated gaze.

I was unnerved as he stared at me and tried awkwardly to cover myself but he kept his hand on the edge of the sheet and wouldn't let go.

"I said I had a surprise and here it is." He handed me a jewelry box that was instantly recognizable as having come from his store. I dreaded opening it.

"Open it."

"I don't want it."

"Open it!" His hair-trigger anger kicked in and I jumped.

I opened it. At first I didn't recognize what it was, simple gold wires about three inches long. I lifted the cardboard insert and saw the solid gold letters, two of them, both Js, both about an inch long. Liquid fire flowed through my veins and short-circuited everything as I realized what these were. He confirmed it.

"They're nipple wires. I brought the equipment I need to install them home. I want my initials hanging from your pretty titties. So, now that you're finished eating, that's what I'm going to do."

"Over my dead body!"

"If need be. But I am putting them on you, make no mistake, and I am putting them on you, tonight."

"Jared No! No! I don't want them!"

"Again, and I'm getting pretty tired of saying this, I don't care what you want anymore. From now on, it's only about what I want!" I saw his fuse was getting short and that he was becoming very angry but I was not going to allow him to do this to me!

"Now, you have a choice, you cooperate or I drug you. Oh, excuse me, I already did that, it was in the spaghetti sauce."

I reached across to smack the smug smile off his face but he grabbed my wrist before I could make contact. He squeezed my hand so hard I thought he was going to break it.

"Ah ah ah, I wouldn't do that, I'm the one who feeds you, remember? And this time I fed you really well. In about twenty minutes you'll be out cold. I'll heat the gold wires until they're red hot, almost blue really and then they'll push right through the tip of your nipple like a . . . well like a hot wire going through butter. I'll attach my initials and then solder the ends together so you can't remove them. You'll look majestic, just like a harem girl wearing sexy dangles for her Sheik. You'll have to learn how to dance with them so they sway together, so you can arouse me." His matter of fact attitude, along with his leering, confident smile scared me. He was really going to do this and I would be powerless to prevent it. I had to try another tack.

"Jared, this is really going to hurt and won't it ruin the sensitivity in my nipples? How will you be able to give me pleasure? *Give him what he wants*, I said to myself, see if that helps any.

"Nah, the wires are very thin and they go through the skin just under the tip, if anything, you'll be more sensitive. The weight of the dangles constantly pulling on your nipples is a great turn on I'm told. Plus, pleasuring you is no longer on my agenda."

No way out there. Another tack was called for but suddenly I couldn't hold my eyes open, my head jerked forward to my chest. "Oh! Jared, please don't!" I whimpered as I slumped back against the sofa cushions and slid to one side. "Please Jared if you ever cared for me, don't do this. Please. I'm begging you, please, please . . . don't."

He came over and lifted me, then propped me in the corner of the sofa. "I'll need you sitting up for this. I don't want them to be crooked." One hand was on my neck, easing it back and the other began fondling my breasts, stroking the undersides, hefting them, then pinching the tips and pulling them out. Over and over, he tugged on them. I saw him bend and examine the underside while holding the nipple taut. "Piece of cake, you'll be wearing my adornments when you wake up and after you get used to them, I'll bet you'll love them. Not that I care, mind you." He leaned in closer and took my nipple into his mouth and suckled it. My head lolled back as his hand released it. I was unconscious and unable to stop this insanity.

Chapter Forty-three

I heard the door open and footsteps coming down the carpeted stairs. Jared was taking care to be quiet; not coming down the stairs as he usually did—thumping down the steps as if wearing combat boots. Occasionally he liked to sneak up on me and scare me, especially if I was asleep, but this slow, drawn out descent was unusual. But he needn't fear that I was sleeping. Who could sleep like this, strapped naked and spread-eagled over a pommel horse, my reddened behind glowing like a cinder? God it hurt, down to the bone it hurt.

For the tenth time in so many days, I regretted my decision to come back into this house, the house that had once been mine that was now my personal chamber of horrors.

My ears pricked; there was more than one set of footprints. Oh dear God, please don't tell me that he's invited voyeurs to watch my humiliation. Tonight he was installing the Gateway in my nether lips and it hadn't occurred to me until now that he might need an assistant or a piercing professional. My ears strained for any sound that would forewarn me, not that I could do anything about it with my limbs chained to each other through the legs of the pommel horse. I was bent over, my abdomen up against the unyielding leather with my wrists attached to my ankles. I could inch up and slide down but I could not separate myself from the heavy contraption that was commonly used for floor vaulting. There was enough slack that I could stand, but not enough to allow me to sit—as if I wanted to put any pressure, whatsoever, on my tender backside. It had healed from my original "punishment," but he was finding new reasons to punish me again almost daily.

I did not hear Jared's key in the inner door, the one that led to this hidden room under the house. Instead I heard the handle rattle and then the deafening sound of gunfire. I looked over my shoulder just as the door was kicked open and sobbed my relief when I recognized Brick in full tactical gear, gun drawn and eyes wildly searching. Six men followed and although my mortification at being seen this way should have been complete, I was beside myself with joy that they had found me, and found me in time.

Brick was instantly behind me, cradling me in his arms and barking out orders accompanied by furious hand gestures. He blocked my nakedness from the others with his body while he shrugged out of his flak jacket.

"Dear God, what has that bastard done to you?" The anguish in his voice broke with a sob as he looked at my shiny, crimson cheeks. You didn't have to see the assortment of paddles on a nearby table to know what had been done to me and how liberally they'd been used. Heat from my skin radiated in waves and each pulse of blood brought fresh pain. When just the slightest brush of his pants against my bottom caused me to whimper, I saw tears flood his eyes.

He leaned over my shoulder and gently tried to take the tape off my mouth. Jared no longer seemed to enjoy my screams and instead wanted muffled moans, plus, I think he was getting concerned that despite the soundproofing, I might find a way to alert the staff that came in and out at various times of the day.

"I need some glycerin here!" His hand ran repeatedly

along my naked shoulder, caressing and lightly squeezing in an unspoken gesture of support. I could tell he was afraid to touch me anywhere, afraid he'd hurt me more. He rattled the chains that were attached to my wrists, trying to see how they were attached. "Bolt cutter! I need some bolt cutters!" He covered me with his jacket as gently as he could, careful not to let it drag against my skin, but just the weight of it caused me to slump and the hem to rub against my tender ravaged skin. I let out a hoarse moan through my gag.

"Jesus Christ! Get the E.M.T.s down here right away. You two, get pictures of the scene, but do not get any pictures of her!"

A woman appeared with a bottle of glycerin and together she and Brick used saturated cloths to ease the tape and gag from my mouth. As soon as it was off, I started coughing and Brick waited until I stopped before holding water to my lips. I coughed some more, having one spasm after another before settling into a regular pattern of breathing. While Brick cooed against my ear, telling me that everything was going to be all right now, two officers showed up at my side carrying huge bolt cutters. I was soon liberated from the sturdy iron legs of the pommel horse but I would not let them pull it away from me. I slid to my knees and wrapped Brick's jacket around me, trying to cover as much of my body as I could while being very careful not to put any pressure whatsoever on my backside. "It hurts," I whispered to Brick as I clutched his shoulders and he nodded with his eyes closed.

"I know it does baby, I know. We're going to get you something for the pain. Just hold on." He hollered again for the E.M.T.s just as they came bounding down the steps. Then I looked up and my tear-filled eyes met his. I sobbed and then wailed into his chest so only he could hear, "He pierced my nipples. I can hardly stand the pain. Can you take the wires out? Now, right now? Please, Brick."

I saw his eyes widen and then fall to the area of my chest.

I was still holding the lapels of his coat together, close to my chest. I had been holding them tightly closed as something to anchor me against the pain. Now I let them fall open between us and Brick stared down at my breasts, at the nipples that were swollen and bruised and covered with dried blood. Slim gold wires were threaded through them, locked in place at the ends with diamond-studded pendants. On each wire a large J was suspended and within each J, the name Jared was etched. Hanging from the very tips of each breast was that monster's name and I could not stand it to be there. More than the pain, I couldn't stand the ornate jewelry that was meant to brand me, to remind me that I belonged to him.

I doubt that I will ever see so much anger in Brick's face ever again. At least, I sure hope not. I watched as his jaw clenched and a vein throbbed in his temple. He rammed his fist into the pommel horse sending it crashing into the cinderblock wall. He pulled the jacket closed, then he stood and walked over to where the bolt cutters lay on the floor. They were way too big for the job, but he used them anyway. As they shielded me, the female officer held each breast in her hand, away from the cutting jaws of the blade and then I held the wire out for Brick. Brick snipped the wires and then demolished the gold pins and settings with the bolt cutter, sending the precious diamonds flying. With infinite care, he pulled the remnants of each wire out of the tips of my breasts. There was a look of satisfaction in his eyes but I knew he was no where near satisfied, heat was now coming off him in waves.

Antiseptic swabs were pressed to my bleeding nipples and even though I had to suck in air to endure the stinging, I was so happy the piercings were out that I didn't care.

I was prone, leaning on my elbows, holding big pieces of gauze to my breasts while the E.M.T.s were securing me to a gurney. I was covered from my waist down with a sheet. Every minute or so, I was told to check to make sure I had stopped bleeding. After a pillow was placed under my breasts, I dropped my head onto my folded arms and I was covered from my shoulders down with a blanket in preparation for the men to take me up the stairs to the ambulance.

Brick was stroking my cheek, rubbing my shoulders, kissing my temple and murmuring so many things that I couldn't absorb them all, when we heard a loud commotion upstairs. Then we heard feet running above us. Brick stood and grabbed his gun and we all watched as Jared, being chased by officers, tumbled down the steps and into the room.

At the door he took in the scene. No one spoke while his eyes searched for me and found me on the cot, covered, my head resting on my hands. I couldn't help myself, despite all the men piling into the room with their guns drawn, I had to show him. I forced myself up on my arms as high as I could, allowing my breasts to sway. I pulled the gauze pads from my chest and showed him my nipples. "As you can see, your jewelry has been removed."

His eyes became hard shards and his shoulders lifted. I noticed his fists clench as he stepped closer. I didn't know if he was getting ready to erupt because I'd removed his jewelry or because all these men were looking at my breasts. Brick moved to stand in his way, barring his way to me.

"She's my wife! This is private property, what we do here is private!"

"Yeah, and this is private, too!" Brick's fist slammed into the center of his face. Blood from his nose sprayed out in a flume and he crumpled to the floor. Brick reached down and lifted him by his throat, propping him against the wall. Then he hit him again, and again, and again. Each contact of his fist to Jared's face and body was solid and brutal, as he pounded into his flesh over and over. I heard cracking noises and knew that either his cheekbone or his jaw was broken. It sounded like one or two ribs snapped also. No one moved to stop Brick until it became evident that he was not going to stop on his own. It took four men to pull him off.

I eased myself back down onto the gurney and felt the woman officer pulling the sheet up over my shoulders. I put my head on my hands and closed my eyes. It was over. I was safe. And I would never have to run and hide again.

Brick sat beside me in the ambulance. He kept kissing my forehead and generally blubbering about how brave I was; how he had been afraid he wouldn't find me in time, how everything was going to be all right now. He promised that I would never have to worry about that sick bastard ever again.

"He's going to prison. Now you can get a divorce without any problem. You can move back into that fine mansion if you want, he certainly won't have any need for it; we'll see to his room and board."

"I don't want that. I don't want to ever live there again."

"Then sell it and buy something you do want."

"I just want my Dolphin. I feel safe and I'm happy there. I just want to go home to my RV."

"Well, that may take a few days, you're gonna need some lookin' after. Good God, if you're not the most troublesome woman I have ever met! Does it ever get easier loving you?"

I laughed before I realized what it was that he'd said. "Love? You love me?"

"Well yeah. Not the you-have-to-wear-my-name-on-your-chest kind, but the really good kind."

"The really good kind?"

"Yeah, the white picket fence kind."

"How does one do that on a motorhome, paint it?" I chuckled. "You know that I'm not ready to settle down and marry."

"I know. You're not divorced yet."

"Even when I am, I won't be ready, at least not initially. It's going to take some time to heal over this and then to make sure that marriage is what I truly want."

"How could I not be what you want? Look at me, I'm prime husband material."

"That may be, but I am no longer interested in being someone's wife, at least not now. I want to be plain ol' Jenny . . ."

"Carrie . . ."

"Actually, it's Debbie . . . "

"No more hiding, you can be whoever you want to be."

"I just want to be your girlfriend for now. Let's see how that goes before we draw white pickets on the Dolphin."

"Let's get you better and resettled and then we'll talk."

"Talk?"

"Okay, that's not the word I'm really thinking but we do have an audience here, you know. And, it appears you're out of action for a little while at least." He'd read the report, he knew I'd been raped and sodomized.

I looked over at the E.M.T. who was checking my blood pressure for the umpteenth time. From the shade of red her face had turned, I knew he was right about the audience part. "You need to have your hands looked after," I said holding one up for inspection. "You were brutal to them."

"Not as brutal as I wanted to be to him, believe me. I think that's the closest I've ever been to being totally out of control. I really could have killed him."

"I'm glad you didn't. I wouldn't want to have to visit my boyfriend in jail." There was silence as we just looked into each other's eyes. "How did you know to rescue me?"

"Your friend Connor tracked me down. He said you hadn't been returning his e-mails or phone calls and that you missed being there for his wedding. He said you had hinted at going back to your house to get your passport, if you could verify that your husband was still experiencing memory loss. I asked a friend of mine who owns a jewelry store in D.C. to call Jared at his office. They spoke at length and my friend said he didn't detect anything other than a savvy businessman. He had no problem recalling specific antique estate pieces that had recently been auctioned at Sotheby's. I smelled a trap. The one you apparently fell into."

I grimaced. Indeed I had. "It was so stupid of me. I guess I should have figured he'd have no problem getting his assistant to lie for him. Women are always falling over themselves to please him."

"Well, there'll be no more of that, unless they're prison guards."

"How long do you think he'll get, what can he really be charged with—after all, I am still his wife."

"We'll let the D.A. figure that out but you just can't chain your wife up in your basement and rape and beat her. And if I'm not mistaken, some of the toys he had were designed specifically for sodomy, which is illegal in the state of Virginia. He'll get jail time."

"He has a whole slew of prominent lawyers."

"So do we. He'll do time, trust me. And the media will crucify him."

"What if he charges you for beating him up?"

"Everybody saw him fall down the steps, no one saw him getting beat up."

The vehicle stopped and the doors were opened. As I was being lifted out and the gurney raised for transport into the center, I heard someone call Brick's name. He leaned down and gave me a quick kiss. "I'll see you in a few minutes. Don't moon anybody."

"Ha ha."

The next time I saw him I was so deep into my pain medication that I wasn't sure I'd heard him right. Something about Jillie, and him having to go, but that he'd be back and we'd *talk*, a lot, because he was a good *talker* and he knew I would be a good *talker*, too.

"You're all *talk*," I managed to whisper.

The nurse checking the IVs over my shoulder must've thought we were crazy.

"I'll call you. Go to sleep now. Dream about me."

"I'll dream about you all right. I'll dream about you painting white pickets on my Dolphin."

The nurse quirked her head and then shook it. Surely she wasn't hearing things right.

"I thought you didn't want that?"

"I've decided I want a cradle with a tiny Angelina in it one day, so we'll have to work on the pickets sooner or later."

"Well then, we will really need to do some *talking* if we're going to make that happen."

"*Talk, talk, talk* . . . when do we sleep?" I was out, not to waken for two days. Brick was gone and I had a slew of reporters and corporate lawyers lined up to see me. I could sit in a chair now with the help of an inflatable donut but it would be several more days before I would even attempt a plane ride back to my Dolphin.

When I finally got the purse I had left in the rental car back, I saw there was a message on my voicemail from a number I didn't recognize. I punched in the codes to retrieve it.

"Jenny, this is Randy. The guy with the four kids and the harridan for a wife that you met in Las Cruces. One of my guys on the setup crew knows this Robert Byrne's guy you're looking for, so give me a call when you get a chance and for Heaven's sake make it during the day, during the workweek. We've talked, and Charlotte's getting better, but I'm still on a very short leash and you're way too pretty by far for her to be comfortable with me talkin' to you."

The next books in the series:

Running into a Brick Wall
Running on Empty

ABOUT THE AUTHORS

Jacqueline DeGroot has published eight novels, a book of short stories and co-authored a local history book. The novels are romances set along the southeast coastline of North Carolina that she calls home. Sexy, witty, and emotionally relevant, the novels bring vibrant characters to life in a coastal community so real you can hear the surf and smell the salt in the air.

To date she has published:

Climax
The Secret of the Kindred Spirit
What Dreams Are Made Of
Barefoot Beaches
For the Love of Amanda
Shipwrecked at Sunset
Worth Any Price
Running into Temptation with Peggy Grich
Widows of Sea Trail-Book One

and contributed to:

Tales of the Silver Coast, A Secret History of Brunswick County by Miller Pope.

Shipwrecked at Sunset, combines forensics, Southern history, and forbidden love. A handsome pathologist and a beautiful Coastal Area Management inspector team up to unravel a mystery that starts with her discovery of a Civil War corpse in the aftermath of a hurricane.

Worth Any Price is set in Wilmington and tells the story of a serial killer who ransoms his victims in a most unusual manner. Three single women, devoted to their children, with nowhere to turn when they discover that their child is missing rely on three strangers. The men, either in the right place or the wrong place, are alerted to their plight and come to their rescue. By doing so, their lives are altered forever. *Worth Any Price* is a romance unlike any other.

Jack lives in Sunset Beach with her husband, Bill. Daughter Kimberly attends UNCW, and two grown sons live in Shallotte, and New York. Formerly an overachieving car salesperson in Vienna, VA—she ranked #6 in the country in Pontiac sales—Jack now lives a less stressful life in a small beach community. She rides bikes, cooks elaborate dinners, decorates lavish cakes, and takes long walks along the beach.

Peggy Grich has been an avid RVer for the past six years, loves the RV lifestyle, and is now a full-time RVer. She and her husband, Jim, are the former inkeepers and owners of Goose Creek Bed and Breakfast in Ocean Isle, North Carolina.

Prior to living in North Carolina, they built, owned, and operated a television station, TV8, in Glens Falls, New York.

Peggy has edited books for several authors and is the former Public Information Officer for a community college in North Carolina. She is also an experienced graphic designer.

Peggy and her husband produce *American RVer,* a monthly Internet Television Show for RVers, which features their RV travels, national rallies, technical tips, and interviews with friends they have met across America. It can be seen at *www.americanrver.com.*

To order additional books or post a message to Jacqueline, visit her website at *www.jacquelinedegroot.com.*

LaVergne, TN USA
15 November 2010
204940LV00002B/14/P

9 781607 025900